Contents

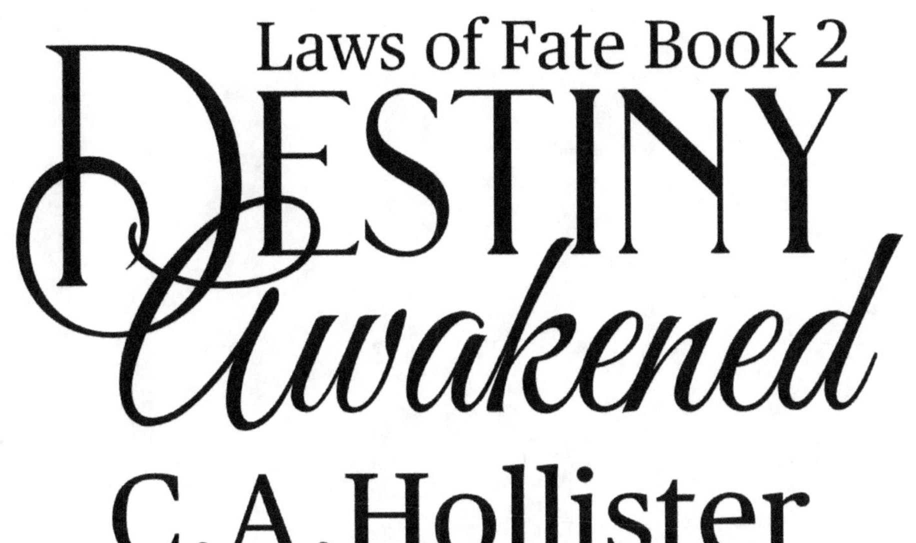

Laws of Fate Book 2
DESTINY
Awakened
C.A.Hollister

Dedication

For Bethany. Your brutal honesty has been invaluable to my writing. Thank you for finding the time to read my awful first drafts and giving me assurance and support throughout my entire journey.

Chapter 1

THE DEAD MAN'S EYES snapped open; his dry, cracked lips sucking in precious life. Faint light stung his newly awakened sight, making him squint against the orange flames dotting the walls. Hoping the sensation was temporary, he ignored the searing pain caused by the flicking candlelight. Beyond discomfort was a sense of relief to feel anything at all.

A dull pressure pulsed in his chest where fingers withdrew from mottled flesh. Segomo watched, transfixed, as the wounds sealed shut almost instantly. The air itself pressed in on him, heavy, stagnant, and reeking of decay. Still, he took in another deep breath despite the stink of rotting meat and fetid death clawing at his throat.

"There you are." The voice sliced through his skull like a newly sharpened blade.

Segomo pushed himself upright, getting a better view of the creature that dragged him from the underworld. A grotesque face, distorted and tilted, studied him from a crouching position on the filthy floor. Shadows writhed unnaturally around the Fomorian, alluding to the power that the ancient being possessed.

Once Segomo's vision sharpened, he examined the dank crypt more closely. "I have to admit," his voice was as unfamiliar as the body he now inhabited, "I had doubts about your abilities. Your underlings did little to inspire confidence when they came to me with your offer."

Indech stood with a fluidity that contrasted his mangled form. "Your father's authority is not as infallible as he believes it to be. There are blind spots that can be exploited. Especially where you are concerned."

Segomo stared at the gnarled hand being held out to him. His face twisted into disdain at the thought of touching the vile creature. But he was still weak, and his newly revived muscles needed time to adjust to the blood now pumping through his veins. It was somewhat comforting to feel a beating heart, even if it wasn't his own.

Taking the outstretched hand, Segomo used his other hand to steady himself against the cold, damp wall. "I was under the impression you would make me whole. Not shove me into some useless human carcass." He spat the words out of his foreign mouth.

"It is within my power to restore your godhood." The Fomorian's smile was sickening. "When the terms of our agreement are met, you will have your mantle restored."

Segomo closed his borrowed eyes. Mortal or not, this existence was better than being banished to the underworld, staring at the same monotonous scenery for the rest of eternity. He tracked the scraping of clawed toes to where Indech gathered bloodied tools from the circle of ancient, misshapen bones.

"Your deeds echo throughout the Weaver's threads." Indech's voice resonated from every corner of the crypt, making Segomo's stomach roll uncomfortably. "We cannot take the chance of betrayal with one such as you."

Segomo pushed himself up straight, embracing the anger that surged through him. "Do not speak to me of Ronwen and her ridiculous tapestry. Just as she no longer controls my path, I will not allow Arawn to dictate my fate."

Indech reached into the pocket of the dark coat he wore. It seemed to be made of fine materials, stitched with great care, and was wholly out of place on his mangled body. He handed Segomo a tarnished medallion that was attached to a thin gold chain. "That suit of flesh and bones keeps you tethered to me. This talisman offers my protection. And it will give you a taste of the power you covet."

Once the pendant rested against his skin, the fatigue weighing Segomo down vanished, replaced with a vigor he hadn't experienced since before being imprisoned all those eons ago. He traced the ancient symbols on the cool surface. "We should get on with the reason you've procured me from the underworld. I would like to have my godhood restored as quickly as possible."

"The awakening is fast approaching. We must prepare the way." A man appeared from within the shadows and whispered something to the Fomorian. To Segomo, Indech said, "I have located a suitable vessel for my father. I expect you to retrieve it for me."

Segomo stared at the demon, insulted to be relegated as a mere errand boy.

As if sensing his ire, Indech went on. "Given your history with these dragons, you will have the upper hand when the time comes to abscond with the child."

"Dragons?"

"I believe you once commanded the army led by their patriarch."

Segomo studied the decaying stone floor. The idea Hengist still lived after so many centuries was daunting. They had rivers of bad blood between them. Looking up from the ground, he asked, "Who is this child?"

Indech made a low, thoughtful sound. "I have waited ages upon ages for one such as he to slip past Arawn's watchful gaze. His birthright is the key to opening the way for my father to retake his lost kingdom."

As curious as he was about why this boy was so special, Segomo wanted to be away from Indech and stretch his unsteady legs in a world he no longer recognized. "Where can I find him?"

"First, you must acclimate to this realm." He motioned to the door, where a man held out a black bag nearly as tall as Segomo's borrowed body. "I have arranged for your transportation as well. My faithful may not be the army you once commanded, but they are quite competent." He paused, then added, "Make sure the vessel is unharmed."

Segomo nodded, already adrift in memories of pleasures long denied. luxuries, bloodlust, and the intoxicating thrum of worship. Outside, he eyed a dark contraption he didn't recognize. Moonlight reflected on the glass-like surface. Some of the dead that passed through the underworld spoke of such things, but his inexperience with the modern world left him unsure of what to do.

A young woman stood at an open door. Her stark blond hair complemented a pair of pale blue eyes. She stepped away, motioning for him to climb inside. Before he could do so, Indech joined him, handing over a piece of white parchment. "Find the warlock, Marshall. He will help you gather whatever it is you need."

Segomo pocketed the paper without reading it, then ran a calculating gaze down the front of the blond woman holding the door. Despite her delicious appearance, the stench of death emanating from her body turned his stomach. He ignored the hunger in her stare. She wanted more than carnal pleasure. If he dared partake in that sweet bounty, the creature inside her would devour his soul. He eased past her and settled into the plush seating, eager to be away from Indech and the crypt.

As the strange wheeled conveyance began to move, a heavy unease descended over him. The drab decor surrounding him couldn't compare to the opulence he was used to. The sound of an unfamiliar rhythmic hum roared in his ears, drowning out the rustle of the wind seeping through open glass windows.

He missed the brisk breeze sweeping across his face as he galloped atop his steed through the hills of his homeland. The sterile odor of the metal box on wheels filled his nostrils, reminding him of the unnaturalness of his situation. He would endure the discomfort if he was to reclaim his mantle. Already, his mouth watered at the thought of the delicious revenge he would take on those who betrayed him—starting with the kin of that sanctimonious Death Dragon.

Uninvited images seeped from the depths of his mind—silken black hair tangled in the wind, wide eyes frozen in terror. He clenched his jaw. He had been a god once, but even gods made mistakes. No. Not mistakes. Choices. And he chose vengeance.

The echoes of desperate screams reverberated through the cramped space around him. Pitiful condemnations haunted his thoughts for too long, bringing the weight of guilt pressing down on him like a heavy stone as he struggled to keep his composure. The pungent aroma of decay hung in the air, a stark reminder of the evil he was bargaining with, giving him the strength to push aside the past.

It was time for him to reclaim his legacy, and no ghosts of those dead souls would stop his ascension. Indech failed to fully comprehend the scope of Segomo's true power and what it meant to set him free. The Fomorian went to a lot of trouble to bind Segomo's soul to this body. There must be a better reason for it than abducting a child.

Pushing deeper into the soft fabric, Segomo peered out of the window, losing himself in the brilliant lights of the upcoming city, excited to experience all that had eluded him for centuries.

"Pink is not my color," Cora said, absentmindedly tucking loose strands of copper-colored hair behind her ear. She skimmed the room with a bored expression, trying to keep the irritation from showing on her face.

Darya cocked her head to one side, lifting a pale rose chiffon dress to Cora's chest, frowned, then held up a delicate sundress with a bright yellow gingham pattern. "I agree. It clashes with your hair. Yellow it is, then."

Cora's expression contorted into what she hoped was disgust, appalled that her so-called friend didn't know her better than that. "Let me make this clear. Over my dead body."

"Oh, come on." Darya shoved the soft fabric at her. "I'm not asking you to toss out your entire wardrobe. I simply want you to try on something that doesn't look like you're attending to a funeral."

Cora pushed Darya's hand away as if the very idea of touching the dress would give her some disease. "That's not the point." She slid a terse gaze down the front of the flowery ensemble before Darya hung it back in its original spot. "Why are you suddenly so concerned with my choice in fashion, anyway?"

Refusing to meet her stare, Darya rummaged through another rack of colorful tops. "No reason. I thought you were tired of wearing the same two colors every day."

"Uh-huh." Cora narrowed her eyes. "You never once, in all the time we've known each other, made a big deal about my style." A terrible thought crossed her mind. "You're trying to set me up on a date again, aren't you?"

Darya lifted a pastel purple t-shirt from the rack and held it up to Cora. "I'm not trying to set you up on a date. I'm trying to broaden your fashion horizons. Mix it up a little. We are living in the nineteen-nineties, not the eighteen-nineties. We can wear whatever we like these days, you know."

Cora plucked the shirt from Darya's hand and put it back where it belonged. "You were lucky you didn't have to live through a time when corsets were mandatory and bold colors were sinful. You would be amazed at how many people nearly fainted at the sight of designs on fabric."

A shadow of sadness passed over Darya. "Sometimes I wish I had the chance." She returned another shirt to the rack. "My mom would be about your age. I mean, you two were born around the same time."

Guilt made Cora turn away and pretend to be interested in a jewelry display. "I would have helped your people if I could. By the time I gained full control of my godhood, your destiny was set in motion. I would have been forbidden from interfering."

"It worked out the way it was supposed to." Darya tapped a pair of petite pearl earrings attached to a thin, white cardboard piece. "These are your style."

The bell over the shop's door jangled sharply, distracting Darya. Cora moved away from the jewelry and the temptation to buy the earrings. They were beautiful, and pearls were her favorite precious gemstone.

A little boy with tousled corn silk hair and bright green eyes bounded inside, his little footsteps creaking over the hardwood floor. He clutched a brown paper sack to his chest and glanced over his shoulder. "I beat you."

Behind him, a girl two years his senior chased him across the dress shop. The newly refinished wood flooring creaked and groaned with each step. She carried a matching paper sack as her brother. Cora recognized Dino's logo. "Only because you cheated."

"Whoa." Darya reached for Bastian, saving him from careening into a display of jewelry. "What are you two doing here? Did you come into the village alone?"

Brigita's smirk was nearly identical to her father. Her eyes held the same bright shade of green as her brother, but shared her mother's dark hair and porcelain complexion. "We came with Grandfather. He is making some last-minute arrangements for his holiday with Ronwen. We saw you talking to Aunt Cora through the window, and Bastian took off across the street before I could stop him."

Darya glanced down at her son. "That was a dangerous thing to do, young man."

Cora stood back, her arms crossed, watching the easy rhythm of Darya and her children. The warmth between them was mesmerizing. It stirred something raw and unwelcome in her chest—a reminder of the life she lived without such attachments.

It amazed Cora just how opposite yet so much alike Brigita and Saebastian were. They both carried traces of their parents inside them, yet their powers were vastly different. Brigita was destined to become a fierce goddess. More so than her mother. And little

Bastian had been communing with animals since before he could walk. On top of that, they possessed the same dragon bloodline that was older than some of the gods themselves.

Cora didn't have to be an oracle to foresee the extraordinary destinies that awaited those beautiful children. Somewhere deep in her heart, in a place she kept hidden, she coveted the love Darya and Edwind shared to make such a wonderful life together. They had overcome seemingly insurmountable odds to reach their destiny.

"Alright, you two," Darya said, shooing the kids toward the door. "Find your grandfather and no more treats from Dino's shop. I don't want your appetite ruined."

"Fine," Brigita mumbled as she took hold of Bastian's hand.

He jerked it free. "I'm not a baby."

Brigita snatched him by his arm. "Then stop acting like one. Grandfather said you have to listen to me."

Darya eased across the room to the long window, displaying mannequins with other odds and ends. When Brigita and Bastian were with their grandfather again, she joined Cora near the back of the shop. "I swear, Horsa spoils those two as if they are his only two grandchildren."

"It's been what, a thousand years since he's been able to take on that role?"

Darya frowned. "I suppose you're right. Sometimes I forget just how long he waited for us." Giving the place one more thoughtful once over, she said, "If you're not going to let me liven up your wardrobe, I guess I'll go home and help my dear sweet husband with dinner. I'll see you later tonight."

Cora narrowed her eyes at her friend. "Tonight?"

"I told you about it a few days ago. Horsa wants one last dinner with the family before leaving for Italy. He acts as if he won't see us again for another thousand years." On her way out, she shot Cora an innocent smile. "Be there around six, and wear something that's not black or brown."

Cora waited until she was alone before searching the rack for the dress Darya picked out earlier. She tried to imagine wearing an outfit so delicate and quickly dismissed the idea. She wasn't made for vibrant, beautiful clothes like Darya. Cora's simplistic choices in fashion and decor kept her life uncluttered and uncomplicated.

Glancing at her watch, she thought about racing home and making up some random excuse to leave town. But blowing off one of her only friends was worse than the prospect of enduring a blind date. Cora resigned herself to the inevitable, climbing behind the wheel of her small Mercedes, a car she knew made her stick out like a sore thumb in a village of practical Volkswagens and Fords.

The drive to her bungalow was a short one. Broughied was the sort of place that seemed frozen in time, its slate-roofed cottages and cobbled streets unbothered by the passing years. She wondered if Horsa and his father had a hand in slowing down the hands of time here, fighting to keep the ever advancing modern world from encroaching on the tiny little village. For them to be as long lived as they were, she would have thought they were more open to change.

On the other hand, Cora's nomadic lifestyle was a way to distance herself from others. Over the decades, she came and went, never opting to settle down in one place. Especially not somewhere as small and quiet as Broughied. Then she met Darya a few years ago.

Their first encounter was brief but tense. Darya had been fiercely protective of Edwind every time Cora came around.

For weeks, Darya refused to interact with her. One night, after copious amounts of alcohol, she confessed that Cora's red hair was a reminder of the woman who tried to steal Edwind away when they were still in nine eighty-two.

After a long bout of laughter that ended with Cora nearly sliding off the couch, she promised Darya there was absolutely nothing to be worried about. She couldn't be more turned off by Edwind and the irritatingly noble Wodehal traits that plagued his entire bloodline. It was the main reason she wouldn't to date Dino when Darya tried to set them up.

Cora parked her car on the quiet side street in front of the quaint little cottage she called home. A cool breeze swept through the still neighborhood, bringing the first hint of fall. She was tempted to take an extended vacation across the ocean in some warm part of the southern United States. Winter was her least favorite season, given how cold-natured she was.

After unlocking the front door, she hung her keys on the hook by the coat rack and headed for her bedroom, where she intended to pick out the most bland, unremarkable outfit she could put together. The clean scent of fresh laundry mixed with a salty breeze sweeping up the coast to the open windows in her room.

She rummaged through her wardrobe, having to fight with the tightly packed clothes. There were many options to choose from. That realization bothered her more than it should have. Maybe it was time to get rid of some things. Staying rooted in place for so long allowed her to accumulate unnecessary stuff, and her house was becoming too cluttered.

A delicate button up blouse a shade lighter than her glacial blue eyes caught her attention among the dark browns and blacks. She snatched it off the hanger, rubbing her fingers against the soft fabric. It would pair perfectly with the black slacks hanging over a chair near the door. The outfit was the perfect petty compromise—not quite the dress Darya hoped for, but a welcome change from the drab shades of boring that made up most of Cora's attire.

Not that a change in clothes would make tonight any less exhausting.

With a heavy sigh, she tossed the blouse and slacks onto the bed. The sooner she changed and left, the sooner she could get through the awkward dinner, and, hopefully, dodge whatever romantic scheme Darya had undoubtedly concocted.

Cora arrived at the Wodehal house a little before six. She sat behind the wheel, trying to peer inside the shuttered windows. She hoped to spot any potential guests who could turn into a prospective date.

The rubber soles of her ankle-high boots slapped against the stone walkway leading to the front door. She kept picking at the satin fabric, already uncomfortable in the loose yet stifling blouse. Maybe she should have chosen something with a less drastic neckline.

She barely had a chance to knock when Darya flung it open, greeting her with a wide grin. She gave Cora an approving once-over. "You're looking lovely tonight."

"I think this was a bad idea."

Darya took her by the hand, dragging her through the living room and into the kitchen. The soft melody of Simply Red drifted from the open door of Edwind's office. "Be a dear and take these to the veranda." She handed Cora a tray of assorted glasses. "Horsa brought an experimental brew he claims to have been saving for a special occasion."

Staring at the mugs thrust into her hands, Cara pursed her lips into a tight scowl. "Is my non-date here already?"

Darya turned her back, shrugging. "Better hurry. You don't want to keep the guys waiting."

Cora had to balance the tray in one hand to open the sliding door. By some miracle, she made it outside without a single cup falling to the ground, despite the acrobatic flips her stomach was doing. She shouldn't be so nervous. Darya knew what she was. Surely, she wouldn't try setting her up with some run-of-the-mill mortal man who didn't realize what he was getting himself into.

As soon as she set the mugs on the table, Cora was met by Horsa's off kilter grin, half hidden behind a neatly trimmed beard. His dark hair was dapper as always, complementing a sun kissed complexion. "There's a ravishing sight for sore eyes," he exclaimed.

"Careful, old man," Cora said, snatching a bottle from the bucket of ice. "If Ronwen hears you talking like that, she is likely to start plucking scales from your body."

His head fell back with heavy laughter, and when he looked at her again, his malachite gaze sparkled in the fading daylight. "She will be helpless to this tongue of mine when I see her next."

Cora laughed. Edwind, on the other hand, shifted in his chair, running fingers through his hair, the last rays of the afternoon shining against the sandy blond strands. "Can you please keep those thoughts to yourself?"

The sound of children laughing brought Cora's attention around to the beach, where Brigita and Bastian ran through the surf. Despite their joyful laughter, seeing them so close to the waves made her skin ripple with an icy dread.

She forgot her fear when she watched an older boy chasing after them, keeping his distance from the water. It wasn't surprising that he would keep so far inland. Not after the last time he went into the ocean.

If Marcos was there, it meant his father was nearby. Behind her, the door from the dining room opened, and Darya walked out, followed by Dino.

Cora's eyes widened, piercing Darya with her stare, trying not to be obvious, but the other woman refused to pay attention to her.

"How are the children?" Darya asked.

Edwind nodded to the beach. "Enjoying themselves."

Dino came around the chair beside Cora. His gaze slipped past her, and the look on his face morphed into the same apprehension that still lingered in Cora's blood. "Should they be so close to the water?"

Darya laid a hand on his shoulder. "We are watching him. Nothing bad will happen here."

The smile that replaced his scowl did little to hide the anxiety tightening his pensive expression. He turned away from the ocean but kept his body positioned to sprint down the stairs at any moment. When he glanced at Cora again, there was no mistaking the shift in his demeanor; and she wasn't sure if he was thrilled about her presence. "Hello, Cora. It's good to see you."

She locked her grin in place, making her cheeks ache. "You as well, Dino. I didn't know you were going to be here."

He glanced to the side. "Darya didn't tell you?"

"Oh," Darya said. "I must have forgotten to mention it. Silly me."

Horsa cleared his throat, turning to his son. "Edwind, I'll be leaving for Italy tomorrow. I'm hoping to convince Ronwen to stay for one more month so we can visit my old place in Macedonia. We should be back before November."

"Do you need me to watch over the Dragon's Rest?"

"Mrs. Beal can handle the Inn. I'll leave a number where I can be reached." He stared at the ocean. "I wish we could have put this little holiday off until winter. I would have loved for Ronwen to experience the solstice fires there. They are almost as thrilling as the ones on Didean."

"Perhaps we should take a holiday there as well." Edwind winked at Darya, who failed to hide the rush of pink that lit up her cheeks.

From the stories Cora was told about Didean and its solstice fires, she secretly wished for the chance to experience them herself. According to both Darya and Edwind, they put to shame anything Cora had been a part of.

Horsa's chuckle faded into thoughtful silence, then he said, "Did I ever tell you of the Winter your nephew married the woman who carried on our bloodline?"

Edwind's smile dropped. "You don't tell me much about Gita and Saebbi's past, even though I ask you nearly every time we see each other. She's my sister. Shouldn't I know how she fared after we left?"

"Take that up with Morigan. She makes the laws. We simply follow them."

"You're practically her son-in-law." Edwind countered. "You should be allowed some kind of leniency."

A hint of sadness washed over Horsa. "It's not that simple. Those memories are sometimes painful for me to relive." With the slightest shake of his head, he went on. "Anyway, it was the year Miller turned twenty-eight. Ten-twelve, I believe. Gita thought she was going to die of old age before he gave her grandchildren."

"I do wish I could have met him," Edwind mused.

Horsa nodded to Dino, then to where Marcos played with the other children. "He lives on in them."

At the door, Darya glanced over her shoulder. "Edwind, would you help me with something inside?"

The lines around his mouth tightened, like he wanted to argue, but whatever he saw in her face made him acquiesce with a nod. "Father, can you go over your itinerary with me?"

Horsa took a drink. "It's not important. I'll write it down before I leave."

"Horsa, come inside," Darya insisted through a forced smile.

He glanced from her to Cora, then Dino, before sighing and following them indoors.

Cora bypassed the chair next to Dino, leaning on the railing where she watched the kids play. After a minute of uneasy silence, she asked, "How's Marcos?"

"Good. He's good. Already thinking about university. Something in the arts. You should see the comics he's created. I wish I had a fraction of his talent."

"That's great." Knowing she was the one who saved Marcos' life made it easier to live with the consequences of stealing a soul from her father.

For the next minute or so, they stared at anything but each other. The sounds of children's laughter mingled with the whisper of the sea. Cora would have been content to exist in the silence between them for the rest of the night, breathing in the soothing brine of the ocean.

This wasn't the first time Darya had tried to set her up with Dino. Cora dodged nearly every opportunity for them to be alone. She just wasn't attracted to him. He was the farthest thing from her type that any man could be. Maybe it was knowing his familial ties. The Wodehal men tended to be too uptight and rigid for her tastes.

When she glanced to the side, he was staring through the window, where Darya gathered cups and plates from the cupboards. Cora may not be the most adept at love, having been stunted in both giving and receiving it, but she recognized the longing etched in his face.

She knew the story of how Dino had fallen head over heels for Darya when she first arrived in Broughied ten years ago, and how he nearly lost an arm because of that infatuation. It seemed he was still smitten, even after all this time.

He went to turn away from the window, so she returned to watching the beach before he caught her staring at him. His footsteps clunked across the wooden deck, and she smelled his woodsy cologne a few seconds before he came into view from her periphery.

"I know this is awkward, having to do the whole dinner thing with Darya and the family," he said. "But if you would be up for it, I'd like the chance to take you out on a proper date. Just the two of us."

Her stomach did a somersault before trying to climb up her throat. It would have been so easy to accept his offer, if only to avoid the aftermath of rejection, but that wouldn't be fair to either of them. Meeting his stare, she tried to soften her expression. "I'm sorry, Dino. You're sweet, and Marcos is such an awesome kid. I just don't see you that way."

He stared at her, his face a blank wall. At first, she thought he was going to be okay, but the serenity of his expression darkened. "I'm sweet. Sweet. Doesn't that take the piss? If you don't see me in that way, tell me, Cora, how exactly do you see me?"

"Dino..."

He held up his hands. "I can't believe—It doesn't matter. I'm sorry if I made you uncomfortable."

The glass door opened and Darya stuck her head out. "The food is ready." She eyed them, her smile fading. "What's going on?"

"I'm sorry, Darya." Cora stepped around Dino. "I should go."

Dino bound down the stairs. "You stay. Marcos and I will leave."

Darya stared after him as headed down the embankment to the beach. "What was that about?"

"He asked me out on a date. I said no."

"Why?"

"He's not my type."

Marcos spotted Cora and ran to her side despite his father's objections, giving her a hug.

She returned the gesture. "Hey, kiddo." Every time she saw Marcos, he seemed to grow another inch. He was at least three inches taller than her five-six frame. It was hard to believe he was two years from being a grown man. Despite the lack of attraction to his father, she shared a special bond with Marcos. Maybe it was stealing his soul back from Arawn, so Dino wouldn't lose his only son.

"Marcos, we're leaving." Dino refused to look at Cora or Darya on his way by.

"But Dad, I thought we were eating dinner."

"We aren't," he muttered. "Let's go."

Shooting Cora a confused look, Marcos headed down the steps, following his dad around the house.

When they were gone, Darya gave her friend an apologetic frown. "I shouldn't have made you come tonight."

Cora met her stare and, keeping her voice low, said, "He still has a thing for you."

Darya grimaced. "I hoped he would be over all that by now."

"I'm sorry I ruined your evening."

Darya backed toward the door. "Will you at least stay for dinner?"

No longer in the mood to eat, Cora considered going back home and spending the rest of the night drinking in her garden. But in the end, she couldn't bring herself to let Darya down after she went to so much trouble. "Sure. Give me a few minutes to gather myself."

When she was alone, Cora stared at the ocean, letting the sound of endless waves wash over her. It was a simple thing; a date. Yet there were so many possible complications she didn't know how to put them into words. She was better off keeping Dino on the outskirts of her life. He didn't fully comprehend who or what she was. Her abilities went far beyond saving a little boy from her father. No one understood the full extent of her powers. Not even Horsa.

Because of Arawn, Cora was cursed with a birthright that she never wanted. Being death's heir forced her into a life of fleeting encounters, so no one ever got close enough to glimpse the monster she kept hidden away.

One day she might find a love as enduring as Darya and Edwind. Someone who could cherish her despite the bloodline she shared with the god of the underworld. All she knew for certain was Dino wouldn't be that man.

STALE SMOKE AND SOURED ale clawed at Segomo's senses upon entering the small tavern. It was a visceral reminder of the mortal world's filth. His shoes crunched across the sticky floor, making his approach to the communal table feel like he was trudging through thick sand. The tavern keeper futilely wiped at the filthy surface, distracted by a tiny screen with colorless people moving back and forth, kicking a ball between them.

Segomo went to rest his hands next to a bowl of what looked like shriveled seeds, then thought better of it, given how disgusting the rest of the place appeared to be. He cleared his throat, hoping to get the other man's attention.

The tavern keeper barely looked away from the black box. "What can I get you, mate?"

"I wish to see Marshall."

Hearing the name was enough to pull his full scrutiny. "And you are?"

"Short on time and patience. He is expecting me."

The scrawny man grunted, clearly unimpressed by the body Segomo inhabited. "Wait here."

When the tavern keeper disappeared through a door on the other side of the bar, Segomo turned his attention to the mirror across from him. Despite the smudged film over the reflective surface, he had a clear view of his wiry frame, understanding now why the tavern keeper acted so unbothered. His hair was the same color as churned mud and lay flat and stringy against his head. Dark eyes were sunken into a narrow face. His ruddy complexion was broken by a hook nose and a thin mouth. He pulled back his lips, showing off crooked, dingy teeth.

Segomo was disgusted by the flesh prison. He wanted to claw away the stranger's face, to have his flawless features restored; but there would be no reprieve from this skin and bone until he satisfied the bargain with Indech. When Segomo's godhood was restored, he would revel in the retribution awaiting his mother and father. He wanted them to plea for their freedom and their lives, just like they made him beg for his sovereignty, and later, death.

For now, Segomo had to play the game. He would stifle the rage eating away at his soul, lest he be found out and returned to purgatory. It was yet another reminder of how precarious his situation was. Every second that passed in the mortal realm meant that his body lay vulnerable in the underworld. Arawn could, at any time, visit unannounced in a futile attempt to salvage their relationship.

Segomo put a hand to his throat, expecting to feel the cold, heavy piece of ethereal metal that had been a part of his existence for longer than he could remember. The instant Arawn locked that damn Qel around his son's neck, effectively severing the ties to his godhood, any hope of reconciliation had been destroyed. It was one thing to hold Segomo captive. Using that torque his mother so graciously constructed to turn him practically mortal was unforgivable. Now, here he was, forced into a state of being where he had little to no control over his autonomy.

The little man returned, motioning to the open doorway. "Through there."

Stepping over the threshold was like entering another plane of existence. The air was crisp and clean, free of the weighty stink from the tavern. There was a hint of something woodsy and sweet that he couldn't quite recall, but it made his mouth water. Though there were no visible light sources, the walls reflected the clear radiance of the sun. The magic that conjured such a place was strong, yet still a simple trick for one with the knowledge of manipulating the elements.

A rather rotund man sat behind a desk on the opposite side of the room. His balding head was bowed as he scribbled furiously on a piece of parchment paper. His lips kept pace with the frantic movements of his pen. Light bounced off the page, making the words appear to be dancing back and forth in the same erratic rhythm of his indecipherable whispers.

Segomo huffed out an annoyed sigh. He didn't care about whatever trivial tasks Marshall was involved in. Time was too precious a commodity.

The warlock held up his free hand. If Segomo had access to his full powers, he would have removed it from Marshall's body and slapped him across the face with it for the audacity. For now, though, he waited impatiently for Marshall to finish.

"Sorry about that. These spells can be a bit finicky, this one in particular. I wouldn't want either of us on the receiving end of the backlash should it decide to unravel unexpectedly."

Segomo approached the desk and dropped a coin on the pristine surface. "You have something I need."

Marshall stared at the silver token briefly but refused to touch it. Disgust soured his expression. "I guess your kind aren't much for small talk."

Segomo narrowed his eyes, his lips stretching into a repulsive sneer. Did Marshall believe him to be a Fomorian? How insulting. "I'm not one of those vile things."

For the first time, Marshall met Segomo's stare. "Well, you're not the owner of that body." Pushing away from the desk, he searched the drawer next to him. "I don't care what you are. I am paid to render a service, not ask questions." He pulled out a satchel and pushed it across the polished surface. "This should get you past the wards."

"Should?"

"The magic that protects the boy you're after is tricky. It's ancient and relatively unknown among my people, but it's the best I can do, given the limited time your patron allowed."

Segomo took the bag and loosened the string holding it closed.

Marshall shot to his feet. "Don't open it yet, fool."

Despite not having his body or his power, the glower he laid on Marshall made the man shrink into his seat.

"If you release the little guys now, you are wasting their magic, and I don't have time to conjure more." His tone was more subdued.

"You cannot be sure they will work," Segomo countered.

"I'm confident in my skills." He waved a dismissive hand. "I believe that concludes our business for the time being."

Segomo didn't care for being disregarded in such a flippant manner, but in his current state, what choice did he have but to concede to the worm for now? He would make note of the encounter, vowing to revisit Marshall and his establishment when his powers were restored.

Once outside, Segomo took a few seconds to watch the busy streets. Everything was so much louder than he remembered. His gaze followed the outline of a building in the distance. Never in his countless years in this realm had he ever seen such marvels. Occasionally, he would converse with those few souls that wandered into his little corner of purgatory. But no words did justice to the enormity of the world he awakened in.

The driver cleared her throat. "Shall we go?"

He stayed in place for a while longer, wondering just how far he could push Indech's minions? She stood by the door he exited earlier. Despite her petite body, the creature inside it might prove to be a worthy foe. It had been too long since he enjoyed a good fight.

Heaving a disappointed sigh, he returned to the metal box. The time for such pleasures would have to wait. He had a dragon to capture.

The shrill ring of the telephone shattered Cora's alcohol-induced sleep, dragging her from the depths of a restless nightmare. She pushed herself upright on the plush sofa cushion, squinting at the clock on the wall across the living room. Her blurred vision and tipsy brain struggled to make out the exact time.

Remnants of her dream hung heavy in her subconscious, but with each jarring jangle, it slid farther into the recesses of sleep, leaving only the vague sense of longing. She blindly reached for the smooth plastic receiver, fumbling past the empty wine bottle she had emptied earlier after returning from the Wodehal house.

"Someone better be dead." Her voice sounded like her vocal chords had been scraped raw.

"Let's hope it hasn't gotten that far."

The remaining vestiges of sleep fled Cora's mind, and she bolted upright. "Raquel?"

"I had a vision. It wasn't clear, but I saw a boy. He was—is—will be in danger." There was a pause, then came the sound of a shaky sigh rushed through the other end of the line. "I didn't get a good look at him, but I heard someone calling for Marcos."

"Wait. Dino's kid?"

"I believe so. I tried to retrieve the vision, but it kept slipping away. Someone or something is fighting hard to keep it hidden. I don't think I was supposed to see it at all."

Cora pushed to her feet. "Raquel, focus. What is going to happen?"

"The boy—Marcos. He was yelling. A black shadow was standing over him. Oh, Cora. It reeked of a power I've never experienced before. You need to go to him. Right now."

Cora slammed the phone back in its cradle and grabbed the first shirt and pair of jeans she laid her hands on. After slipping into her boots, she threw open the wardrobe and opened the hidden compartment to retrieve the onyx blade that lay in a crimson silk lined box.

The black dagger hummed with an ancient magic, light glinting off the ethereal metal, reflecting a rainbow of colors. She tucked it into the sheath at her back. Even with the barrier between the blade and her body, its power seeped into her skin.

The dagger was crafted from the same otherworldly material that her father's death knights used for their weapons. Arawn had gifted it to her when she was still in his charge in the underworld. Knowing the dangerous power imbued within, she sometimes wondered if her father had a lapse in judgment, given the tumultuous nature of their strained relationship.

Tucking the death blade into the leather pouch, she rushed outside. She was halfway to her car when she thought about calling Edwind or Horsa, but the urgency and fear in Raquel's voice left no room for wasting time waiting for backup, so she jumped into the driver's seat and took off through the quiet streets of Broughied.

Being the middle of the night, it meant traffic was practically nonexistent. She made it across the village to where Dino's little cottage sat on a cliff overlooking the ocean.

She skidded to a stop in front of the house to find it devoid of any light. Nothing seemed out of place. There was no shouting. No ransacking of his house. She climbed out of her car, breathing in the pungent odor of earth and sea. A breeze swept through the surrounding trees, whispering through late summer leaves, but there was no hint of danger as far as she could tell. What if Raquel had been wrong about her vision? Or her timing was off. It wouldn't be the first time.

A light sprang to life on the front step, casting an orange glow on her from where she stood at the base of the stairs. Too late to turn back now. She had only a few seconds to come up with a believable excuse as to why she was there at such an ungodly hour. Perhaps she could try convincing him she wanted to continue their conversation from earlier.

She made the short climb to the front door. When Dino opened it, she was taken aback by the sight of him, wearing only a pair of green and black plaid boxers. Though he wasn't as defined and sinewy as the rest of the Wodehal men, he still had the right amount of muscle in all the right places to make her wonder just how dangerous he could be if pushed to his limits.

"What the bloody hell are you doing here?" He peered at her through tired eyes, then leaned back and glanced at the wall behind him. "It's nearly one in the morning."

"I'm sorry, I got a call—" So much for the lie. "I thought you and Marcos were—" Pushing out a breath, she searched her mind for an explanation that wouldn't make herself sound like a complete loon. "Raquel called. She had a vision."

Dino ran a hand down his face and took a step to the side. Cora expected him to slam it shut. Instead, he said, "You know I don't believe in that rubbish."

She wanted to point out that the rubbish he was referring to was way more believable than, say, shapeshifting dragons, but kept that observation to herself. "I wouldn't have come if it wasn't serious." Her attention wandered past Dino, to the set of stairs leading to the second floor. If only she could put her eyes on the kid, she would call Raquel back and tell her the vision was a dud. Turning to Dino, she added, "It's about Marcos."

At the mention of his son's name, Dino tightened his grip on the door. He looked like he was ready to shut her out, but the irritation in his features vanished. Stepping aside, he said, "Come in."

Cora had been in his house only once, and it appeared nothing had changed since then. He shuffled to the sink, filled a kettle and set it on the stovetop before joining her at the table.

"What is this vision you are so concerned about?"

She sat forward, not knowing where to begin. "Raquel wasn't very clear about what she saw."

Dino speared her with suspicion. "Why does that not surprise me?"

"I know how it sounds, but I've never heard her so desperate and scared." Taking a moment to gather her thoughts, she went on. "She said Marcos is in danger. Something is after him. Something more dangerous than she's ever encountered."

For a second, Dino's expression shifted from irritation to fear. He stood and gathered a couple of cups and pulled out two tea bags from a tin on the counter. "What is supposedly after my son?"

"I wish I knew. She only said he is in danger."

Dino pushed himself away from the cabinet, his head dropping to his chest. "I can't believe—"

There was a loud crash from above their heads, followed by a boy's shriek. Cora shot up the stairs, the violent beating of her heart echoing each frantic step. All she could think about was the horrible images Raquel recounted.

Please let Marcos be safe. She repeated the mantra for the length of the hallway to the last door on the left, where something heavy thudded to the ground. She twisted the locked doorknob and panic flared hot in her chest. From the other side came another strangled cry.

Cora drew on both the goddess inside her and the suffocating panic lighting her veins on fire and kicked the door, ignoring the sharp pain racing up the nerves of her leg. The wood creaked and splintered, coming loose from the frame before crashing into the room. It was dark beyond the threshold, but the faint glow of moonlight illuminated the space enough for her to see a woman dressed in black, struggling to pull Marcos off the bed.

Acting without thinking, Cora lunged forward. She latched onto the interloper's arms, yanking her backward so hard they both nearly fell to the floor, then used the momentum to slam the other woman to the ground and straddled her chest, drawing the dagger from its sheath.

Wide, fearful eyes tracked the onyx blade as it came to rest on the soft bronze flesh at the base of the woman's neck. Because of her connection to the dead, Cora caught the reflection of the entity behind a wary gaze. Coming face to face with a creature no longer welcome in this world distracted her enough to loosen her grip. Raquel had been right. Whoever or whatever ordered the attack was indeed dangerous.

The other woman took advantage of Cora's momentary distraction, shoving her to the side. She slammed into the corner of the bed, her left shoulder-blade exploding in sharp waves of lightning traveling down the length of her arm. Cora scrambled to her hands and knees, going for the woman's ankles. She flipped the entity on its back and dug her fingers into the soft flesh of the creature's neck. Careful not to pierce the skin just yet, Cora tucked the blade against the fragile spot between the jawbone and left ear. "Who gave you that body?"

The chuckle that escaped the dead woman's lips sent finger like chills climbing up Cora's spine. It was far from anything human. Cora leaned forward. "Tell me, and I'll make your return to the afterlife a quick and painless one."

The woman dropped her head back and let out a piercing bellow that reverberated through Cora's bones. That wasn't just a soul in a stolen body. The power that resonated in the wail was something ancient and savage. Behind them, a trembling cacophony of footsteps bound up the stairs. Cora shoved the blade sideways into its neck, destroying the body and whatever occupied it.

Her breath came in ragged gasps as the creature stilled beneath her. The visceral howl still echoed in her mind like an unwanted caress. Cora squeezed the dagger until her knuckles whitened, and she forced herself to crawl across the floor to the bed. The door to the bedroom slammed shut, and she was on her feet within the span of a heartbeat, only to find Dino covered in sweat and blood. There was a butcher knife in one of his hands that dripped with a dark, almost black ichor.

"Where's Marcos?" he demanded.

She searched the room and nearly fell into another bout of panic when she didn't see him. A hand latched on to her ankle from underneath the bed, prompting her to kneel. The fear in Marcos' pleading stare gave her the strength to pull him out and yank him to his feet. "Thank the gods you are safe."

Dino stood frozen in place, his eyes locked on Marcos, as if afraid to move and shatter the illusion that his son was still alive. Then, in a single desperate motion, he grabbed the boy and pulled him against his chest. After a few seconds, he loosened his grip and asked Cora, "What are those things?"

Rushing across the room, she threw the curtains to the side and peered out of the window. "Abominations."

Dino shoved a chest of drawers in front of the door, bracing against the heavy pounding from the other side. Despite his heightened strength, he was being moved with each hit. "We need to get out of here. Now." His voice cracked on the last word.

She stuck her head out of the open window, calculating the distance from the outlying roof tiles. She'd easily make the drop without hurting herself too much, giving Dino and Marcos a chance to fly to safety. "How many are out there?"

"I don't know. A dozen. Maybe more. Everything happened so fast. As soon as they were inside, they ignored me and ran for the stairs. I tried to head them off." He eyed the butcher knife in his hand. "I'm not sure how I got here before they did."

Cora's chest twisted tighter. She knew exactly what he was feeling. He probably never experienced actual combat when he served in the Royal Naval Reserve. No amount of training could prepare someone for the adrenaline surge that pumped through their veins when faced with true danger.

Movement from the sky drew her attention to the moon. An enormous shadow blotted out the faint light, making her blood ice over. "Shit."

"What?" Dino's voice echoed the fear she fought to suppress. The door shook again, this time accompanied by a loud crack.

She met Dino's stare. "I was hoping you two could fly away from here, but they have their own dragon."

His gaze landed on his son.

"But," Cora said, dragging his attention back to her. "I have an idea. I'm going to need your trust and your body."

He frowned at her but said nothing.

"I need you to be a distraction. Maybe if they see you, they will think we escaped too. I'll get Marcos to safety. Take him somewhere they'll never find him."

Dino opened his mouth to argue, but relented when the door took another splintering hit. "Fine. Whatever. Just make sure he is safe."

Marcos shook his head. "I'm not leaving my dad."

Cora peered out of the window again, craning her neck to the side to make sure no one waited for them over the steep pitch of the roof.

"Don't worry about me," Dino said, his voice taking on a calm bravado. "Go with Cora. I'll be right behind you."

Another few seconds passed, and when the intruders attacked the door again, pieces of wood shot into the room. Taking Marcos by the hand, she stepped onto the rooftop shingles first to make sure there was no one waiting for them before helping him outside. She carefully led him to the edge of the shingles, keeping her back to the log siding. There was a loud crash from somewhere inside the bedroom, and she jerked Marcos around the corner out of sight of the window and watched Dino fly into the air. She hid in the shadows as guttural shouts emanated from inside.

Only after she heard the stampede of heavy footsteps fade did she inch forward, keeping to the shadows.

Marcos' chest rose and fell in quick breaths. "Why are they after me?"

Despite how hard she tried, she failed to keep the worry out of her expression. "I don't know, but we need to move fast. I'm going to open a portal that will take us to someplace safe until I can figure out what's happening."

"A portal? Like what Aunt Darya and Uncle Edwind traveled through?" He shook his head. "Aren't they dangerous?"

"So are the monsters after you," she snapped. Sucking in a soothing breath, she squeezed his hand. "As soon as it's safe, we will come right back."

"What about Dad?"

"He's a lot stronger than you realize, kid. He will be fine." Ronwen was going to kick her ass when she found out about the portal. "This might be uncomfortable."

Cora didn't have time to fully consider where she wanted to go, so she latched on to the first place that came to mind. Somewhere that would get them as far away from there and ensure their safety when they arrived. Pouring all her power into the black blade, she sliced at the air, creating ethereal lines that formed faint symbols that would tear a hole in reality.

She'd attempted this only once before when she tried to visit her brother before the falling out with their father. That was her first and only warning of Fate's laws and the consequences if she broke them. She only hoped Ronwen would show her mercy. Cora was trying to save a life, after all.

Again.

The air split apart, revealing a breathtaking sight of shimmering opalescent colors. They swirled and expanded in a mesmerizing aura that beckoned her to go through. As she gripped the dagger in her left hand, its hum resonated throughout her body, draining her energy with each passing moment. The scent of ozone filled her nostrils, and a crackle of energy swelled around her. The portal was a beautiful yet dangerous gateway, and she was well aware she lacked the strength to keep it open for very long.

She squeezed Marcos' hand. "Okay, kiddo. Hold tight."

A sudden, brutal shove against her spine stole the breath from her lungs. She reached out, instinctively grasping for Marcos, but he slipped through her fingers as she stumbled forward, tumbling into the past.

Chapter 3

THE SOLSTICE FIRE BLAZED against the night sky. Embers spiraled upward, mingling with the twinkling lights blanketing the heavens. Miller leaned against a tall oak tree, watching the people of his tribe celebrate the heart of winter. The ale flowed freely among the revelers as the flickering glow of the pyre illuminated their flushed faces. Sporadic bouts of laughter drowned out the crash of distant waves.

The thick, smoky aroma of burning wood hung in the air, and as Miller breathed in the crisp night, a pang of longing pulled at him to be with his people so he could lose himself in the festivities. This was likely the last time he would be witness to the sacred ceremonies. And with that knowledge, guilt ate at his resolve. After the solstice fires, he planned to leave the island and find the life that awaited him beyond the shores of Didean, but he dreaded the coming talk with his mother.

Every time he attempted to broach the topic of his departure, he stared at the sorrow that haunted a woman who still grieved for her husband. Saebbi left in the spring of ten-ten, expecting to return that same summer. Now, nearly two years later, there was no sign of the ship. Night after night, the whispering waves echoed the ache in their hearts. The pain of the unknown fate that befell his father was palpable.

Despite the guilt that held him captive, Miller dared not stay much longer. His destiny waited for him beyond the sea. It sang to his blood, beckoning him to heed the call. Surely, his mother understood the adventure that enticed his dragon away.

"Why are you not celebrating with the others?"

Miller glanced over his shoulder at the woman, who seemingly appeared out of the dark. Her pale green eyes regarded him with concern and grief.

"I'm not up for the dance."

Gita nodded to the pyre. "You used to love the solstice fires."

Turning his attention to the men and women losing themselves to the music that carried their bodies around the blazing circle, he uncrossed his arms and pushed off the tree, only to be halted by a raised arm.

"Go. Choose a woman to dance with. There is no expectation of commitment. Not tonight."

He blushed. "Some other time, perhaps."

He tried to ignore her unwavering stare, but his gaze was soon drawn to hers. The hardened lines around her mouth and eyes softened. "I wish I could give you solace in your father's absence."

"Have my grandfathers still not found any sign of him?"

She shook her head. "If there was anything to find, they would have done so by now." She urged him toward the others. "I am sure Ester is looking forward to dancing with you."

He didn't have the heart to tell her that what she believed was a strong bond between him and Ester was simply an infatuation they both grew out of. At one time, he thought he loved her but realized his feelings for Ester were that of a dear friend.

Ester spoke of her need to escape from the island and her family's traditions. Her mother lamented the decision to remain on Didean. By the time Winfred made up her mind to leave, she was already pregnant with Ester's older brother. So she chose to stay with the man she loved and abandon her desire to find a life beyond the banks of his home.

That was the trap Miller feared he would fall into if he didn't get away soon. He attempted a smile, but it felt out of place. "Not tonight."

Leaving his mother to stare after him, he wandered into the trees, keeping the sounds of the celebration behind him. He hoped his grandfathers would have found some kind of wreckage to give them closure. It would make his departure more bearable.

The pressure thrust on him to walk the same path as his uncle, a man he never met, was unbearable at times. To live in the shadow of Edwind Wodehal seemed an impossible feat. Miller's father understood the need to escape such a demanding legacy. Saebbi fled from his birthright many years ago, renouncing his claim to an earldom better left to his younger brother.

Before Saebbi's ship disappeared, he kept his mother's expectations manageable. Now that Miller was alone to take on the role of patriarch of Didean, he was drowning in the sheer responsibility of legacy he didn't want.

His grandfathers understood the desire for a life free of Didean. Hengist often told Miller to follow his dragon heart, and in doing so, he could not stay on Didean.

Letting his senses guide him, Miller wove in and out of the trees, unbothered by the darkness or lack of direction. He knew the island well enough that he could have found his way back, even if he had been struck blind and deaf. The freshly fallen snow padded his footsteps, making his voyage into the forest quiet, lost in the fading laughter behind him.

Winter had always been his favorite time of year. The bitter cold was a sharp reminder of nature's ruthless temperament, a stark contrast to the months spent toiling under the sun. Everything they cultivated, everything they bled for, would inevitably be swallowed by ice and silence.

He was so lost in his thoughts that he wasn't prepared when the night split apart with a searing flash, as if the sun had risen in place of the moon. He lifted a hand to his face to block the assault on his eyes. The sound of a someone in distress bounced down the hillside behind him, coming to an abrupt halt when something—or someone—crashed into his chest, sending them both to the frozen ground. Instinctively, he reached around the woman to protect her from the fall. His hands landed on a pair of breasts that fit nicely in his palms.

A sharp elbow jabbed into his side, followed by an even sharper voice. "Get your hands off me, you pervert."

The bite of her words made him release his hold on her. "Forgive me, my lady." He got to his feet, ready to help her up as well, but she was already standing.

"No, no, no." Wild, pale blue eyes searched the darkened woods. "Where is he?"

Miller studied the strange clothing she wore, noting the thin fabric of her dark shirt and the short sleeves that left her arms exposed to the cold. Her breeches were made of a more substantial material but were still insufficient to keep her warm in the snow.

Her gaze landed on him, the intensity of her stare sending a shiver down his spine. "Did you see anyone else come through the rift?"

His skin prickled at the mention of that word. His parents spoke of one that took his uncle into the future to be with his wife and unborn child.

The woman began to shake as she turned in a slow circle, taking in the dark landscape. "I had him in my hand." Her voice quivered as the cold sank deeper into her bones.

Miller removed one of his furs and held it out to her. "Here. This will keep you warm until we reach—"

"Miller!" His mother sprinted into the clearing, breathless. "Thank the gods you are safe. I saw a bright light." Her gaze landed on the woman before him, and her proud posture wilted. With a weary sigh, she muttered, "Not again."

"Again?" Miller said. "Do you know her?"

Gita took the fur from his hand and slung it around the shivering woman. "I do not, but I recognize someone who does not belong in our time. Come," she said. "We should get you inside before you freeze."

The stranger sidestepped his mother's grasp. "I need to find Marcos. He should have come through with me."

Gita nodded to Miller. "Search the island."

He hesitated, eyeing the newcomer.

"I imagine if she has the power to traverse time, she knows what we are."

He met the stranger's pleading gaze for a breath too long before spiraling into the sky.

Cora remained fixed on the crimson dragon, mesmerized by the striking resemblance it bore to Horsa. She marveled at the sight of its massive wings, graceful and silent as it soared off into the distance. When he disappeared from view, she shifted back to a set of sea foam eyes studying her.

The musty scent of the forest invaded her senses, overpowered by the tension in the air. Cora came around, getting caught in the inscrutable gaze of the Wodehal clan. If the man that just leaped into the sky was Miller, then the woman in front of her must be Gita.

"Follow me," the dragoness said.

"I have to find Marcos." Cora meant to follow the rut dug into the ground leading into the darkness of the trees, but Gita blocked her path.

"You know nothing of this island, and your clothes are insufficient to protect you from the cold. If Marcos is lost in these woods, he will be found." The hardness in her gaze left no room for argument.

Desperation clouded Cora's judgment and was tempted to ignore the other woman's commands. She wasn't sure who would emerge the victor in that fight. The wind's frigid bite pushed her to follow Gita through the trees.

Not far into their walk, they came upon an open valley where a blazing bonfire licked at the sky as men and women celebrated among the warmth of its heat. Beyond the fire, she saw an outline of a tall stone tower attached to the infamous castle Darya and Edwind spoke of.

It loomed overhead, sparking something inside her, deep within that place where her powers dwelled. As she passed through the open gate, her skin tingled like the very air around the stones was alive with an ancient energy welcoming her. She paused at the double doors, the golden light promising respite from the bitter cold.

"Does something trouble you?" Gita asked.

Cora's gaze wandered over the gray stone and the glowing candelabras inside the doorway. "Not really. I just got a creepy sense of déjà vu." When she looked at Gita again, the dragoness had a confused expression on her face. "Nothing. I'm fine."

Gita nodded and continued to lead her to a small room where a fire waited for them. She swept her arm toward the chair near the hearth. "Sit. I will have some tea brought to us."

The warmth of the flames was a welcome sensation on Cora's chilled face, but it did little to take away the icy dread that ate at her guts. She kept going over the last few seconds before she fell through the doorway into the past. She was sure Marcos had been right there behind her. The damn portal jumbled her memories, yet she had a lingering sense of being pushed from behind.

"Drink this." Gita's silent approach snapped Cora out of her thoughts. After setting the cup on the table between the chairs, she sat down, her stare holding Cora still. "It will take the chill from your blood."

Cora stared at the dark liquid briefly before bringing it to her nose. The cinnamon-ginger blend was soothing, yet there was another unfamiliar scent tickling the back of her mind. The warm tea trickled down her throat, banishing the shiver rippling through her muscles. She closed her eyes, appreciating the calming effects of the herbs. It was a brief sensation, however. Sooner than later, she would have to explain her presence.

"When you're ready," Gita began. "You can tell me your name."

Cora set the cup down and met Gita's stare. "You didn't have to put those herbs in my drink. I am more than willing to be honest with you."

For the first time since their meeting, Gita's calm facade slipped, and her expression shifted to surprise. "Who are you? Why are you here?"

"My name is Cora. As I'm sure you've already guessed, I'm like Darya. Although I was raised to control my magic. What they did to her was stupid and dangerous. Letting her live her life, ignorant of the power she wielded, nearly got her killed." She blew out a hard breath. "As to why I'm here, I didn't know where else to go. Who else to turn to."

Heavy footsteps echoed down the hall, drawing her attention to the doorway. When Miller entered empty-handed, her heart sank.

"There are no other strangers on the island, aside from you, my lady," Miller said.

Cora stood, narrowing her gaze, trying to discern whether he was telling the truth. The fire cast flickering shadows across his face, sharpening the angles of his jaw and glinting off the russet threads woven through his beard. His sea foam eyes, set beneath thick brows, held the same noble integrity as the rest of his kin. He had no reason to lie. Her fear was messing with rational thought.

She started pacing the length of the room. If Marcos wasn't there, he had to be in nineteen ninety-two. "One of those monsters must have taken him." She spoke more to herself than the others. Lifting her stare to Gita, she said, "I have to go back."

"Go back where?" Gita asked. "Is Marcos a lover? Your husband?"

She shook her head, appalled at Gita's questions. "Goddess, no. He's only a child. I was trying to protect him."

"Protect him from what? Where is it you come from?"

Cora chewed at her lower lip. What harm could it do to tell them some of the truth? "Nineteen ninety-two."

Gita's mouth lifted into a wide smile. "That is where my brother traveled. Can you tell me of Edwind and Darya? How are little Brigita and Saebastian?"

Cora stared at the dragoness. "How do you know about the children?" Waving a dismissive hand, she said, "Never mind. It doesn't matter." After a brief hesitation, she went on. "Edwind and his family are great. Happy as can be."

"Is Marcos your child?" Miller asked.

"No. He's your—" She pressed her lips together, worried she was about to say too much.

Miller straightened. "He is my what?"

"I hope I don't get in trouble for this," she mumbled to herself. After a few seconds, she met Miller's stare. "He's one of your descendants."

Gita clasped her hands together. "So, you do give me grand-children."

A bright hue of red ran up Miller's neck while, at the same time, the color drained from his face.

Cora took the opportunity to slip past him, heading outdoors. Her skin crawled at the thought of having to open another doorway home. She didn't think she had the strength, but what choice did she have? Taking the dagger from her belt, she drew in a steadying breath, gathering what magic she could grasp.

"What are you doing?" Gita asked.

"I have to go back." Cora moved the blade with purpose, ready-ing herself for the amount of energy it would take to tear open the hole through time and space.

Miller was at her side as the world split wide, making them both squint against the brilliant shimmering lights. "I'm coming with you," he announced.

"You will do no such thing," Gita demanded.

"Whatever danger Lady Cora is facing is perilous enough for her to risk wandering through time. If she is to keep this descendent of mine safe, she will need another ally by her side."

"She does not need your sword." The panic in Gita's words was palpable.

His expression hardened, but Cora cut off his next thought. "Your mum is right. You will only get in the way."

While he was distracted, Cora rushed forward, knowing it was only a matter of seconds before her strength dissipated. The last thing she heard before plunging into the portal was Gita shouting Miller's name.

The ground heaved beneath Miller's feet as he stumbled free of the swirling rift. Harsh, unnatural light pierced his vision, making his head spin like the world itself was being ripped apart. He fumbled for something—anything to keep himself upright, gripping the first steady object within his reach.

All around him, odd flickering lights burned his sight. The air smelled of something sharp and metallic. The ground beneath him was too smooth, too perfect. This was not his world. His heart pounded in his chest as his senses fought the reality of the unfamiliar surroundings. Sharp angles, glowing rectangles, and a deafening stillness were unlike anything he'd ever known. After a while, his vision cleared, and he studied the foreign confines of the small space. His fingers brushed over the soft fabric of the chair he clung to, the sensation as exotic as the strange sights around him.

Sounds of hurried footsteps above his head drew his focus away from the new surroundings. "Lady Cora," he called. Pain lacerated his mind from the effort of speaking, but he ignored the discomfort and rushed up the set of stairs to his left. He stumbled along the railing, trying to keep his vision from clouding over again.

He reached the top of the landing and sensed someone just out of his periphery, catching a wooden stick with one hand before it made contact with his head. He yanked the object out of the stranger's grip and, with a swift motion, pulled the man off balance, causing him to stumble. Then Miller shoved his shoulder forward. The impact was accompanied by a loud thud against the far wall, but he was then knocked backward from a punch to his chin, giving the other man the opportunity to run them both down the hall, sending them tumbling through an open window to the ground below.

As soon as Miller landed, he was crushed by the heavy weight of a black talon. A pair of fierce, flaming orbs glowered at him. The dragon's lips peeled back, revealing a set of curved teeth ready to bite off his head. His own dragon emerged, and he flipped his foe backward, rolling him past the house. He saw Cora round the corner, skidding to a stop at the scene before her.

Her gaze darted between them, then landed on the man who was picking himself off the ground. "Dino, what's going on?" She glanced to her left. "What are you doing here?"

"You know him?" Dino asked, taking a slow step forward.

Miller released his dragon.

She moved in between the two men. "Yeah, kind of. It's not important right now. Where's Marcos?"

Anger melted into dread. "I thought he was with you. You told me you'd get him to safety. Somewhere they wouldn't find him."

"I tried. I had him in my hands. When I got to the other side, he wasn't with me."

Dino's jaw went slack. "The other side of what? Did you take him through a portal? Oh my god, Cora. What were you thinking? He could be anywhere. He could be in any time."

She shook her head. "He's not lost in time. I don't think he made it through with me."

"That's not any better." Dino ran his hands through his hair, his face pinched with fear. "You should have taken him to Edwind and Darya. He would have been safe with them. How could you do something so reckless?"

Miller stepped up beside Cora. "Calm yourself. Lady Cora went to a lot of trouble to save the boy, and you treat her as if she made this happen."

Dino glanced between them. "Who is he?"

Unable to meet his stare, Cora waved a hand at Miller. "Your great, great, great whatever, grandfather."

"You brought one of my ancestors here? From when?"

"Ten-twelve."

Dino's mouth dropped open again. "Ten-twelve? That would make him..." He let the sentence fall off.

"Gita and Saebbi's son. Yes." She finished.

"Jesus Christ, Cora. Do you understand how dangerous that is? You could have killed my whole family line."

She shot a frustrated glare beside her, sending a not so unpleasant shiver down Miller's spine. "I didn't plan for him to follow me."

"Well, send him back before something happens and we no longer exist."

"I will. First, tell me what happened after I left."

"I tried to lead those goons away. When I returned, everyone was gone. I went to look for you and Marcos." He pointed to Miller. "That's when he appeared. I thought he was one of them."

"We are going to find Marcos. I promise."

"Just like you promised to keep him safe. They have my son."
Dino's voice cracked despite the fury in his words. He doubled
over, pressing his hands onto his knees, his breath coming in
short, ragged bursts. He looked past Cora, past Miller, as if
trying to will Marcos back into existence. "He's just a kid," he
whispered. "Alone. Terrified."

She squeezed her fingers into fists. "I will find him," she whispered.

Dino's eyes shimmered with a dangerous crimson glow. "I
don't care what you must do or who you have to ask for help.
Find Marcos and bring him back to me." He sliced the space
between them with a glare, landing on Miller. "And send him
back to where he belongs."

Miller crossed his arms. "I'm not going anywhere until I am
sure Marcos is safe."

"You aren't staying here and potentially killing my bloodline."

Until that moment, Miller was content to keep out of their
fight. It wasn't his place to insert himself into the bitter nuances
of these peoples' lives. There was obviously more to their past
than a missing child, and as much as he loathed the way his own
blood spoke to Lady Cora, he was not there to disrupt whatever
path they had chosen together. Yet if Dino thought he would best
Miller in any form of combat, that was the line not to be crossed
lightly. "I do not like how you speak to me, nor do I care for how
you are treating Lady Cora."

"Lady?" Dino scoffed.

Miller dropped his arms and stood to his full height, bringing
himself to tower over the other man. "Do you wish to continue
our fight?"

Dino grabbed his side, wincing from the blow Miller landed. "I'll see that Edwind puts a stop to this."

Miller froze at the mention of that name. "Uncle Edwind is here?"

Cora blocked Dino's path. "If you do that, you're only going to make things harder to find Marcos."

"It doesn't matter if we get wiped out because of your stupidity." He saw the darkness fall over Miller's face and rushed around the house.

She made a full circle before saying, "This isn't good." Heaving a weary sigh, she mustered a tired smile. "I need to send you home."

"Lady Cora—"

"Just Cora," she said. "I'm not royalty."

He set his mouth into a determined scowl. "I will not be bullied by that arrogant ass of a man."

"He's not wrong. You don't belong here. There's no telling what kind of damage we've already done."

"I wish to help save this descendent of mine. Dino still lives. My presence has changed nothing thus far." He frowned at her. "You risked the wrath of the gods to keep Marcos from harm. That alone speaks volumes about the danger you face."

She started walking away, silently dismissing him. He caught up to her and noted how her lips were drawn into a tight, puckered grimace. He watched her eyes tracing something unseen while her muscles wound ever tighter. Her gaze drifted to the darkness of the surrounding forest. "Edwind is going to lose his mind when he finds out what I've done." She pushed past him. "At least you can meet your uncle before he murders me."

"Surely, Uncle Edwind will be reasonable when you explain your actions."

Cora paused. The look on her face was stunned disbelief. "Reasonable? I inadvertently dragged his nephew a thousand years into the future, potentially screwing up whole generations of his bloodline. I think the best I can hope for is something just shy of homicidal."

Miller's mouth fell into a pinched expression. He wasn't sure what to make of her answer, but judging from her tone, he had a feeling she knew Uncle Edwind well enough to be afraid. If his uncle could strike that kind of fear in a woman such as Cora, perhaps his parents didn't know the true man behind the name Edwind Wodehal.

Chapter 4

Cora whipped the Mercedes onto the narrow, two-lane road that would take her to Edwind and Darya's house. Miller was in the passenger seat, latched on the dash as if expecting to be thrown through the windshield at any moment. His eyes darted from side to side as the scenery flew by. She recognized the panic of a man who didn't have a clue about what modern transportation was all about.

Tempering her anxiety, she lifted her foot off the accelerator, letting the car slow to a normal speed. "Sorry."

"For what?" he asked, keeping a watchful stare on the darkness outside the windows.

"I forget that you've never experienced this kind of travel. Though I'd imagine these speeds don't compare to flying."

He tore his gaze from the windshield. "I am in control when I fly."

She saw his fingers unclench, so she kept talking, grasping at any subject to keep his mind off the drive. "From what I've been told, it took Edwind a while to get used to the future. I guess I was lucky. I got to ease into modern marvels such as cars and electricity."

"Are you from another time?"

She leaned back, easing up her own grip on the steering wheel. "In a way. I was born in the early nineteen hundreds."

Miller pulled his hands from the dash and relaxed into the seat. He stared at his lap for a few seconds. "You are not much younger than my mother."

That drew an embarrassed laugh. "I guess being compared to your mum is better than being called an old hag."

"That is not what I meant."

She shot him a cheeky grin. "I'm just giving you a hard time. It's been interesting watching the world grow and develop over the last handful of decades. I can't begin to fathom the changes Hengist and Horsa have lived through. They've witnessed entire civilizations rise, fall, turn to dust, then start all over again." She grimaced at the thought. "To have loved and lost as much as they have is incomprehensible."

"Have you not experienced such affection in the last century?"

She glanced to the side, not meeting his stare. "You don't live as long as I have without developing feelings, but it never lasts."

"Do you think that one day you may find a love like Uncle Edwind and Aunt Darya? Or my mother and father?"

Frowning at the odd question, she said, "That kind of love isn't meant for everyone."

He sat back, staring out the window for a long time. A sharp exhale broke the silence. "I would rather live a life free to explore, to experience adventures of my own making."

"I hate to burst your bubble, but eventually, you find someone who tames that adventuring spirit of yours."

He snorted out a scoff. "One day, a woman may do just that, but for now, I plan to make my own way in the world before I have to be tied down to the responsibilities of a wife and children."

She didn't have the heart to tell him that, according to Horsa, it was going to happen when he returned to Didean. "You make it sound like a curse to be saddled with a family."

"Do you wish to be tethered to the monotony of such an existence?"

"Who's to say it has to be so boring?"

"You don't understand. The woman I am destined for may not share my desires for a life outside the island. Once I am committed, I will honor my vows, even if it means my own misery. I would like to have had a taste of what the world can offer before I resign myself to that fate."

Understanding tugged at Cora, but she knew more than anyone that Fate's will was not a mere suggestion. Whatever escape Miller hoped to find was only a brief reprieve from his final destination.

To her relief, Darya's drive came into view so she didn't have to continue what was turning out to be an awkward exchange. "We're here."

She shifted the car into neutral, then set the hand brake, but hesitated before getting out. The door to the Wodehal house loomed ahead like a waiting predator, ready to devour her whole as soon as she stepped over the threshold. Pushing aside her nervousness, she climbed out of the driver's seat and started up the stone walk. She hadn't gotten within a few feet of the oak door when it was yanked open, revealing a scowling Edwind.

"What have you done?"

The force of his anger made her take an involuntary step back into Miller's unmoving frame. He touched her shoulders and gently moved her to the side.

"Uncle Edwind?"

Edwind's angry features softened at the sight of the man now standing at her side. "You have your mother's eyes." He pulled his nephew into a tight embrace. "I never thought I'd have the chance to meet my sister's child." With an arm still around his neck, he walked Miller inside, ignoring Cora for the time being.

Darya stood beside the three-seater settee, where Dino sat staring into a cup of dark liquid.

"My love," Edwind said. "This is Gita and Saebbi's son, Miller." He turned to the young man. "How old are you, boy?"

"Twenty-eight."

"How is your father? How's Saebbi?"

Miller's smile melted into confusion. "I thought Grandfather Horsa would have told you."

"Told me what? Did something happen to him?"

Miller glanced between his aunt and uncle. "His ship was lost at sea. He will have been gone two years next spring."

Darya took Edwind's hand. "I'm so sorry. I know how close you were." To Miller, she said, "How is Gita?"

"She tries to be strong for me, but I see how much she misses him."

Edwind shook his head. "Why didn't Father tell me any of this?"

Darya patted his arm. "He knows you were like brothers. Maybe he wanted to spare you that pain."

Cora watched Dino fidget with his cup. His eyes flicked from Edwind to Miller, the struggle not to jump into their conversation etched in his weary expression. At one point, he set his tea on the coffee table, but every time he opened his mouth to cut in, he squeezed it shut again, unable or unwilling to interrupt.

Taking in a steadying breath, Cora said, "As much as I'd love to stand here and listen to you two reminisce about your lives and families, we should get on to finding Marcos."

Edwind's glare threatened to suffocate her with the sheer weight of it. She didn't mean to pull the full force of his wrath, but she wouldn't let Dino take the brunt of his anger.

"You shouldn't have brought Miller here. It's dangerous for him in such an unfamiliar environment. Not to mention what it could do to his descendants."

Miller's pleasant demeanor vanished. "Do not put the blame on Cora. I snuck into the portal. She tried to stop me."

Cora crossed her arms, fighting to keep her gaze on Edwind. "I'll let you flay me alive later. Right now, we have more important things to worry about."

"Marcos would still be here if you hadn't taken him through that fucking portal in the first place." The vitriol in Dino's tone pierced Cora's heart.

"There was no other way." Her voice was barely above a whisper.

"You should have run while I distracted them."

"That would have never worked. They had us surrounded."

Darya stepped in between them. "You both did what you thought was best for Marcos."

Cora glanced from Dino to Darya. "As soon as I got a glimpse of the monster trying to get at him, I knew I didn't have a choice. Somehow, someone figured out a way to snatch dangerous creatures from the underworld and shove them into mortal bodies like meat puppets."

Darya made a face. "I imagine Arawn isn't happy about that."

"I doubt he knows. Hell, I didn't know what I was up against until tonight. If I had, I could have been more prepared."

"Are you one of Arawn's Death Knights?" Miller asked. "Grandfather Hengist told me stories about them."

Dino snorted, but Darya silenced him with a single glare.

Cora ignored the question and paced the length of the settee. The smart and easy thing to do would be to make a quick trip to the underworld and tell her father what was happening to his precious souls, but after their last altercation, she had no way of getting there. Even if she managed to open a doorway to his realm, she wasn't sure he wouldn't lock her away like he did other unfortunate individuals who garnered his wrath. Besides, other than her word, what proof did she have?

Coming around to face Edwind, she said, "There's a shit hole pub in the city. The guy that runs it has his hands in some shady business, both in the mortal and supernatural worlds. He owes me a favor. I can ask him to poke a few holes and see what he can stir up."

"We don't have that kind of time to waste." Dino's tone was just short of pleading. "We need to find my son."

Edwind held up a hand, cutting off Cora. "What else do you suggest we do? We have zero leads. At least Cora is offering to do something."

Dino's shoulders fell, and he dropped his head. "Fine. Let's fucking go, then."

Miller followed Dino and Cora to the front door, but Edwind stopped him. "What are you doing?"

"I am going with them."

"Absolutely not," Edwind and Dino said in unison.

"You are too important to my family to take the chance of anything happening to you," Dino added.

"And to your mother," Edwind said.

Miller's shoulders tightened. "I am not a child. I wish you and this pompous descendant of mine would stop treating me as such."

Edwind refused to relent. "You have no idea how to survive in this world. Things are so much different here."

Dino motioned toward the door. "In fact, Cora should send you home before we leave. Just to be safe."

Cora looked between the three men and shook her head back and forth. "Have you all gone mad?"

All eyes turned to her.

"I may not be familiar with the eleventh century, but I'm pretty damn sure it's a lot more wild and untamed than nineteen ninety-two." She motioned a hand up and down Miller's broad frame. "And have you seen your nephew? Not only does he share your dragon blood, but he's also built like a Viking god. He can take on both of you without breaking a sweat."

Edwind folded his arms, ready to argue, but she cut him off.

"The creatures who took Marcos are dangerous. Who or whatever snatched them from the underworld without Arawn noticing is even more so. Right now, we need all the help we can get. Miller is a grown man who can take care of himself. Or do you think you aren't strong enough to protect him?" As soon as she said those last words, her skin prickled with unease, fearing that she had pushed Edwind too far.

Miller broke the silence that grew to a dangerous level. "I like her. She speaks with sense."

She opened the front door. "I'm going to search for Marcos. You're all welcome to join me."

Edwind sighed, then nodded to the open door. "I suppose it will be safe enough to take him into the city."

Dino rushed in front of the men. "I'm not letting him go out there and risk his life and our lineage."

"He won't be alone. We will be there." Edwind said. "Besides, I doubt you can stop him even if you tried."

Dino raised his gaze to Miller, who stood two inches taller. "Fine. Try not to die and kill off our entire family line."

"I'll do my best," Miller said.

Cora climbed into the driver's seat, disappointed when Dino joined her up front. Edwind and Miller folded themselves into the cramped back seat, appearing uncomfortable. "We can take your car," she told Edwind.

"This will do."

Dino glared at her from the passenger seat. "I swear, Cora, if anything happens to Marcos, I will never forgive you."

She gripped the steering wheel, biting back a terse reply. If anything happened to that kid, she'd never forgive herself. She flipped the radio on before shifting into reverse, forgetting she'd been blasting at nearly full volume earlier that evening. Miller jumped and pushed himself back in the seat, his eyes wide with wonder.

Dino turned it back off. "Are you trying to deafen us?"

"Turn it back on," Miller said. "I like it."

She reached for the knob again but dialed the volume down to a more acceptable level.

"What is this called?"

"Music. Rock and roll, to be more exact." She eyed him in the rearview mirror. "You have good taste."

Segomo stared out of the darkened window of the vehicle, ignoring the glistening swamp water eyes that scrutinized him through malformed lids. The air reeked of damp rot and oiled leather, mixed with the faint metallic tang of something far fouler. Long, twisted legs stretched awkwardly across the small expanse between them, forcing Segomo to hug the door so as not to be touched by the Fomorian. He wondered how Indech was comfortable folding himself into such a confined space, yet there he was, lounging like a king.

A gnarled, bony hand stroked the pale hair of the boy who lay unconscious next to Indech. "You are much more efficient than I could have hoped. I expected more losses, the way you spoke of those dragons."

Ignoring the preening of his ego, Segomo struggled to keep from drumming his fingers on the door. It was an impatient habit he'd picked up in his youth and one that he had never outgrown in the thousands of years since. The appearance of the little goddess had been nearly as jarring as waking in such a strange new world. Her presence greatly complicated things.

Yet, when he thought about spending one more second trapped in that endless purgatory, his endearment for her wouldn't dissuade him from his path. He had tasted the sweetness of freedom, and no one would stand in his way. Not even his little sister.

"You look worried."

Segomo forced his gaze to the ruined face of the demon. "You don't understand the pandora's box you've unleashed, taking the boy."

Indech shifted in the seat, and the leather groaned under his oversized frame. "Yet here you are, unharmed. Hidden from their wrath."

Segomo's mouth twitched as he fought a sneer. "The dragons you stole from are more formidable than most. As you pointed out, I once commanded their patriarch. The Death Dragon will not take this slight against him lightly."

"I fear neither gods nor dragons."

Segomo tilted his head slowly, a faint smirk tugging at his mouth. "Your kind rarely feel fear until it is far too late."

Indech matched his grin. "I expect you to be as diligent in your next assignment. The tome is of utmost importance in opening the way for my father to walk once again among us."

"The grimoire has been lost for eons. I do not believe Fate herself knows of its location." Lucky for Segomo, he spent most of his time imprisoned in the underworld, gleaning information he shouldn't be privy to. "When I find it, I expect my mantle restored."

Indech stopped petting the boy's hair, the twisted smile fading. "You are in no position to alter our bargain. You will reap your rewards only when Tethra is freed from his prison.

Segomo exited the vehicle but bent down, meeting the Fomorian's sickly gaze. "I have had a long time to reflect on my past mistakes. I think hubris was my biggest downfall. It brings even the strongest of us to our knees."

Indech made a dismissive motion with a gnarled finger, and the door shut on its own, leaving Segomo to watch the red orbs disappear over the hill.

Behind him, dim yellow lights painted the wet pavement with muted streaks. He was glad he hadn't mentioned Cora. If she was involved with the boy's family, there was no doubt in his mind that she would fight for him with the ferocity of the warrior goddess he trained her to be. Yet it was that stubborn, unyielding fire that was her most fatal flaw. Despite the simmering resentment he still held for the gods, Cora was as much a victim in the tapestry as every other poor soul trapped in the confines of Fate's grand designs.

And that was why she must be kept far from this war.

"We should go."

Segomo glanced over his shoulder at the woman leaning on the vehicle. Pushing Cora to the back of his thoughts, he climbed into the seat, the glossy material cold against his palms. Seeking out Marshall again wasn't ideal, but given the little resources he had to work with, what other option did he have? His jaw tightened as he stared straight ahead, already regretting what came next, but regret didn't change necessity. "Take me to the warlock."

Cora did her best to ignore the pointed stares from Dino, focusing instead on the boisterous conversation between Edwind and Miller. They shared stories of their time on Didean, comparing their experiences. Miller spoke of his parents and how their lives had changed since Edwind's departure, and in turn, Edwind told him of his life in the future and his new role as a husband and father.

When the discussion turned to Hengist, Dino shifted in his seat, staring over his shoulder in disbelief.

Edwind chuckled at a particularly gaudy tale of Hengist and his unseemly conquests. "Sometimes I wonder how that old dragon has survived this long."

"Is it possible to see my grandfathers while I'm here?" Miller asked.

"I hope you will be long gone before they return."

Cora pulled into a dark alley, its slick pavement glittering faintly under the dim streetlight. A three-story industrial building loomed ahead, with a rust-streaked facade slouching under years of neglect. Trash and forgotten debris littered the cracked asphalt. "We have arrived, gentlemen."

Edwind stared at the faded sign of the only business left in the outdated building. "The Snake Pit?"

"Real classy, yeah?"

Dino snorted. "You weren't kidding when you called it a shit hole."

She peered past Edwind to Miller, who studied the surrounding high-rises across the street. "I'm sorry for getting him mixed up in this. I had no intention of bringing him here. He's as pushy and stubborn as the rest of you Wodehal men."

Following her gaze, Edwind's pensive scowl vanished. "I have to admit, I am grateful to have met him. I want so badly to take the children back to the Didean I remember, but I dare not risk it. What if something terrible happens to them while we are there?"

"For once, your paranoia is a good thing. Time travel is dangerous, despite how carelessly the gods like to trample along its threads. I suppose when Morigan tires of undoing their meddling ways, she will put an end to it."

"Hopefully not before Brigita comes into her powers," he said with a half grin.

"You're still here, so that fate is already woven." She nodded to where Miller was walking toward them. "As is his. So long as Dino continues to exist, all is right with the grand scheme."

She pushed off the car and headed for the door. "Anyway, I'll go in, talk to my guy, and be out in ten minutes, tops. You boys enjoy the ambiance."

Miller made a move to follow. "You're going in alone?"

She raised a coppery eyebrow at Edwind. "He's just like you. Overprotective to a fault." To Miller, she said, "I'm a big girl. If I need help, I'll let you know. Enjoy your little adventure." Then gave him a quick wink.

Dino met her at the door. "I don't care if you think you want help or not; if this man of yours knows anything about Marcos, I'm going in with you."

"If I need a master of strategic retreats, you'll be the first person I call. Wait here."

She wasn't surprised to walk into a near-empty bar. The smell of stale beer and mildew made her stomach lurch, but she pushed down the pang of nausea and weaved through the vacant tables to the back of the asymmetrical room where a man leaned against a dingy faux wood bar that had at one time been polished to a mirror shine. Now, it looked as old and tired as the surrounding buildings.

"Where's the boss man?" She asked, pulling the bartender's attention from the telly.

Teodor flicked a bored gaze at her and turned back to the football game. "He's with someone."

"It's important. I need to speak with him now."

"I can't say when he will be free."

"Well, tell him I'm here and that it's urgent."

He kept his focus on the black-and-white screen. "You're not that important."

She loathed that golem with a passion. He was given the same arrogant personality as his creator. "And you," she hissed, "are a useless waste of magic and body parts."

Ignoring his protests, she squeezed around the bar, the putrid smell of the place further invading her nostrils. When she reached the door that led to Marshall's back office, she pushed it open with a sense of relief.

The clean air was an oasis from the pub. As much as she despised Marshall and his little pet, he was a powerful warlock and a well of information both in the mundane and metaphysical worlds.

Marshall sat forward in his chair. "Isn't this a lovely surprise?" His body was coiled tight, as if he was ready to bolt to his feet at any second. He glanced between Cora and the fellow sitting across from him.

She took a moment to survey the stranger, scanning his appearance before cautiously making her way toward the desk. The man had an unremarkable appearance about him, as if he was intentionally blending in with the rest of the room. His flat brown hair was slicked back and revealed a glimpse of the slightly darker shade of brown in his eyes.

He turned in his seat, and she noted he had a thin, wiry frame. But she saw past his unassuming facade. He was more dangerous than he appeared by the way his gaze held on to hers for longer than was comfortable.

"Who's the goon?" She asked, keeping herself far enough away that he couldn't reach out and touch her.

"I do have other associates. And we were in the middle of a meeting."

She shot the other man one last wary look before returning to Marshall, "I need to speak to you. Alone."

Marshall leaned back in the chair and reached for a lighter for the ever-present cigar hanging from his mouth. "Whatever you have to say to me, you can say in front of my new business partner."

"I don't think so." She didn't bother hiding the disdain in her voice.

The wiry man stood, holding out his hands in a placating gesture. "I'll step outside and let the lady have her privacy. Her business sounds more urgent than mine."

When they were alone, Cora turned back to Marshall. "You keep good company."

He shrugged and, with the slightest movements of his fingers, produced a single flame and lit the cigar's tip. After taking a few quick puffs, he said, "It takes all kinds, love. What can I do for you?"

"Have you heard of anything weird going on in the city lately?"

He blew a perfectly round smoke ring. "I deal with a lot of weird shit. You need to be a little more specific."

"There's a group of—" She bit at her lower lip. "I'm not sure what they are—were. All I know is that they don't belong in this world. Not anymore. Has anyone been trying their hands at summoning the dead?"

"As in a medium?"

"No. Not just talking to them. I mean, pulling their dead asses from the underworld and putting them into bodies up here."

Marshall took the cigar from his mouth and set it in the ashtray on the corner of the desk. "That's going to take a very powerful entity. Is Arawn aware of this?"

"Do you see the city overrun with Death Knights?" She crossed her arms. "Can you put some feelers out? See if you can turn up anything for me?"

"Sure. What exactly am I searching for?"

She considered how much she should tell him. It was one thing to utilizing his expertise now and then, but he wasn't trustworthy. "Someone took a kid. I want him back."

"That's not a lot to go on."

"It's enough."

He snuffed out the cigar and stood. "Because I like you, I'll see what I can turn up. I'll give you a call if I hear anything." She was at the door when he added, "Send my associate back in on your way out."

The creep was sitting at the bar, swirling a glass of light amber liquid, sharing a snarky grin with Teodor. When he saw Cora, his lips widened into a genuine smile.

"I hope you two had a productive chat." His voice had a subtle brogue that made the hair on her arms stand on end. It was as if a slithering serpent had wrapped itself around her mind, squeezing at memories she had long tried to bury.

"Marshall is asking for you," she muttered.

He tipped the glass at Teodor and sauntered past Cora toward the back room. On his way by, she caught the unmistakable hint of the same magic she sensed on the creatures who attacked them at Dino's house.

Her reaction was swift. One hand went for the dagger, but the man saw her intention and threw the liquor aside, using his free hand to stop the black blade from piercing his chest. He slid his other arm into the crook of her elbows, locking it against her back and pinning her to the front of him. She clamped her mouth shut, fighting against the pain of his ruthless grip.

"Now, now, Little Goddess. We can't have you mussing those delicate hands of yours."

A wave of nausea swept over Cora, making her skin grow cold and clammy. She wanted to vomit, but not from the stench of the cheap whisky on the man's breath. What sickened her—no, what frightened her to the core was hearing that pet name. Only one person ever used it, and he was supposed to be locked away in the underworld for the rest of eternity.

No matter who was being slipped out from under her father's nose, her brother should not have been so easily stolen from the underworld.

His voice softened. "I've missed you, Coramagda. We have so much to catch up on."

Chapter 5

"CORA SHOULD BE OUT by now." Miller paced back and forth in front of the metal entrance, willing it to open and have Cora join them. The thought of her alone in such an unsavory place sent chills of unease through his blood. The very air reeked of rot, and not just from the filth that littered the surrounding area. For a moment, Miller wondered if he made the right choice, following Cora. What if his presence simply made things worse for his descendants?

Dino caught his attention by tapping a round jeweled bracelet on his wrist. "It's only been fifteen minutes."

Edwind frowned. "I agree with Miller. She isn't one to tarry in times like these."

That was all the permission Miller needed. He ignored the doubts circling his mind and pushed his way inside. A putrid stench permeated the air inside the small tavern, but his sights were focused on the short, rounded man half hidden behind the ale-board. Though the construction was much more refined than some Miller had seen in his travels, it was not well cared for. He couldn't imagine actually eating or drinking from such a disgusting surface.

The stout man's dark eyes flicked to the door to his left him, then back to the newcomers. "What can I do for you, gentlemen?"

Miller tracked the hand that slipped beneath the stained wood. Moving on instinct, he shot forward, snatching the little man by the throat. "I suggest you keep your hands where we can see them."

Edwind eased up beside Miller. "Where is she?"

"Who?" His voice trembled against Miller's hold.

Miller squeezed harder, stopping short of cutting off his air supply.

"Oh, her." The tavern keeper rasped, flicking his eyes behind him again. "In there."

"Stay with the bartender," Edwind told Dino.

Edwind approached the back room. Miller didn't hesitate before kicking in the flimsy piece of wood, nearly splintering it in two. Before they were over the threshold, the man closest to them drew Cora from the chair. He held a black blade to her delicate throat. Miller recognized it as the one she used to open the portal.

Cora tested her captors' hold as she glared at Miller and Edwind. "I told you to wait for me." Her tone was as angry as her expression.

Miller eyed the other men. "It seems we are here to rescue you."

"This asshole won't do anything." She shoved back at her captor. "Or maybe you will. Go on, Segomo. Do it. Arawn's not here to stop you."

Miller studied her, trying to decide if she was more furious or scared. She struggled to hold on to her captor's arms so that the blade wouldn't pierce her flesh. For a brief moment, their eyes locked, and he knew it was fear that gripped her.

"This isn't about you, Coramagda." The man she called Segomo moved the knife away from her skin but kept it near her
throat.

Miller took a step forward, and Segomo tightened his hold on
both the dagger and Cora.

"Do not move, boy," Segomo warned, pressing the blade just
enough to indent the flesh on her neck.

Edwind snatched Miller's arm, drawing him back.

"I am going to drag you to your prison myself," Cora seethed.

"You can try." Segomo shifted, pulling Cora closer. "The little
goddess is coming with us. As long as you two keep your distance,
she will remain unharmed."

She relaxed into his arms. "Segomo."

"Yes?" he cooed.

"You're a bloody idiot."

His smile faltered.

"Whoever broke you out of your prison didn't trust you any
more than the rest of us. That's why you're stuck in that pathetic
body."

Understanding flickered across his face a second before she
flung her head back, sending his arms flailing wildly. He quickly
recovered, putting a hand to his nose. Before she could grab onto
the dagger, he brought up a foot and shoved her with just enough
force to send her flailing forward.

Miller reached her before she fell to the ground, and as soon
as she got her footing, she whirled around. He tried to hang on
to her, but she slipped free, bolting for the door in the room's far
corner. Segomo slammed it shut after him, but Cora was quick
enough to keep it from hitting her.

Miller made it outside in time to see Cora disappear out of
sight. He shot forward when he heard her voice break through

the silence of the cramped space. It wasn't a cry of panic or pain, but of sheer frustration laced with rage.

A few seconds later, she came stomping back toward the bar, her fists pumping open and closed. "Where is he?" she demanded.

Edwind followed behind her. "Who?"

"Teodor. The bartender." She pushed past Miller. "He is going to tell me everything I need to know."

Cora had an arm around Teodor's neck, dragging him out of the tiny storeroom into the main pub when Miller and Edwind returned. Dino struggled to his feet, rubbing the back of his head. He glanced down at his shirt, futilely brushing at the grime that stained his clothes. She met Miller's stare for only a heartbeat before heaving Teodor on the bar top. Using a stool, she climbed up and swung her legs over the golem, straddling his chest. He squirmed until she latched onto his throat, squeezing.

When she glanced to the side, Edwind stared at her, wide eyed and unsure. Knowing what she was about to do broke through the rage that threaten to burn her from the inside out. Keeping her voice low, she said, "I suggest you take a walk. I'll be done with this meat suit shortly."

Miller crossed his arms. "I'm not leaving."

"None of us are," Edwind agreed.

She set her mouth in a determined frown. In the back of her mind, she knew the dangers of letting them stay, but she didn't have time to argue with those stubborn men. Turning her attention to Teodor, she muttered, "Fine. Have it your way."

Teodor grasped at the hand at his throat. "Please, I don't know what's going on. I'm just a bartender. Marshall doesn't tell me anything."

"You are a slimy weasel who hears everything. That's the thing with arrogant witches like Marshall. They go around summoning and binding golems as if there are no consequences to giving life where it doesn't belong." She put a finger on his forehead. Tiny tendrils of ethereal glowing crimson light snaked out from where her finger touched his skin, burning her as much as it did him, but fear and anger washed it away as quickly as it came. "They treat you like you have no feelings or wants or desires. Like you can't feel pleasure or pain."

He mewled out a moan when she drew her finger along the side of his face, leaving a streak of fading light in its wake.

"But we know better, don't we, Teodor?"

He nodded vigorously.

"You experience everything we do, don't you?"

Again, his head bobbed up and down.

She mimicked his actions, her mouth drawn into a mocking frown. "Marshall isn't strong enough, nor smart enough to be the mastermind behind all this, so who's pulling the strings? Is it Segomo?"

"No." Teodor's voice was barely above a whisper. "He was promised freedom for his help."

"Help with what?"

Teodor squirmed beneath her, but she grasped tighter. She pursed her lips together, fighting her temper. "Come on, Teodor. I'm trying to be nice."

"He is looking for something."

"Something? What something?"

"I—I don't know. A book, I think."

She leaned in closer. "What is it called?"

"I don't know." His voice broke under the pressure of fear. "I swear."

She sat up, her frustration tangible as she hissed out an exhale. "Fine," she said through gritted teeth, "the hard way it is."

She slammed her hands to the sides of his face; the sound of her palms slapping against his skin echoing throughout the room. Light flared, mingling with Teodor's shrill screams. He arched so suddenly and, with so much force, he nearly bucked her off. The distinct crack of bones snapping and rubbing against each other sent shards of fire along her skin. She knew the pain she was inflicting on him, because she felt it, too. Every torn tendon. Every fractured bone. Her body screamed with agony from within, but she kept it locked behind gritted teeth.

Everything calmed.

Cora leaned forward, staring into the golem's blank, dead stare. She began whispering ancient words of power to bind him to her. Each syllable scraped against her tongue like razor blades cutting into her flesh, and she had to cling to him, fighting the urge to throw herself off the bar. Teodor jerked and spasmed, and his eyes went wide. Pools of black filled the once-pale gray of his irises.

"Now," Cora said, patting his cheek. "Let's try this again." Her stomach churned, threatening to upend itself.

Teodor's head lolled to the side, eyeing the men staring at him in stunned silence.

She yanked his focus back to her. "Your ick is nauseating me. Tell me who took Marcos."

"You already know who has him."

"Don't play word games with me. Who put Segomo in that body? What do they want with the boy?"

The golem laughed, his voice reverberating against his vocal cords. "You underestimate your enemy. My knowledge is limited to what will assist my master. All else is wiped from my mind."

She leaned in closer, ignoring the sharp smell of liquor and peanuts on his breath. "Then tell me what you do know."

"The tome is the key to unlocking the prison. When Segomo finds it, they will have all they need for the awakening."

"Awakening?" Dino asked, moving a little closer to the bar.

Cora shot him a warning glare, then went back to Teodor. "Who are *they* and what are *they* trying to awaken?"

"No one can stop what is coming. Tethra will take his rightful place on the throne that was stolen from him. His children will lead his armies, and they will bring the world back to a glorious time before."

Cora's breath caught in her throat. She'd only ever heard a whisper of that name, even among the dead. Teodor twisted under her grasp, so she squeezed every so slightly. "Before what?"

Teodor again dropped his head to the side, his gaze landing on Edwind. "The Death Dragon remembers."

Cora smacked his face, bringing him back to her again. "Where are they keeping Marcos?"

Teodor shook with silent laughter. "Not even Segomo knows. The Fomorian doesn't trust him. Why do you think he was put in a such a weak body?"

"How did they get him away from Arawn?"

"That's a good question, Little Goddess. Perhaps he should be the one asking it."

"Cora." Edwind shuffled forward, keeping a table between them. He motioned toward her and tapped a finger to his nose.

She wiped the blood from her upper lip, smearing it across her palm. When she crawled off the bar, she swayed to the side and had to steady herself on the barstool. After a few seconds, she grabbed Teodor by the shirt. "Come on."

In the back office, she led him to the safe behind the desk. "Open it."

Clunky fingers turned the dial.

"Hurry." Cora's voice wavered. Her head felt like a hot-air balloon being inflated until she thought it would float off her neck.

There was a muted click, and Teodor pushed down on the lever, swinging the door open. No longer needing him, she severed the tether keeping him alive. As soon as her hold on him was gone, so was he. Her gut heaved seconds before she threw herself at the trash can beside the desk.

"Don't touch her," Edwind barked.

A hand swept loose strands of hair out of her face while her body clenched from another bout of vomiting. Minutes passed, and when she was sure she wasn't going to be sick again, she tried to get to her feet, but her legs couldn't to hold her weight.

"Grab what's in the safe." She thought she spoke aloud, but her pulse pounded inside her ears, muting the rest of the world.

Miller loomed over her, his powerful arms lifting her from the hard ground. She strained to comprehend his words, and her vision began to shrink until there was nothing but Miller's malachite eyes brimming with concern. As darkness devoured her, she fought against its iron jaw. She couldn't afford to lose another precious moment when Marcos was still in danger. He was out there somewhere, scared and alone. No matter how much she struggled, there was no staving off the unrelenting pull into the unwanted bliss of unconsciousness.

Chapter 6

THE MEMORY OF THE summer storm hung thick on the warm breeze that swept loose strands across Cora's face, drawing her from the half-sleep of contended musings. Bruised clouds steadily retreated from the valley, heading east out to sea. The surrounding stalks of tall, reedy grass swayed over her bare skin, tickling her round, taut belly. The babies shifted and kicked inside her, restless in anticipation of their upcoming birth.

Footsteps crunched over the rocky terrain. She rolled to her side just as a man crested the hill, his face hidden in the deep shadows of the sunset behind him. The scent of roasted meat drifted toward her, and her stomach rumbled. He always brought her something for her cravings after satisfying her need for him.

"I wish we had ice cream." She reached out an arm, her lips parting into a lazy smile. "That would make this day complete."

His rich laughter sent a delicious shiver across her bare skin. He stepped closer, his fingertips brushing against her. The world around her warped and pulsed, slicing at her vision before everything faded into darkness.

Blinding pain wrenched her from the dream.

Cora's mouth opened, and she squeaked out an anguished grunt from the sudden and unwelcome torment of reality threatening to split her head in two. There was a faint scent of lavender in the air, a sharp contrast to the acrid taste coating her tongue. Every muscle in her body screamed in protest at the mere thought of moving.

But pain was good. Pain meant she was alive.

Cautiously, she explored the back base of her skull, looking for what felt like a blade lodged deep in her neck. When she opened her eyes, tears filled her vision. After the third attempt, she was finally able to focus. She recognized the dainty floral decor of Darya's guest room. She'd slept in that same bed a few times before. The Wodehal house was one of the few places that offered her safety.

Memories from the night before trickled into her mind, and her gut clenched at the realization that Edwind, Dino, and Miller had witnessed the full force of her godhood. There was a reason she kept that part of her life a secret. What she did to Teodor was nearly as unhinged and dangerous as taunting Segomo into killing her. She was surprised Edwind brought her back to his home instead of her place, or worse, leaving her in the pub.

It took a few solid attempts to push herself upright in the bed. She eased her legs over the edge at a measured pace so as not to jostle her still queasy stomach. The picture window on the other side of the room faced the ocean, and the sheer curtains that draped over the glass glowed with the faint light of the impending dawn. Knowing she had only been out for a few hours was a small comfort.

She pushed to her feet, praying her legs would hold her upright, and when she didn't fall back onto the plush duvet, shuffled to the bedroom door left slightly ajar. Low murmurs drifted through the opening.

"Keep your voice down," Darya's hushed whisper held a dangerous undertone.

"You didn't see what she did to that man." Dino's words were laced with anger.

"It wasn't a man," Edwind said.

"I don't care what it was. I can't believe you let her around your children. I can't believe I trusted her with Marcos."

There was a sharp cut-off in the conversation, and then Darya spoke. "I am going to have to ask you to leave our house before I show you what I am capable of."

"I didn't mean—"

"It doesn't matter what you meant." Darya snapped. "Cora grew up knowing who and what she is and taught to control her magic. She has done nothing but show kindness to us. Especially you."

Not wanting the conversation to continue, Cora took in a deep breath and pulled the door open. She ignored the pointed glare she got from Dino and headed for the fridge, where she grabbed a bag of frozen peas from the freezer. "Do you have anything for my head?" She asked.

Darya nodded and disappeared upstairs.

Cora sat down on a barstool, relieved to be able to put her back to the other men. She noticed Miller wasn't among them. Edwind probably hid him away at the Dragon's Rest for his own safety, but Cora was too exhausted to be insulted. If she was in his shoes, she wouldn't want him in the same room as the crazy death goddess, either.

A minute later, Darya returned with a bottle of aspirin and a glass of water. Cora chewed a couple of pills, wincing at the bitter taste, and washed them down with the tap water. Looking past Cora, Darya said, "I thought you were leaving."

Cora looked to the side. Dino shot her a disgusted glare before whirling around and storming out of the front door. The sharp sound of it slamming echoed inside her head.

The room filled with an uncomfortable silence. Darya returned to the kitchen, grabbing a kettle from the stovetop. "I'll make us some tea."

Cora shifted the frozen peas. "I understand why Dino is upset. What I did was—It's a lot to process." She glanced over her shoulder at Edwind, who avoided eye contact like his life depended on it. Despite knowing what she was, he didn't know the full extent of her abilities.

Darya rested a hand on Cora's arm. "We are more than the blood that runs through our veins."

Easy for her to say. Darya didn't have the power to snuff out a person's life with a touch of her hand. Turning her attention to Edwind, Cora said, "Did you grab everything from the safe?"

He nodded. "There were a handful of texts." He disappeared into his office and came back with six leather-bound journals. "I glanced through them, but I don't recognize the language."

Cora turned to a random page and frowned. Though she couldn't decipher the text, the writing was vaguely familiar. Her heart sank when she realized what Marshall had done. "This is going to be a chore. It looks like a hybrid dialect. There's a mix of Latin, Gaelic, and a sprinkle of Ancient Greek."

The door to the downstairs loo opened, and Miller stepped out wearing a snug-fitting, plain gray T-shirt and a pair of matching, knee-length shorts. His hair was freshly toweled from the shower. When he saw Cora sitting at the bar, his expression brightened.

"How was your first experience with modern plumbing?" Edwind asked.

He dragged his gaze from Cora. "Interesting. Much like our waterfalls, but I do enjoy the ability to control the temperature."

Cora turned her attention back to the journal, flipping to the first page. A phrase caught her eye, and she said, "I need a piece of paper and something to write with."

Darya slid an unlined pad across the smooth surface, along with a pen. "I can't believe you can actually read that."

"It's not easy. I'll have to do a lot of paraphrasing."

Leaning into her, Darya said, "Edwind told me about Segomo."

Cora glanced up, the dread of hearing that name reflected in Darya's worried expression. "I was hoping that was a terrible hallucination."

"Surely Arawn knows he is missing by now."

"If so, he hasn't said anything to me about it, although we haven't spoken in decades. I doubt if he would tell me, even if he knew."

"Do you think you should contact him? He can send his Death Knights to find Segomo and anyone else helping him."

Pointing to the page in front of her, she said, "According to this, they are Fomorians. And I don't want the Death Knights involved. Not yet. If Arawn unleashes those psychopaths, they will cut through everyone, innocent or not, who gets in their way."

Darya's eyebrows scrunched together. "Fomorians? There's a name I haven't heard in a long time. I thought they were fairy tales."

"More like nightmares. I've seen the shadows of what they used to be. I don't want to imagine what they could do if they were made whole again."

"What do they possibly need with Marcos?"

"Hopefully, these books will tell us something."

Darya glanced over Cora's shoulder, her mouth working into a tilted frown.

"What are you thinking?" Cora asked.

"Doesn't this all feel scripted to you? Like how I went to nine eighty-two. It's all happening as if it was planned; your journey into the past, Miller following you back here. What if he is meant to help find Marcos?"

Cora glanced to where Edwind and Miller sat opposite each other at the chessboard. "It's possible. Dino hasn't vanished, so the grand plan is still intact." She returned to the mangled penmanship, wondering what was worse, Marshall's handwriting or the ridiculous made-up language?

Darya eyed the scribbled writing, her eyes narrowing. "Do you really think there's something in there that could help find Marcos?"

Cora shrugged. "I have to look. If nothing else, maybe I'll figure out why they snatched Segomo's soul from the underworld."

"If I can help with anything, all you have to do is ask."

It was hard to muster even the slightest of smiles, but Cora pushed her lips into a tight grin. She had no intention of getting Darya's family further embroiled in whatever madness was going on. Cora was the one who let those monsters take Marcos.

"Edwind," Darya said, gathering an armload of blankets from the couch. "Can you spare a few minutes to help me finish hanging the shelf in Brigita's room?"

Cora waited until they were upstairs before opening the notebook to the first page. By the second paragraph, she was ready to throw it at the wall. She leaned back, tapping the end of the pencil on her lower lip, searching her rudimentary grasp on Greek so she could figure out the closest translation to English.

Her gaze wandered across the room, and she found herself drawn to the chess board. Miller sat hunched over, scrutinizing each polished piece. The shirt he wore hugged his upper body in a way that told of someone who'd spent his entire life working the land. Thick arms stretched the fabric, which was surprising since that was most likely one of Edwin's shirts. Her eyes slid down his torso, past his waist, to where the loose shorts stopping just above his knees. His legs flexed when he repositioned himself, muscles rolling with each subtle movement.

It was amazing how a man like Dino came from the same bloodline as Miller Wodehal. Even their demeanor was light years away from each other. Maybe if Dino exuded half of his ancestor's fierce prowess, she might have accepted his proposal for a date—possibly something a little more intimate.

She snapped herself out of those dangerous musings and lifted her eyes from the floor. A heavy blanket of heat rose on her neck and face when she met his malachite stare. One side of Miller's mouth turned up into a half grin that sent the flutter of excitement through her chest.

She whirled around, trying to refocus on the page in front of her. What was already a difficult task of deciphering nearly illegible text was made even more so by his presence. Not only was her concentration lost, but she also had to fight with herself to keep from glancing in his direction.

Maybe after she got something on her stomach, she'd be more clear-headed. Later, she would head into the city and take the journals to Raquel. Perhaps if she could get her hands on the texts, they would give her the means to find Marcos.

Excited squeals distracted Cora from the notebook. It was a welcomed distraction from the maddeningly incoherent scribblings. She wondered how someone as incompetent as Marshall managed to claw his way up the ranks of his coven to command so much authority. If the hastily written ramblings were any indication of what waited in the other texts, she would be better off setting them on fire in the hopes of appeasing the gods, praying they would grant her clarity and understanding.

Cora pushed the book aside, opting for the now lukewarm tea. She watched Edwind introduce the kids to Miller. Brigita practically bounced off the ceiling with excitement over meeting her cousin, but Bastian only gave a polite show of interest before his attention shifted to the stack of blueberry pancakes waiting to be devoured.

Darya intercepted him before he snatched the whole plate. "There's plenty for everyone," she said, setting two pancakes in front of him, along with eggs and sausage. Ignoring his exaggerated frown, she added, "You need to eat more than pancakes."

As the family gathered around the table, Cora took the opportunity to slip outside to not intrude on their meal. Though Edwind wasn't as vocal as Dino had been, she sensed the unease in his tense body language. Not to mention, he kept eyeing her, as if expecting her to morph into some sort of two headed monstrosity.

The soothing whisper of the ocean caressed the beach, helping to unwind the tension that had coiled inside her mind. She tucked her legs underneath her and laid out the journal, ready to dive into another round of delusional ramblings of a sanctimonious warlock. So far, all she'd been able to find were useless spells and incantations. Nothing that mentioned Tethra or Marcos or a ritual. She was starting to think she was wasting her time, but she refused to give up until she scoured each and every last page.

The glass door opened, and Cora glanced up from the notebook. Miller carried a plate stacked with delicious breakfast foods. He set the bountiful spread on the table beside her chair. As soon as the smell hit her nose, her mouth watered in anticipation of the first bite.

"Brigita insisted I bring you food. She said you wouldn't think to eat otherwise."

Cora smiled. "That girl is too much like her mother; always thinking she knows what's best for other people."

"I can take it back if you're not hungry," he said, reaching for the plate.

Cora lunged at the table, hovering protectively over the food. "Don't you dare. I mean, you went to all this trouble."

His toothy grin was contagious, and she couldn't stop her own smile from breaking her stony expression. Instead of leaving like she expected, he sat down next to her, nodding to the book in her lap. "Can I help?"

"I doubt you can read this mess."

He studied her for a few seconds, his face losing its cheerfulness. "I may not be as worldly as you or Uncle Edwind, but I am not an ignorant man. My grandfathers taught me many languages."

Cora rolled her eyes. "I wasn't insulting your intelligence." She grabbed the fork and stabbed at a perfectly browned piece of sausage. "You men are so delicate when it comes to your egos."

She took her time chewing, then nodded to the table where the stack of notebooks waited to be read. "Go on, then. Have a look."

He picked up one of the journals, flipped it open to a random page, and began reading. After a few sentences, his brows slowly stitched together. His lips moved with the effort to understand the words until he finally set it aside and shook his head. "How can you possibly read this? The dialects are mangled beyond recognition."

"I can read it well enough. If there's any reference to Marcos or Tethra, I'll see it." She lifted her tea and froze when she spotted Edwind watching them through the window. "You should probably go inside."

Miller followed her stare. "He acts as if it's not safe to be around you."

"After last night, a lot of people might consider being in my presence unsafe." She set the plate back on the table, no longer hungry. "That's ridiculous, of course. I've never lost control, but for some reason, everyone is scared of the girl who plays with dead things."

When the silence stretched out between them, she looked up to find him staring at her. "Not everyone."

The door opened again, and Edwind stuck his head out. "Miller, would you care to finish our game?"

He kept his eyes locked on Cora for more than was comfortable before following his uncle inside. She could still feel his eyes boring into her very soul, and it wasn't an altogether unpleasant sensation.

After a few minutes of scanning the next page, a single word shattered her concentration, and she shot to her feet. Her heart thudded against her chest as she read the passage surrounding

Tethra's name. She reread the paragraph a few times, making sure she was interpreting it correctly.

Book in hand, she rushed inside. "I found something." Her elation soon turned to panic, and the food she'd just eaten threatened to crawl back up her throat and land at her feet.

Dino stood in the entryway, his haggard appearance a testament to his current state of being. The hopeful expression on his face made her want to open a hole in the floor and disappear rather than tell him what she found.

"What is it?" he asked, rushing to her side. "Did you find Marcos?"

Cora shot Darya a pleading look, then eyed the kids.

"Alright, children," Darya said, motioning to Brigita and Bastian. "Gather your things and meet me in the car. Your cousins are looking forward to your visit today."

Darya approached Cora, keeping her voice low, despite the kids being out of earshot. "What did you find?"

"I still don't know where they took Marcos," Cora began.

Dino's face fell.

"But I know why they want him. Why they chose him."

The scrutiny of everyone's gaze was nearly too much. Her eyes fell to the ground. "When Tethra was banished, his body was destroyed, leaving his essence trapped in another realm. To free him, they need a vessel for him to inhabit. One that is powerful enough to sustain him."

Dino took a step back. "They are going to put that thing in my son?"

"They will try." She closed her eyes so she wouldn't have to see the devastation in Dino's eyes.

"What will happen to Marcos?"

Cora couldn't bring herself to say the words.

"What is going to happen to my son, Cora?"

Instead of answering his question, she tried to give him a glimmer of hope. "The timing has to be right. Certain criteria have to be met. According to the notes, there is a tome that holds the key to opening Tethra's prison and bind him to his vessel. No one knows where it is or even if it still exists." She looked up. "That might be why they went to so much trouble to free Segomo. He must know its whereabouts."

"I failed him," Dino whispered. Then he turned a disgusted frown on Cora. "You failed him."

The venom in his words made her flinch.

Darya stepped in front of Dino, arms crossed. "She hasn't failed anyone. If not for Cora and the magic that scares you so much, you would have lost Marcos a long time ago."

"It doesn't matter now, does it? He was still taken." Backing to the door, Dino whirled around, leaving them to stare at the empty space he left behind.

Cora went back to the veranda and gathered up the journals. Darya tried to grab her arm, but Cora shied away from the touch. "Dino's right. I failed Marcos. I couldn't save him."

"He's angry and scared." She followed Cora into the house.

Cora paused at the front door. "I'm going into the city. Raquel sent me to Dino's before the attack, so she can find a way to locate Marcos." Outside, she threw the books in the passenger seat of her car, taking a few deep breaths to ease the tightness in her chest.

The passenger door opened, and Miller snatched up the books before dropping into the seat. The small car rocked with the weight of his solid frame.

"What do you think you're doing?" The bite of her words didn't seem to faze him.

"Going with you. After last night, I am not letting you face this danger alone. Especially with the likes of Segomo loose in the world."

She glanced at the front door where Edwind stood with his arms crossed, a stony frown etched onto his face. "I can deal with Segomo." Although, the thought of what he would do to her if they saw each other again scared her more than she wanted to admit.

"Is that how you ended up unconscious in my arms?" He motioned to the remnants of the cut on her neck. "And nearly died?"

"He wouldn't have killed me. Besides, Edwind isn't going to like the idea of you traipsing all over the city by yourself."

"You will be with me."

His grin cracked her determination. The argument she had ready to unleash faded to mild irritation, but there was a part of her relieved not to be doing this alone.

He relaxed into the seat. "I am a grown man who can make my own way in the world. What is it you said? Dragon's blood and built like a god?"

Viking god, she mused to herself.

Only after Darya dragged Edwind inside did she finally relent. "Fine, but you better keep that precious cargo safe at all times." Her gaze slid down between his legs. "You're carrying the next generation of Wodehal's."

He dipped his head, catching her attention. "I will gladly entrust my future generations in your very capable hands."

She fought a flustered sigh. "Just—Keep yourself alive, okay?"

Chapter 7

BY THE TIME CORA reached the bustling city streets, Miller failed to hide the unease crackling through him. She tried to keep her chaotic driving to a minimum, but his right hand gripped the door so tight, his white knuckles were a stark contrast to the dark interior. The cheap plastic handle creaked and underneath the pressure of his fingers as they tightened and released again and again.

She down shifted, slowing her approach as they entered the city limits. Traffic wasn't too terrible this time of the morning. There were more pedestrians clogging up the pavement and roads. Glancing to the side, she reached over, giving him a reassuring pat. "Relax. We're almost there."

His eyes moved to her hand, then to the door, and he dropped his arm into his lap.

The car drifted through the city streets at a pace that was a little too slow for her liking. She had to stop herself from blaring the horn and screaming at people darting into her path. She didn't want to add to Miller's tightly wound anxiety. After turning down a side street, she found an empty space and parked. Raquel's place was tucked into a forgotten corner of a narrow alley accessible only by foot.

She stepped onto the pavement and glanced behind her, where Miller lingered near the car. He watched the constant movement around him, eyes darting back and forth. Each time someone honked or shouted, he flinched, his muscles winding even tighter.

"The villages in my time aren't as congested and loud," he said.

She eased to his side and laid a hand on his arm, squeezing gently to break his concentration. "You're going to give yourself a stroke. I'm pretty sure we aren't in any immediate danger at the moment."

He tore his gaze from the traffic, eyeing her hand. When he lifted his eyes to hers, the tight lines around his mouth faded, but didn't disappear completely.

"Will you be okay?" She nodded to her car. "I can take you back to Edwind's place if it's too much for you."

The remainder of his anxiety melted into exasperation. "I will be fine." He carefully removed her hand from his arm.

Unable to resist one last poke at the proverbial bear, she said, "There's that big brave dragon adventurer." Before he could follow through with the retort that flashed through his eyes, she went back to the car and grabbed a journal before continuing down the alley.

He jogged to her side. "Where are we going?"

"The night I tried to bring Marcos to you and your mother, I got a call from a psychic friend of mine. She warned me about the attack, so perhaps she can help me find him now."

"What is a psychic?"

"You may be more familiar with the term oracle."

His pace slowed, and he frowned at the ground. "I see. And you believe in such a person? I thought you were more sensible."

"Says the dragon."

He shrugged. "Still, I am flesh and blood. Oracles spout riddles and nonsense, giving false hope with their lies."

"I take it you've had a run in with one?"

Instead of answering, he turned his attention to the surrounding cityscape.

Cora waited a few more seconds for an answer. When she didn't get one, she kept walking. Given that he had lost his father at sea, surely, he and his mum used every resource available to find him. Had she been on speaking terms with Arawn, Cora might have gone to the underworld to see if she could locate Saebbi. It may be hard news to receive, but it would provide them with much needed closure.

The thought of talking to Arawn again, asking him for any kind of favor, made her skin prickle with a cold dread. Not even the flesh and blood of the keeper of souls was beyond his wrath. The fact that she'd went twenty-seven years without so much as a whisper from him was a relief.

At the next intersection, she turned into a narrow alley that dead ended into a plain wood door. There was a freshly painted sign hanging above it, denoting the shop as an apothecary. The bright colors were the only attempt at advertising Raquel made. Whoever needed or wanted her help found their way to her.

Before Cora could knock, it swung inward, revealing a petite woman wearing a vibrant pink and yellow robe that looked unbelievably soft and fluffy. Her caramel skin contrasted with the fabric, making her Mediterranean complexion appear even darker.

"I wasn't expecting you until later. You caught me fresh out of the shower." Raquel's honey-colored eyes reflected the mid-morning light, giving them an eerie glow. Her accent reminded Cora of Horsa and Hengist, and she wondered if Raquel was as old as they were. That was a subject Raquel was masterful at avoiding.

"We can come back later." Cora offered.

"Don't be a smart ass. Tell your friend to wipe his feet. I don't want to have to clean up the sludge he has on his shoes."

Miller picked up one foot at a time, then dutifully scraped his boots on the industrial rug before following Cora over the threshold.

Once inside, Raquel led them down a short hallway, past an open door to the tiny room where she conducted seances or readings or whatever a woman of her paranormal skill did. Cora had known her for decades and still didn't know exactly where Raquel fell on the otherworldly spectrum. It was easier to call her a psychic, although Cora speculated there was much more to her than the power of second sight.

The sweet cinnamon scent of baked goods filled the air, making Cora's mouth water in anticipation of getting to partake in something gooey and delicious. The kitchen looked exactly as it had the last time she visited. There was a single window near the table that had a bland view of the next building over, but a soft, gauzy like light lit the small space from an unseen source.

"Cora has no manners. My name is Raquel." She held out a hand to Miller, but he tucked his arms behind his back.

"Miller," he said.

Unfazed by his actions, she nodded. "I knew it started with an M."

"Of course you did."

Raquel's smile widened. "How can a man of your lineage be such a skeptic?"

He lifted himself upright, staring down his nose at her. "I am not one to believe every charlatan that crosses my path."

She cocked her head to the side, studying him for a long time. "I'm sorry you had such an unpleasant experience with one fraud. It doesn't mean we are all frauds taking advantage of a widow and her son."

His eyes widened, but he kept quiet.

Raquel motioned for them to sit. "As I said, I didn't expect you until later." She took the steaming kettle from the gas burner and set it on a pewter serving tray, along with three dainty tea cups. "I don't have everything in order. The cinnamon rolls won't be ready for another five minutes or so."

Cora grinned. She turned into an excited little girl at the prospect of sweet treats. "We can wait."

Raquel brought the tray to the table, taking her time setting them in front of her guests and poured the hot water over the tea bags already waiting in the cups. "If you're here early, then you must have uncovered something important."

Before Cora could answer, Miller said, "You're the oracle. Shouldn't you know why we are here?"

"What is your problem?" Cora asked. "Why are you being so hostile?"

Raquel took a seat between them. She tested her tea, then added a cube of sugar from the bowl in the center of the table. Her unbothered demeanor carried over to her voice. "Did you tell your mother of your plans to leave the island before rushing after Cora?"

Miller's hand froze, the cup halfway to his mouth.

"I didn't think so. Your departure will deeply sadden Gita, but she understands your need to travel the world. Every youngling hears the same call. She, too, made her mark as a young dragoness."

His arm sank to the table.

After another tentative sip, Raquel went on. "Her pain and suffering will remain hidden in her heart, as it has since the moment she opened it to love your father. But you do what makes you happy, Miller Wodehal; selfish child."

Cora recognized the struggle to keep his emotions locked away behind a mask of indifference. The muscles in his jaw flexed as he chewed on his words. He pushed up from the chair, eyes averted from either woman, and stormed outside, leaving Cora to stare after him.

Turning an exasperated frown on Raquel, Cora said, "Did you have to be so blunt?"

"He has a destiny, and it's not the grand adventure he's expecting. The sooner he accepts the path laid out for him, the quicker he can come to terms with his fate."

Cora let go of a long sigh. "Well, I'm not here about his destiny." She set the journal on the table. "I got my hands on some information that has changed everything."

Raquel leaned into her, eyeing the notebook as Cora went over the passage she'd found earlier. Raquel's expression went from unease to disturbed.

"I was hoping you could use the journals as a way to locate Marcos," Cora said.

Raquel stared at the journal with blatant disgust, refusing to touch it. "I'm not laying a finger on those pages. The vile magic imbued inside can't help us."

"I have to find Marcos."

"It will take time, but I have some potent allies that can help get through who or whatever is blocking my vision."

"Unfortunately, time is not a luxury we can afford."

"That's all I can do at the moment."

Frustrated, Cora nodded and went to stand, but Raquel reached for her hands, the warmth of her palms seeping into Cora's skin. She studied Cora, her mouth twitching as if to speak, but let her go without saying a word.

"Is there something you're not telling me?" Cora asked. "If it's about Marcos, I don't care how bad it is. I have to know."

"It has nothing to do with the boy. I'm concerned about your wellbeing. You need to stop shutting yourself away from the rest of the world."

It was an odd segue, but Cora couldn't afford to waste time pirouetting around Raquel's cryptic messages. "You worry too much." She stood, eyeing the oven where the delicious smells emanated. Other, more urgent matters overshadowed her love of sweets. "I'm perfectly content with the friends I have now."

Raquel's expression didn't change. "Keep an open mind and an open heart going forward."

Cora's lips pursed into a flat grin. "You bet. Open mind. Anyway, I need to get on with my search. I'll ring you up later, yeah?"

Miller leaned against a faded brick wall with his arms crossed over his chest, peering down the alley to the street beyond. His profile was suitably broody for his bloodline, but Cora couldn't blame him for his reaction. She stopped beside him, keeping her tone neutral. "Ready to go?"

His answer was to push off the building and take his place behind her. At the end of the alley, she paused. "Raquel can be abrasive."

"She claims to know my intentions, but she is mistaken."

Cora nodded slowly, watching the passing traffic. "So, you aren't planning to leave Didean?"

His lips pinched together as if he had something sour stuck in his mouth. After a few seconds of chewing on his response, he dropped his arms to his side. "I was going to wait until after the solstice fires to tell Mother of my plans."

She slid a questioning look his way, but kept quiet. It wasn't her place to pick apart his life choices. Goddess knew she'd made a plethora of horrible mistakes in her lengthy lifetime. Peering up and down the street one last time, she turned left. "Marshall has a warehouse not far from here. It's worth checking out."

They walked in mutual silence for the next few blocks until Cora glanced over her shoulder. Her stomach dropped; Miller wasn't there. Panic flared in her chest, but then, farther up the pavement, she spotted his silhouette slipping into a building. She hurried to catch up, annoyance warming her skin.

A newly bolted hand-painted sign hung above the door, the fresh wood stark against the weathered facade. The Gaelic script was familiar: Bùth na Neònachais. Roughly translated, A Shop of Curiosities.

"What are you doing?" she said, rushing in after him. "It's not open for business yet."

Her gaze drifted over half empty shelves and displays. The distinct, tangy scent of fresh paint hung heavy in the air.

Miller pointed to the wall behind the counter. "That sword—The craftsmanship is impeccable."

She eyed the steel blade, immediately thinking of the one Edwind kept in his office. It was indeed a fine specimen of the marvels of what a pair of hands could create with the right tools and talent.

Miller went to retrieve the sword, but before he reached the other side of the counter, she latched onto his arm. "You can't just walk back there." The frustrated look on his face made her scowl melt into amusement.

"Where is the shop owner?" he demanded. "I wish to see the blade. I will need one if I am to protect you."

She stared at him for a few seconds. The last thing she needed from him was protection, but given how he reacted to the notebooks, telling him as much would further prickle his sensitive ego.

With a shake of her head, she lifted a hand and tapped the bell on the edge of the glass counter.

From somewhere in the back, a muffled voice said, "Be with you in a minute."

"He'll be here in a minute," she echoed.

"I heard the man."

Satisfied with her smartassery, she turned her attention to the rest of the shop's wares. At first glance, nothing seemed particularly special—just a collection of mismatched items that looked more out of place than intriguing. For a shop of oddities, there wasn't anything really that odd. Half-filled shelves held rusty keys, tarnished compasses, and relics so unremarkable they were hardly worth displaying.

She was sifting through some of the stranger pieces when Miller's voice broke the quiet, greeting someone behind her.

"I'd like to see that blade you have on the wall," he said.

"You have a good eye. That piece of steel has a lot of history."

The shop owner's voice was clearer now, and there was no mistaking the hint of an Irish brogue rolling off each syllable. It was the same tongue that whispered sweet promises of carnal pleasures only his kind could give. Hearing it again sent chills down her spine, and not in a good way.

It had been decades since they last laid eyes on each other. Not nearly long enough to forget his betrayal. She wanted to disembowel him for bringing another woman into her bed. It was one thing to sleep around on her, but to have the audacity to do it in her home—in her bed, was more than she could forgive.

She glanced at the door, calculating her chances of getting outside before he spotted her. No sooner had she taken a step toward the exit, Emmett laughed.

"Would you look at that? I never thought you'd darken my doorstep again."

She conjured the most venomous sneer she could manage, turning it on him. "Had I known this was your shop, I would have lit myself on fire rather than set foot inside."

Emmett shot Miller an amused smile. "Take your time with that sword, mate."

He sauntered over to where Cora stood with one hand on her hip, the other ready to rake across his face. "It's been a long time," he purred. "Gods, you still look amazing." He bit his lower lip and added, "I bet you taste just as sweet."

The sneer puckered into disgust. "And you're still a creep."

His laughter came easily. "Come on. Surely you're not bitter after all this time." He reached for her, but she smacked his hand away.

She looked past him to where Miller ran a finger against the fine edge of the weapon. "If you're done ogling that sword, we need to go."

Emmett glanced between them. "You're with this daftie now?

Miller laid the sword on the counter with great care and joined Cora at the door.

She rolled her eyes. "Let's do this again, in say, another twenty-five years."

"I see you're the same frigid bitch you've always been. Why do you think I wanted you to catch me with that woman? It was the only way I could get a genuine reaction out of you."

There was no warning before Miller rounded on Emmett, slamming him against the far wall, knocking a box of random keys onto the floor. "Do not speak so cruelly to Lady Cora."

Instead of being cowed by the show of aggression, Emmet chuckled. "She does like her men to be forceful, doesn't she? That girl has a ferocious appetite in bed. I mean, who else but the daughter of Arawn can fuck like she does?"

Miller pushed off him, glancing back at Cora. She wanted to rip Emett's tongue right out of his mouth. Instead of bloodshed, she chose to walk away, throwing open the door and storming outside. She stomped down the pavement while trying to swallow down her fury before it consumed her.

But beneath the rage was something far more dangerous—an unfamiliar warmth curling up inside her ribs. No one had defended her like that in years. She didn't need it. She didn't want it. So why did Miller's actions shake her more than Emmett's words?

The familiar presence of Miller settled in beside her. "That was disgusting what he said to you."

"He's a prick." She pushed out a heavy breath. "Well, you were curious about my affiliation with Arawn."

"Why would you feel the need to keep your father a secret?"

She finally met his stare. "You saw what I did to Teodor. Usually, when people find out who my father is and what I'm capable of, they tend to either fear me or they are disgusted by me. Which category are you in?"

He stepped in front of her, halting them both. His eyes took hold of her as if he'd grabbed her by the arms. "Neither."

It took a great deal of effort to break his intangible hold, but when she did, she turned away, muttering, "Then you really are a daftie." After a few steps, she whirled around, poking a finger at him. "And for the record, I don't need your protection. I'm not some fucking damsel in distress. I can fight my own damn battles."

He pulled himself straighter, his relaxed features hardening into a granite wall of cold indifference. "Forgive me, goddess. I meant no offense."

She leaned into him, pushing her finger into his chest. "Don't call me that. Ever." Despite her anger, or maybe because of it, heated tears blurred her vision. She whirled around and started walking before he could see them spill over the dams of her lashes.

Cora held two ice cream cones in her hands, carefully making her way to the park bench where Miller sat watching a family of ducks playing in the water. He had a bland expression on his face that may as well have been a scowl from a man who, like his great-grandfather, wore a dozy smile most of the time.

She purchased the frozen treats with the intention of taking the sting from her outburst. Miller had done nothing wrong. In fact, his attempt to defend her honor caught her off guard. She wasn't used to having someone else fight her battles, and she didn't know how to gracefully accept his well-intentioned actions.

A simple apology wouldn't cut it, so she decided to try to make amends with the one thing that always made her feel better. She approached the bench and held out a cone.

Miller eyed her suspiciously. "What is it?"

She sat down beside him. "Ice cream. It will change your life."

He took the cone and watched her lick her frozen snack before bringing it up to his nose. To her horror, he stuck a quarter of it into his mouth before she could stop him. Cora tried not to laugh at his strangled outburst.

He squeezed his eyes shut. "Why does it hurt?"

She reached for his hand before he threw the precious delicacy. "You're not supposed to take such big bites." Patiently, she demonstrated the proper way to eat the ice cream. "Small licks. It's a lot less painful."

He watched her for a few seconds before mimicking her actions, more cautious that time.

"See?" she said.

They sat in silence, eating their frozen desserts, watching the sun glitter across the water's surface. After a few failed attempts at trying to break the stalemate, she took one last deep breath. On the exhale, she said, "I'm sorry I yelled at you. What you did—" She held out the last two bites of her cone. "I guess in a way it was sweet of you."

He took the offered cone and popped it into his mouth. After it was gone, he shook his head. "I couldn't stand to hear that man say those things to you, but I overstepped my place."

"He's a nob who thinks way too highly of himself."

"Why do you let people treat you so badly? You do not deserve such vitriol."

She stared at the water, trying to come up with a believable answer to his question. The truth was, she locked away her feelings for fear of being betrayed like so many times before. "I learned a long time ago to ignore people's misconceptions of me."

Another minute of silence passed, and he said, "You don't have to worry about that shop owner speaking ill of you again," he said casually, as if talking about the weather.

She raised a suspicious brow. "Is that so?"

He nodded. "I took that sword of his and ran it through his foot."

"You did what?"

"I told him if he so much as looked upon you with anything but the reverence your bloodline demands, I will come back and skewer him and take his ears for trophies."

She stared at him, open-mouthed, unsure of how to respond. Part of her wanted to yell at him again for acting like some kind of overprotective man-child, but his intentions came from a good place. She wished she could have seen the smug smile wiped off Emmett's face. "You should have aimed higher."

The laugh that burst out of Miller struck another sense of déjà vu, sending a swell of an unexpected emotion through her. Lust? No. What he made her feel was something more profound than attraction. And far more dangerous for them both.

"Perhaps if I meet him again, I will indeed aim higher." When his laughter fizzled, they hung onto each other's gazes until the awkwardness became too much. He glanced down at his hands. "I already knew Arawn was your father."

She gaped at him. "How?"

"Dino told me while we waited for you outside the tavern."

She relaxed into the back of the bench. "Of course he did."

"It doesn't make you a monster, this magic you wield. What you do with it defines who you are."

"You saw what I did with it."

When he lifted his eyes again, the sun reflected in his gaze, and he trapped her within their sea foam depths. "You did what you had to for the life of someone you love. Never be sorry for making those impossible choices others are too afraid to consider."

As quickly as that dangerous man Miller kept hidden appeared, he was gone again. "We should get to this warehouse you spoke of. I shouldn't have distracted you from it."

Cora took a few seconds to gather her thoughts. "It's a waste of time. Segomo won't let Marshall leave anything lying around for me to find. I'm going to take the notebooks home and finish reading through them."

"I can help."

"We've established how well that's going to work out. Besides, you're missing a once in a lifetime opportunity to spend what little time you have left here with a part of your family you'd otherwise never have the chance to meet. I'll have to send you back soon, anyway."

"You can try."

She pushed to her feet, ignoring the taunt. They were almost to the pavement when she spotted a tiny clump of brown fur laying in the grass beneath a maple tree. She knelt, gently scooping it up. Its body wasn't quite stiff. It hadn't been dead very long.

"You poor thing," she cooed, cradling the limp squirrel in her hands. A soft warmth bloomed in her palms, glowing with a faint crimson hue that pulsed gently, like a heartbeat. The magic tingled beneath her skin, subtle but alive, threading through her fingers and into the tiny body.

At first, nothing happened.

Then, a whisper of movement. A flutter of fur tickled her palms. A spark ignited in the stillness. The squirrel jerked and spasmed, then settled, its nose twitching as it peeked out from between her fingers, dazed but alive.

"There you are," she whispered, smiling. "Let's get you back to your nest."

Before she could stand, Miller cupped his hands around hers. "Let me." His grip on the squirrel was surprisingly gentle for a man his size.

He scaled the tree with the ease of someone who'd spent his whole life climbing. He found the nest and placed it back with its family, then jumped to the ground, landing more gracefully than expected.

"Thank you," she said.

He stared at her with a boyish fascination. "That was amazing. Can you do the same with people?"

"I can, but Arawn tends to frown on that sort of thing." She avoided his gaze, focusing on her feet until they reached the car.

They were nearly to the city limits when Miller spoke again. "I think it's unfair how people treat you."

She was glad she had to focus on the heavy traffic, so she couldn't glare at him. The weight of his stare was hard enough to ignore, and she knew if she looked into his eyes, she would be trapped once again.

"If they took the time to get to know you; the woman you hide behind that mask you wear, they would see what an amazing person you really are."

Checking the side mirror, she said, "Good thing I have you fooled."

"I think it's the rest of the world you have fooled."

She struggled to keep her eyes on the road. His stare was like a caress on her cheeks and all she wanted to do was get lost in it. He saw beyond her ruse and glimpsed the woman that so desperately sought to be acknowledged.

Fate had a messed-up sense of humor, sending a man who was already spoken for. One day Cora would have to send a personal thank-you card to her along with a box of angry vipers.

Chapter 8

THE DRIVE FROM THE city was awkward and quiet. Now and then Miller shifted in his seat, poised to speak, but each time he tried, she preemptively shut him down. After his third attempt, she flipped on the radio, drowning out whatever else he wanted to say.

She parked in front of the Wodehal house and stared out of the driver's window, hoping he would take the hint and get out of her car without striking up a conversation.

"Are you not coming inside?" Miller asked, holding on to the open passenger door.

She motioned to the back seat where the notebooks were sprawled haphazardly. "I have a lot of reading to do. I'll call if I find anything."

He was slow to move away and even slower to shut the door. As soon as he did, she shifted into reverse and whipped the car around to leave. She kept glancing in the rearview mirror until Miller finally disappeared inside.

The excuse to search the journals had been a flimsy one. Whatever lay in those books wouldn't give them the answers they needed, but that didn't mean she wasn't going to keep trying. Currently, she knew the who, when, why, and how, but the where was still a mystery. Even with what information she had gleaned from those pages, there were no leads that would help them find Marcos, much less save him from the horrific fate that awaited him.

Cora glanced at the analog clock on her dash. Each tick of the second hand was more time wasted. Sleep was no longer a luxury she could afford. She would go through every single word of those journals for even the smallest bit of information, whether it was helpful to her cause or not.

The silence of her house pressed in on her when she stepped over the threshold. On her way to the kitchen, she dropped the notebooks on the coffee table. The heavy stack of books rattled the cheap wood. She eyed the kettle, then drifted to the unopened bottle of vintage port waiting to be uncorked. She needed something stronger than tea to see her through. Drink and glass in hand, she returned to the living room, where she plopped down on the couch, ready to dive into another round of near indecipherable text.

For hours, she lost herself in the abhorrent ravings of Marshall's private thoughts. Had she known he was capable of such atrocities, she would have cut him out of her life years ago. She read the last line of the second book, and having learned nothing useful, leaned back into the plush cushions, letting her head fall to the side. The sun was nearly gone from the sky, leaving only a faint glimmer of starlight twinkling through the sheer curtains.

Pushing off the couch, she stared into the kitchen. Not really up to cooking an elaborate meal, she went to her room and grabbed the tin of chocolate she kept inside her bedside table. It had been a spur-of-the-moment buy when she visited Dino's shop. She planned to save them for a lonely night of watching whatever old movie was on the telly.

When she returned to the couch, she poured herself another glass of wine and slid one of the dark chocolates onto her tongue, savoring the sharp bite of the bitter treat. Her thoughts kept slipping back to earlier in the day with the incident at the pawnshop and later at the park.

Miller's face haunted her, and no matter how hard she tried, she couldn't dispel the intense attraction she felt for him. He witnessed the full scope of her godhood, and it hadn't scared him away. A dangerous ache bloomed in her chest, prompting her to take a long drink, hoping to dismiss the feeling.

There was a sharp rap on her door, and she jumped, nearly spilling her the dark liquid on the open journal in front of her. She glanced at the clock on the wall beside her. It was well after seven o'clock, and she wasn't expecting anyone. Her heart thudded against her chest with each step she took. When she opened the door, Miller stood half hidden in the shadows of the dim light above his head. She stuck her head outside, looking down the path to the road.

"What are you doing here? Did something happen at Darya and Edwind's?"

"Nothing is wrong. I was out for a walk and ended up here." His gaze flicked down her body before snapping back to her face.

A wave of goosebumps bloomed across her skin where his eyes had gone. "Alone?"

"Yes."

"How do you know where I live?"

"I came into the village earlier with Aunt Darya. She showed me."

"I see. So, you walked? All the way from your uncle's house?"

"I'm a capable man."

"Why?"

He shrugged. "That house is too confining."

"You wanted to get out of one confining space and into another?"

His mouth tightened into what could best describe as a poor attempt at a scowl. "May I come in?"

Moving aside, she waved him over the threshold. "Sure. I'll call Darya and let her know you are safe."

He ignored her comment and stepped past her. "Have you found anything else in the journals?"

"Nothing useful."

The phone call to Darya went better than expected. At least Edwind wasn't on his way to her place. Not yet, anyway. After convincing Darya to keep Edwind home, Cora returned to the living room to find Miller sticking the last of her chocolates between his lips. "Sure, help yourself," she grumbled.

He held up the empty tin. "Do you have any more of these? They are delectable."

She snatched the box from him. "No. That was my emergency stash."

"My apologies. I will replace them. Where can we find more?"

He went to stand, but she put a hand on his shoulder, holding him in place. "Don't worry about it. I can get more later." If Dino would even sell to her anymore. "Edwind is furious that you came all this way by yourself, but he's not rushing over to pick you up."

"I wish he would stop treating me like some inept child."

"Well, you are out of your element." She went back to the kitchen to grab an extra glass. "Here, I have plenty of wine."

While she filled his glass, he asked, "Do you still care for your brother? Segomo, that is."

She lifted the bottle and stared at him, unsure of how to answer.

"My grandfathers were excellent teachers of history. I've heard Segomo's name before. He is the son of the keeper of souls and was once a ruthless leader of Arawn's most feared Death Knights. Great Grandfather once served under his command."

Though Cora knew Hengist's past with her family, it was difficult to wrap her head around just how old the ancient dragon really was. She nodded. "Who better to give you a lesson in history than those who lived it?"

Miller relaxed on the couch, and his unwavering stare made her shift uncomfortably. "We have a complicated relationship," she said. "He would have killed me if he didn't need a hostage. I'm Father's half mortal child who gets to live the life denied to Segomo. He's always resented me for that. I tried to prove to him I wasn't the bratty, spoiled little goddess he thought I was. Eventually, I had to accept there was nothing I could say or do to change his mind."

Miller reached for the bottle, refilling her glass as she had done for him. His gaze wandered over the room, landing on a group of photos on the wall across from the couch. "Aunt Darya told me of these photographs." He stood and strode to the frames. "I am hoping to take a few with me when I return so I can show Mother." He pointed to the frame. "Who is this woman with you?"

"That's my mother, Magda."

"Does she still live?"

"She does, but I haven't seen her in a long time. It pains me to watch her body wither away while I remain the same." She swirled the wine, staring intently as if it held the answers to the universe. "Does that make me a terrible daughter?"

"If it does, then I must be a terrible son. I occasionally find myself relieved that my father disappeared at sea, so time would not ravage his body. I know my mother feels the same way, though she would never say so aloud."

Cora nodded solemnly. "Sometimes, we bury the truth to cope with life's unfairness." Refusing to travel any further down that road, she gathered the journals into a neat pile. To change the subject, she said, "I bet it's a relief to have the knowledge that your destiny is waiting for you when you return home."

He frowned at her. "What do you mean?"

"Your future, my past, everything that will come to pass. It's been written already. The woman you marry. Your children. All of it."

His eyes went out of focus for a few seconds. "To some, the certainty of one's future would be welcomed, but it absolutely terrifies me to think I have no control over my destiny."

He came around to the couch and plopped down. "What if I'm not the one destined to carry on the Wodehal legacy? What if Mother has another child? She is still young. Grandfather Horsa could have more children we do not yet know of. Why is everyone so sure it is I who must make this sacrifice for the sake of our family?"

Cora sympathized with his reluctance to be burdened with such a heavy responsibility. "You realize Horsa has lived through this, right? He hasn't exactly given us all the details, but he mentioned Dino being a direct descendant of Gita by way of her son. Her only son."

He leaned forward, elbows braced on his knees. "Coming here has shown me how much of what I would be missing if I'm forced to stay on Didean."

A terrible thought occurred to Cora. What if, by trying to take Marcos to ten-twelve and letting Miller slip through the portal, she irrevocably screwed up the Wodehal bloodline? There was no telling what kind of mess this was going to make of their past, or what Morigan would do to her.

The dread festering inside her must have shown on her face, because Miller sat forward and said, "You had no influence on my decision to leave. I've felt this way long before you ever fell into my life. I have lived under the pressure to carry on the traditions of my family and live up to a man I've never met. Now that I have, I question whether I want to become the same man as Uncle Edwind. He is not who my mother thinks he is."

Cora's brows rose in disbelief. "Edwind is one of the kindest, most loyal men I've ever known. He can test one's patience, sure, but there is no one else I'd rather have on my side." She reached for his hand, squeezing gently. "If you were in his place, wouldn't you be so fiercely protective of your family?"

Miller narrowed his eyes at her. "Do not use your sensible logic on me."

Taking up her glass, she said, "Look, I understand more than anyone the pressure and expectation of family. As the daughter of a god and a druid priestess, I had a lot of expectations growing up. I spent most of my childhood in the underworld learning to control my magic. Arawn made it clear that one day I was to take my place at his side as heir to his throne. Until then, I was allowed to live among my mother's people."

She tipped her head back, downing the rest of the tart wine. "I don't want it; any of it. I want to forge my own path and not have to walk in someone else's footsteps."

Miller took the glass from her hand and set it on the table, doing the same with his. Cora tracked his movements, her pulse doubling when he leaned in, his lips brushing against hers. She tasted the tart hint of port mixed with the memory of the chocolate lingering on his breath. Her exposed flesh rippled with goosebumps when he pressed into her, his tongue joining hers in a seductive dance that built slowly while their hands explored as tentatively as their kiss.

He pulled her deeper into his embrace and she gave into him, helpless to his touch, despite the voice in the back of her mind begging her to stop, to get away from this man who could never be hers. But the dangerous desire he kindled earlier now raged out of control through her blood. She worked her fingers into his hair, deepening their kiss. His hands moved slowly, urging the strap off her shoulder. Lightning followed in the wake of his fingertips, making both her pulse and breath quicken.

His calloused palms found their way under her shirt, fingertips brushing against taught nipples. There was no biting protest to stop him this time. Instead, she arched into him, aching to feel him against her bare flesh.

In between the ebb and flow of their kiss, images swept through her mind. A moon hung full above them. Miller stared down at her, silhouetted by the ethereal glow. His eyes flared in the dark of the night as if intending to devour her with sight alone. The scene shifted, and she was under a waterfall, an arm anchored around her waist as Miller pushed inside her. She screamed his name, but her voice was lost in the cascading water.

Cora opened her eyes, and she was back on her sofa, resting against the worn fabric. Miller had broken from her mouth and was now exploring the supple softness of her breasts. She tried to speak, but her lips moved in wordless cries of pleasure. When at last she found her voice, she squeezed his shoulders, urging him to move away. "What are we doing?"

He hovered over her. His irises burned like white-hot embers with his need for her. "Making our own path."

Reality came crashing into her. His words sliced through the haze of desire, and she pushed at him, wriggling free, then yanked the strap over her shoulder. She squeezed her eyes shut, shoving down the warring emotions on the cusp of swallowing her whole. "I—We—" Her chest heaved with the effort to speak.

Miller sat up. "Did I say something wrong?"

She scrambled to her feet and grabbed the glasses from the table. "As an amazing a lover that I'm sure you are, I won't be used as a means to spit in the eye of fate or destiny or whatever it is you are trying to escape. You will have to find someone else for that."

He followed her to the kitchen. "Is that what you think I want?"

Struggling to hold a neutral tone, she forced a smile. "I think we've had too much to drink and let it get to our heads."

"What I said just now—"

She whirled around, keeping her eyes locked on his chin. "Can never happen. You have your destiny, whether you want it or not. It's the reason Marcos exists. We nearly screwed up everything, and for what? Because we don't like the life that's laid out for us? At least you have a family to look forward to."

"Cora—"

She motioned for the door. "Please, go."

"Will you let me explain myself?"

"You need to go." She dug her fingers into her palms, desperately clinging to the knowledge that what she was doing was the right thing.

For Dino.

For Marcos.

Miller blew out a harsh breath. "Let me explain," he begged again

"Leave," she snapped.

He stared at her for a long time. She wondered if he would fight her like he had done since arriving in nineteen ninety-two. At last, he dipped his head, his mouth set in a tight grimace. "As you wish."

She flinched at the sound of the door slamming shut. Despite what she said, every part of her being wanted to race after him and give him an escape from his destiny. She wanted Miller all to herself; this man who stood unafraid against the darkness inside her.

Maybe he was simply using her. Just like everyone else. It was easier to think he was yet another person in her life stringing her along until she was used up, but she knew better. There was nothing in this world or the next that could convince her that a blood relative of the Wodehal clan would be so fundamentally cruel, for cruelty's sake.

In the end, it didn't matter how they felt about each other. His path was set in stone, and there was no room for her on it.

She swiped at her eyes, but the tears kept coming. In her bedroom, she dug out a t-shirt and jeans from the laundry she hadn't yet put away. She couldn't stay there alone with her thoughts. If she let herself think—if she let herself feel—it would break her. She needed a distraction to quiet the guilt clawing at her insides. A stupid, meaningless, self-destructive distraction. And there was no better place than the pub down the street.

The man behind the wheel of the town car tensed when a tall figure stomped down the walk to the street. Segomo leaned forward. "Do not make a move against him. We need not invite trouble when it is walking away."

Marshall eyed Segomo in the rearview mirror. "That bitch killed my golem. It's only fair that I return the favor."

Segomo rested a hand on the back of the passenger's seat, ready to latch onto Marshall's throat. "If you so much as hint at a threat to Cora, I will make you beg for the sweet taste of death."

Marshall met his stare in the mirror again. Satisfied with the fear he glimpsed in the warlock's shadowed gaze, Segomo relaxed. "We are not here to spill blood. You were a fool to leave those tomes so easily accessible. If the Little Goddess or her dragon companions use them against us, we will both be at the mercy of a monster even more dangerous than myself."

"If you had kept your guise in place, she wouldn't have had a reason to suspect me."

Segomo stared out of the window, watching the house. "That couldn't be avoided. Cora is much more clever than you realize." More so than he wanted to admit. She had come a long way from the temperamental young woman that abandoned him all those years ago.

Marshall snorted. "I doubt Cora is going to hand over my journals, not even if we ask nicely. What do you suggest we do?"

Before Segomo had the chance to voice his uncertainty, someone else appeared out of the gloom. Cora followed the same path as the other man, but instead of turning right, she kept walking forward. Having her gone from the house made things easier. He waited until she was out of sight before exiting the car.

Marshall's constant presence irritated him. By the time they reached the front door, Segomo's blood tingled with the need to shove an elbow into the warlock's gut to make his feelings clear.

Before his imprisonment, Segomo would have made an example out of people like Marshall. There was no room in his army for pathetic, power-hungry creatures that fed on the misery of others for the sake of their own amusement. He most certainly would not abide conjuring an abomination like that pitiful golem. Cora had shown mercy by killing it.

His frustration doubled when he realized the door was locked. Such things wouldn't have stopped him had he not been cut off from his birthright.

Marshall sidled up next to him. "Allow me." He whispered an incantation. The air stirred around them, sending an icy finger down Segomo's spine. The faint click of the lock releasing broke through the silence. Marshall pushed the door open, allowing Segomo to go in first.

Maybe the worm could be of use after all.

Marshall flicked his hand, and all the lights sprang to life at once. "There they are." He rushed to the small table in the middle of the sparsely decorated room.

Segomo turned his attention to the wall to his left with hanging images adorning the white surface. The faces were too crisp and clean to be paintings, yet he knew of no such magic that could create such a marvel. One in particular caught his eye. It was a depiction of Cora and another woman. They both shared the same dimpled smile and petite noses. Her mother, no doubt. Cora often spoke of her. The priestess was a kind mother, but a shrewd leader. It pleased him to know that such a commanding figure remained in Cora's life.

"Those are photographs." Marshall's voice broke through Segomo's thoughts. "They are quite the invention. We use what is called a camera to capture whatever subject we want instantly. Better than having to sit still for hours at a time to have someone paint your likeness."

Indeed. Segomo wondered if he could find one of those cameras for his own use. His gaze wandered to the side, where another image portrayed a different family. The mother had dark hair and pale skin. He recognized her man from the bar. As soon as he saw those emerald eyes, Segomo knew he was the progeny of Hengist. He had felt the death dragon's power coursing through the man's veins. A little girl and boy were standing in front of their parents, their wide smiles lacking the wariness of those who had experienced the hardships of life.

Backing away from the wall, Segomo headed down the narrow hall to the open doorway on his right. He stood at the threshold, struck with a sense of unease. Breaking into Cora's home was one thing. Probing into her sacred space was an entirely different form of intrusion. One he wasn't comfortable with, given how private he had been when she invaded his life for the sake of helping her control her powers.

He was about to leave the bedroom when he glimpsed a small wooden box sitting on a table near the bed. From where he stood, he recognized the deft carvings from a hand that had spent millennia practicing the art of what his father sometimes referred to as whittling. For some reason, using that term amused Arawn.

To Segomo, however, it was a way to pass the time. He made that box with Cora in mind. He placed a pink pearl inside before giving it to her. His mouth twitched at the memory of her excited squeal when opening it. It was one of the last times he saw her so happy.

Curiosity got the better of him. He lifted the lid, surprised at what he found. Not long before Cora stopped visiting, she'd gotten angry at him because he wouldn't tell her about his past and the events leading to his imprisonment. If she knew what the horrors his deeds had wrought, she would treat him as the monster everyone else did.

The next time they saw each other, she claimed to have thrown the pearl back into the sea, but she held on to it. He picked up the gold band and studied the precious stone. Perhaps after he completed his bargain with Indech, he would have the chance to ask her what he did that had driven her away.

"We need to go."

Segomo glanced over his shoulder where Marshall stood in the doorway, holding the tomes close to his chest like a lost lover.

"My ravens spotted Cora returning."

Ring still in hand, Segomo started for the door, then thought better of stealing it. A bitter part of him wanted her to know that he was aware of her lie, so he left it on the table beside the box.

"Where is she?" Segomo asked.

"Not far." Marshall closed his eyes. "And she isn't alone."

"We need not complicate things. Now is not the time for confrontation." Even as he spoke the words, he made up his mind about his next move.

Cora didn't set out to pick up the guy at the pub. He was a local she'd seen hanging around and tried to ask her out a few times before, but she had no interest in a man who cared more about his appearance than most women. After the first round of shots, she successfully dimmed the memory of Miller's disappointed expression when she kicked him out.

That was about the time she got distracted by Will. Or was his name Daniel? It didn't matter. He was simply a means to rid herself of the nagging ache in her chest.

She offered to bring the guy to her house for a night of noncommittal drunken debauchery. He'd been more than willing to take her up on the proposal. On the way back to her house, Will or Daniel drew her into his arms, pressing his mouth to her neck. His breath was heavy with expensive whiskey. "I can't wait to bury my face between those beautiful legs of yours."

"We're almost at my place." She stopped him short of her mouth, not ready to wipe away Miller's kiss just yet.

They rounded the corner of her street, and her blood turned to ice in her veins. The body Segomo inhabited was walking down the stone path from her house and climbed into a black town car.

She threw herself and the man around the five-foot brick retainer wall. "Shit."

"What's wrong?"

Without taking her eyes off the car, she said, "I'm sorry, but I have to cut tonight short?"

He moved into her. "You're not going to turn me on like this and expect me to walk away."

She patted his face. "No, of course not." Then ran a glowing finger down his cheek.

His eyes rolled back, and he fell to the pavement. He would wake in a few hours with a massive headache, but he'd be alive.

At the corner, she chanced a look around the brick building as the town car pulled away. When it disappeared over the hill, she rushed to her front door, finding it still locked. Once inside, she flipped on the living room lights. Something was wrong. Not in a way she could pinpoint, but in a way that set her nerves on edge. She was drawn to the coffee table. The notebooks were gone.

A mixture of emotions flowed through her, rage being the strongest. Now she wished she'd stayed home. Maybe then she would have had the chance to extract some answers out of Segomo before sending him back to the underworld. The audacity of invading her home and touch her things was infuriating.

She went to her room to make sure nothing else had been taken. At first glance, everything looked in order. Then she spotted the ring sitting on the nightstand beside the little jewelry box that housed it.

Another wave of unwanted emotion rampaged through her. She snatched up the ring. It was a warning. He wanted her to know that he had been inside her home, her room. She should have thrown it away like she wanted to when she left him behind, but that silly sentimental girl couldn't bring herself to do it. The box and the pearl had meant the world to her because it came from Segomo.

"I should have known you lied about getting rid of it."

Cora turned to find Segomo standing in the doorway of her bedroom. He was across the threshold faster than she could close the distance between them. He wrapped his fingers around her wrists, holding her arms away from him.

"Where's Marcos?" she demanded.

Unfamiliar eyes searched her face. "Why do you care so much about one insignificant child?"

"He's not insignificant."

He studied her for a long time before saying, "The boy is safe. In fact, he is being treated like a little prince. He has everything his dragon heart desires."

She jerked against his grip, surprised at how strong he was, despite his mortality. "If you give him to me, I'll beg Father for leniency."

His laughter lacked any mirth. "Not even you could save me from his wrath, Little Goddess. I've come too far, sacrificed too much to go back to that gilded cage. Until now, you've been but a nuisance. If you continue to get in the way of my plans, I will have to take more drastic measures." He glanced at the photos on the chest of drawers of her and Daraya at the beach with the kids.

"Don't you dare threaten my friends."

When he looked at her again, there was genuine concern touching his features. "I don't make threats, Coramagda." He bent forward and laid a gentle kiss on her forehead. "I am giving you this warning because of the past we once shared and because of the blood we still do. Leave me to do what I must."

He released her wrists, but the familial affection she'd craved from him for so long paralyzed her. Never in all the years that he was her guardian had he ever shown her such overt tenderness.

The sound of the front door slamming closed snapped her out of the shocked state and she bolted after him. By the time she made it to the street, the car was already speeding away, leaving her to stare dumbly after him.

Remembering the not-so-subtle threat to Darya and her family, Cora ran back to the house to grab her keys before taking off toward the coast.

Chapter 9

MILLER LAY IN BED, unable to sleep. His mind refused to quiet, replaying the conversation with Cora over and over again. Did he misread her intentions? Surely not. She reciprocated their kiss just as enthusiastically.

What are we doing? Her voice rasped into his ear.

Making our own path.

It was a simple answer to her question. Yet, she reacted as if he had insulted her.

The sound of frantic pounding brought him upright. He eyed the door, listening to the muffled voices on the other side. Cora's panicked words drew him from the bed and across the room. He slid closer to the opening, peering into what his aunt and uncle called the living room.

"—back from the pub down the street and spotted Segomo coming out of my house," Cora said. "I thought he left, but he was only waiting for me to return."

"Did he take anything?" Darya was facing away from Miller, but he heard the brittle edge of fear in her voice.

"He took everything. The journals. My notes. All of it. Apparently, there was something important inside them after all."

"What about the guy you were with? Did Segomo hurt him?"

Cora ran a hand through her hair. "I didn't have time to un-ring that bell. I sort of knocked him out before we got to my place. It was the easiest way to keep him out of danger."

Miller frowned. He wasn't sure how to feel about the thought of Cora with another man.

"And," she continued, "Segomo made a thinly veiled threat toward you and your family if I didn't back off."

Darya urged Cora toward the couch. "Don't worry about us. We're protected here." She studied Cora's face, then frowned. "You look exhausted. When was the last time you slept?"

Cora turned her head to the side, avoiding eye contact. "I don't need sleep. I need to find Marcos."

Darya looked over her shoulder and Miller thought she was looking at him, but his uncle came into view.

"What's going on?" Edwind took one look at Cora's face and his sleepy demeanor disappeared.

"Segomo took the journals. He threatened to hurt you, Darya, and the kids."

"But we are safe here," Darya reiterated.

"Darya is right," Edwind agreed. "You will not be harmed among these walls. Segomo isn't the scariest foe we've faced. He isn't even fully alive."

"Alive or not he's a master of strategy and manipulation." Cora crossed her arms. "That makes him even more dangerous."

"I'm not arguing with you anymore." Darya started for the stairs. "You're not leaving this house again tonight. You can sleep in Brigita's room."

Cora's shoulders slumped forward, arms dropping to her side. "Don't disturb the children. I'll sleep on the couch."

"Fine. As long as you rest. I'll be right back with a pillow and blanket."

Edwind followed Darya upstairs, leaving Cora to collapse on the plush cushions. Her eyes fluttered a few times before drooping closed, her body sagging into the cushions.

Miller slipped out of the bedroom room. Cora's chest rose and fell in the steady rhythm of slumber.

"Did we wake you?" Darya was at the top of the stairs, holding a blanket and pillow.

"I haven't been to sleep yet." His gaze flicked to the couch. "Why does Cora think she is the only one who can fight this battle?"

"She feels responsible for what happened to Marcos."

"But it wasn't her fault. I don't care what that pompous descendent of mine says."

The corners of Darya's mouth twitched. "As much as I agree with you, it still weighs heavily on her conscience."

He turned back to Cora, his chest tightening with regret. "I wish for her to sleep in my bed."

Darya smiled at him curiously.

"Alone, I mean. What kind of man would I be to make a woman sleep in such an uncomfortable place when there is a much more suitable bed for her?" He didn't mention how much he wanted to join her.

Once downstairs, Darya set the blankets on the back of the couch. "I'll wake her and help her into bed."

He held up a hand. "Let me." Miller gathered her up in his arms, pausing when she stirred. Maybe it was imagination or desire, but he could have sworn she relaxed into him.

Once he got her settled into the bed, he unlaced her boots and slipped them from her feet, then pulled the soft blanket over her body, and while he was bent over her, he ran the back of his fingers down the side of her face, wishing to undo tonight. He hadn't meant for her to feel like a means to break free from his destiny. Far from it. He had wanted to kiss her since their time in the park. When he worked up the courage to finally do so, he knew she was the woman he wished to wed.

After following her through the portal, he dreamed of Cora in his homeland. He wanted nothing more than to take her back with him. He would be content to spend the rest of his life on Didean as long as she was by his side.

Fate was indeed cruel to put this beautiful woman in his path, only to steal her away again and force him into a miserable existence, knowing what he was missing. And he would miss Cora when he was gone.

By the time he returned to the couch, his aunt had gone upstairs, leaving him alone with his thoughts. He relaxed, letting his head fall back. Movement on the top landing caught his attention, and he spotted Brigita peering around the banister.

"Where's Aunt Cora?"

"She's sleeping," he said. "Like you should be."

"Why aren't you in bed too?"

He patted the cushion beside him. "I'm trying to get comfortable."

A frown worked onto her face. "But—"

"Brigita Diane," Darya whispered. "Back to bed."

The little girl whirled around and ran for her room.

Darya looked over the railing. "I'll make sure she doesn't bother you again."

It was a struggle, but eventually he wedged himself into the cushions, finding a comfortable spot that allowed him to drift into dreams of Cora's beautiful face and tender touch.

Gulls cackled against the darkness of the early morning sky still dotted with stars. They illuminated a dead seal that had washed ashore. The stink of decay was strong in the air, but it didn't come from the half rotted carcass. Segomo stood at the edge of the dock, staring into the dark abyss of the waters below. Shards of sunlight cut through the dusk, slicing through the choppy water. He drifted into the past he'd spent centuries trying to bury, yet the memories always returned.

The smell of smoke and despair filled his senses, making his gut clench. Faint screams echoed inside his head. He squeezed his eyes closed, willing the faces to recede into the farthest corners of his mind.

Behind him, the sound of heavy footsteps broke the spell, and he was again on the docks overlooking the sea.

"Did you clean up your mess?"

Segomo clenched his fists at his side, angered by the Fomorian's petulant tone. "Your people's incompetence is no fault of mine."

The grotesque monster laughed. "Perhaps you do not know how to properly motivate them."

Ignoring the blatant taunt, Segomo turned, coming face to face with misshapen features. "I have kept my end of our bargain."

"You will have your freedom when my father walks among us again. Until then, you are leashed to that mortal's body."

Segomo looked forward to flexing his godly powers and showing Indech just how dangerous a creature he could be. "You are going to find the family of that boy you've taken will not be so easily brushed aside. They will tear this world apart to get Marcos back."

Indech's face twisted, the too small sockets of his eyes pinching inward. "They are but a nuisance. As for your dear Coramagda, if she gives you too much trouble, get rid of her."

Segomo's jaw clenched, trying to hide his shock. He went to great lengths to keep her presence hidden from Indech. It must have been that worm, Marshall, who put her name in the Fomorian's ear. Segomo vowed to destroy the warlock and everything he held dear.

When Segomo spoke, his voice was surprisingly steady. "She is not to be harmed."

"I care not for what you do with our enemies as long as they do not get in our way."

A thick mist rolled inland, stopping just short of land. Indech stepped past Segomo. After a few seconds, a modest sized boat came into view. It slowed to a stop at the end of the pier, the single sail folding in on itself. There were three men aboard, all of which stank of rot. Segomo didn't want to imagine which putrid pit of the underworld Indech found them in. One day, he would have to ask the Fomorian exactly how he managed to penetrate Arawn's realm so easily.

Segomo waited until the ship disappeared into the fog before returning to the car. His warning to Cora would go unheeded. She was too stubborn for her own good. It was one of the many traits he instilled in her when she was in his care. He made sure she fought for everything she wanted. The irony wasn't lost on him. Cora was determined to save the boy, though he didn't understand why she went to such measures for the child.

Marshall waited in the driver's seat. "That is one scary beast."

Segomo drove his stare into the other man's skull until Marshall's smile disappeared and he looked away, glaring out of the window as the ship disappeared into the mist. There was another option to make sure Cora wasn't a threat to their plans and ensure her safety at the same time. "I need you to locate an artifact for me." Finding the torque wasn't going to be easy, but Marshall had proven himself resourceful.

For Cora's sake, Segomo hoped it would be enough to keep her alive.

Tiny fingers pushed at Miller's cheeks, rousing him from slumber.

"Is he alive?" Saebastian asked.

"Let your cousin sleep." Darya whispered from somewhere behind the couch.

"Bastian." Cora's whisper caressed Miller's ears, making the hairs on his neck bristle. "Check his eyelids."

The little boy dutifully obeyed and poked at Miller's face, trying to reach his eyes, only to be snatched up and brought into a hug before the tickling began. Bastian squealed with delight as he squirmed and rolled, trying to get free from his tormentor.

Miller finally relented and let him go, then sat up so he could turn his sights on the woman who had sent her minion to do her bidding.

Cora was at the bar, a stack of parchment sitting before her. Soft, fiery curls cascaded down her back in loose waves. His fingers itched to caress those silky locks again. The shirt she wore draped over her, showing off slender legs.

He swallowed back a moan at the images that swirled inside his mind. He imagined how easily her muscles would yield under the pressure of his palms when he slid them in between her legs and up the inner parts of her thighs—

"Since you're awake," Darya's voice shattered his thoughts, "you can grab breakfast. Edwind took Brigita into the city to do some shopping, so I thought I would take Bastian into the forest to commune with the animals. I can wait for you to eat if you would like to join us."

Miller shrugged, tearing his attention away from Cora. "I don't see the point. I cannot speak to them."

"What about you, Cora?"

She shook her head, eyes never leaving the page. "I'd love to, but I'm trying to jot down what I remember from the notebooks." She scribbled something, then said, "What are the words?"

"What words?" Darya asked.

"That's one of the questions that kept popping up over and over. I didn't think much about it until I started writing everything down." Cora glanced up. "Don't mind me. I'm just rambling to myself. Enjoy your walk."

Miller went to the kitchen to fill his plate with the savory meats and eggs left out. He gathered the remaining three round pieces of bread his uncle called pancakes before taking a seat beside Cora. "Is there anything I can help with?"

"Can you tell me where they are keeping Marcos?"

He turned his attention to the food before him.

Her sigh was weary. "I'm sorry. I'm still shaken from last night. There was an incident at my place."

"I know." He took a bite of the sweet pancakes, meeting her stare. "I heard everything. It was smart of you to leave when you did."

A hint of red colored her cheeks, and she turned back to the notebook. After a few seconds, she said, "You didn't have to give up your bed. I was perfectly fine on the couch."

He poked the fork at her. "Would it kill you to simply tell someone thank you?"

Her mouth moved up into a slight smile and her eyes narrowed. "It might," she muttered.

He stared at the plate, hoping she didn't see his own cheeks flush. Her grin had a way of sending flutters through his stomach. After another minute of silence between them, he said, "I must explain what I meant last night—"

"It's fine. Really."

He leaned over, ready to make her hear him out, when he saw a familiar drawing. "What is that?"

She looked down. "A doodle I noticed. It's not exact, but as close as I can remember."

"I've seen it before." He went to his uncle's study and grabbed the glass case from the wall. He slid the encased map in front of Cora. "Uncle Edwind showed it to me yesterday. He said Grandfather Hengist drew it himself a few hundred years ago."

"Be careful with that thing."

He pointed to a symbol in the top right-hand corner of the aged parchment. It resembled a crest he once saw on the sail of Grandfather Horsa's ship. "Does this look like the same marking?"

She stuck the paper on top of the glass and her mouth dropped open. "It's almost identical. Oh my god. This must be important."

"Perhaps this is the place Marcos was taken?"

"Maybe. It's more than we had."

The look in her eyes seized his heart, and when she threw her arms around him, it took every ounce of willpower not to grab hold of her and bury his face in the delicate crevice of her neck. He lifted his head, searching her gaze for any sign that she wanted him to move away. The second her lips touched his, there was no holding back, and he crushed himself against her, desperate to be consumed by her fire.

They drew back from the kiss with an audible gasp. He moved into her again and she took hold of each side of his face like a possessive lover, refusing to relinquish her man.

There was a loud clearing of a throat behind them. Miller glanced over his shoulder to find Edwind holding two cloth bags of food in his arms. His uncle's brows were creased together, and his mouth was set in a tight scowl. Brigita stood beside him. Her expression morphed from shocked to joy. She clapped her hands and squealed with excitement before running upstairs.

Edwind approached the bar and dropped the bags beside the map. "Miller, gather the rest of the groceries from the car."

He hesitated, but did as he was told. He could still hear them from outside.

"Before you get angry and protective," Cora began. "That was a celebratory kiss."

"What is this map doing out of my office? Did you go in there without my permission?"

"What? No. I was trying to recreate what I could remember, and Miller recognized—"

"It was a mistake letting you stay here. How can you be so reckless? You know how important Miller is to this family. What were you thinking?"

"Edwind, would you listen to me? This map of yours—"

"I will not have this family's lineage jeopardized because you can't keep your damn legs closed."

Miller rushed into the house in time to see Cora's head snap back from the viciousness of his words. "What did you just say to her?" He let the bags fall to the floor.

Edwind swung around. "You have a duty to this family. I will not let her destroy your destiny."

Tears clouded Cora's eyes, reflecting the mid morning light spilling through open windows. She jumped off the stool and snatched her keys from the hook by the door. On her way by, Miller reached for her, but she jerked away from him. "Everything I've recreated is there on the bar. If I remember something else, I'll call Darya."

Miller rushed after her. "Please don't go."

Her lips trembled with the effort to hold in her pain. "I'm sorry."

"You did nothing wrong."

"He's right. You're already spoken for." Her eyes flicked to somewhere behind him and she threw herself into the car, refusing to meet his gaze.

"Cora, please."

Ignoring him, she sped out of the driveway, disappearing in a cloud of dirt.

Miller started to run after her, but Edwind grabbed his arm. He used the momentum of Edwind's grasp and swung a fist across his uncle's face. The impact of his jaw on Miller's closed hand sent a shockwave of pain through his wrist that he easily ignored. "How could you say such hateful things to her?" he yelled.

Edwind stumbled to the side, clutching his face. His eyes flashed with something dangerous, and for a second, Miller thought he might strike back. But then, just as suddenly, the rage flickered out, replaced by something far worse—disappointment.

Miller went on. "I never wanted any of this. Even before I came here." He took off for the road again.

"Where are you going?"

"Away from here. Away from you. Away from the life fate has been so cruel to curse me with."

"You could get yourself hurt or killed."

Miller whirled on him, his anger breaching the logical man who only chose violence as a last resort. "If you dare try to stop me, I will show you just how soft you've grown over the years, old man."

Edwind's fist clenched at his sides. "Bah. Be gone with you, then. Ruin your life and destroy that of your descendants. Your mother will not only have lost her husband, but a stubborn child as well."

Miller's jaw worked in tight contractions, but he didn't give in to his uncle's guilt. "You are despicable."

Chapter 10

CORA PULLED UP TO the curb and stared at her house, gripping the steering wheel so hard her knuckles turned white. Her chest ached with hollowness, his mind fogged with guilt and humiliation. She wanted to scream, cry—something. But instead, she climbed out of the car and dragged herself inside.

She made a slow, deliberate circle, taking in the sparse space, the silence reflecting a life that was just as empty. Aside from the few photographs of her mother and Darya's family, blank walls stared back at her. Even the light filtering through the curtains was dim, casting faint, lifeless shadows on the floor.

In her bedroom, she threw off the t-shirt Darya lent her. It still smelled of Miller, making her chest contract. On her way to the bathroom, she sloughed off the rest of her clothes. The sound of water bouncing off tile was a slight distraction, and when she climbed under the heavy stream, she set the temperature as hot as she could stand it.

For a long time, she stood there, letting the heat sink into her skin. Maybe the steam could scald away the guilt that had rooted inside her like a twisted tree. When the water cooled, she reluctantly turned off the faucet, wrapped a towel around her and went to her bedroom. She searched through the mountain of clothes still sitting in the laundry basket, where she picked out a plain black t-shirt and dark jeans.

By the time she was dressed, she had made up her mind to go into the city. Maybe Raquel had some luck with her spirits. If not, then she would call Dino about the island. He may be pissed at her, but he would jump at any chance to find his son.

She snatched up her keys and headed out the door. On her way down the path, she spotted a man coming toward her. Her heart skipped a beat, and she stopped mid stride.

Miller looked between the keys in her hand and her face. "Where are you going?"

"Into the city. Maybe Raquel has some good news for me." She tried to go around him, but he kept blocking her way. "Would you let me by?"

"Not until we speak."

She stared at the ground, unable to look at him. "Look, it's not the first time I've been called a whore, and I'm sure it won't be the last. Edwind was just trying to keep your destiny intact. I don't blame him." Her gaze crawled up his body to his face, but stopped at his chin. "Let it go, please."

His reaction came so fast, and his cry was so loud, her blood resonated with its ferocity. One second, she was standing on her walk and the next she was being carried inside by a pair of hands, both forceful yet gentle at the same time.

In the living room, he set her down on the couch and when she tried to stand, he pointed a finger at her, forcing her to stay put. "You will sit there and listen for once, you stubborn, willful woman. No one, not even the great Edwind Wodehal, gets to speak to you like he did today."

She shot to her feet, a renewed anger filling her. "Like how you are talking to me now?"

"Because you refuse to listen to reason."

"It's always about reason and logic with you, isn't it? Well, let me fill you in on some cold hard facts, Miller Wodehal." She ignored the blurred vision and kept her eyes locked on his, no matter how badly she wanted to shy away. "You speak of this life you so desperately want to escape. A life free from responsibility and the burden of family, but I promise you, one day those lonely nights start getting longer and colder. You keep telling yourself the bodies that fill your bed can make up for the connection your heart craves, but it doesn't."

She dropped to the couch again, resting her head in her hands. "You don't know how lucky you are to have the certainty of someone waiting to love you. I'd give anything to have that. I'd give up everything to trade places with her."

Miller's presence was like an anchor in the storm of her emotions. He knelt down in front of her, pulling her hands away from her face. "From the moment I followed you here, you have filled my thoughts and my dreams. I didn't kiss you to escape my destiny on Didean. I want you to be part of it. Why can't it be you I go home to?"

She rested her forehead against his. "You've already chosen her. She is in my past. She waits for you there."

He caressed her cheek, and when she saw he meant to kiss her, she stiffened against his touch. She stared at him, torn between desire and the crushing weight of reality. This wasn't supposed to happen. He wasn't supposed to love her. And yet...he did. And gods help her, she wanted to love him too.

His lips hovered next to hers. "If we are destined to part, let this moment be ours. To hold until we meet again in the next world."

Her resolve crumbled, dissolving into their kiss. She let him pull her off the couch. Taking him by the hand, she led him to her room, brushing off her jacket and kicking off her boots along the way.

In the bedroom, Miller hiked her up over his hips before following her onto the bed. The weight of his body cocooned her against the duvet. She urged him off her so she could wriggle out of her shirt. There was a fiery glow simmering in his gaze that heated her bare flesh. He climbed on top of her again, and she was struck by another sense of déjà vu, like she had been in this moment before. A smile parted her lips.

"What amuses you, sweet goddess?"

"I feel like we've done this before."

"Perhaps we have." He moved a hand inside her jeans, testing the heat of her desire, drawing a muffled whimper. His fingers nimbly unbuttoned her pants and worked them down her legs, along with her panties.

He bent over her, kissing her only briefly before moving down her neck to her breasts, taking his time, caressing each one with both his hands and lips. She writhed underneath him, burying her fingers deeper into his hair. The coarseness of his beard tickled her belly, then her thighs. His mouth enveloped her, forcing a wordless cry. He used his tongue to drive her to the edge of carnal bliss, and just before sending her over that cliff, he pulled back, holding her stare in the expanse between them.

"You are so beautiful." Then kissed her one last time, and she rocked forward, diving into the torrent of ecstasy that he called forth, crashing into him again and again.

She didn't realize he joined her at the head of the bed until he hovered over her, a satisfied grin on his lips.

She delicately ran her fingertips along his beard. "Make love to me."

He flung off his shirt and shimmied out of his jeans, then settled on top of her, drawn to her heat like the waves of the ocean to the moon. They both tensed when he arched into her, eliciting a quivering moan from Cora.

She dug her fingers into his bare back. "Again," she sighed.

He pulled back and repeated the motion, getting the same pleased response. With each repetition, he quickened his pace. When she was on the cusp of release, she drew him deeper into her embrace, giving in to the rush of pleasure that coursed through her body. She screamed his name as she worked herself against him for every ounce of rapture he allowed.

Miller rolled her over on top of him, his chest rising and falling in quick succession. "I tried to hold on, but you carried me away with you." He traced her breasts with his palms, then dropped them to her hips. "Though I am far from finished."

She took one of his hands and brought his palm to her mouth, caressing it with her lips.

For the rest of the day and into the night, they imprinted each other into their memories. Precious pockets of beautiful moments they hoped would sustain them. But in the back of Cora's mind, she clung to the truth that eventually she was going to have to let him go. No matter how much it tore her heart to shreds, Miller Wodehal was not hers to keep.

The sun hung heavy in the late afternoon sky, sending streaks of fire across the rolling waves of the ocean. Cora stood at the top of the hill overlooking the long stretch of beach where two children frolicked through the frothy surf.

"Don't go too far into the water," she called across the expanse of white sands.

Two cherub faces turned toward her, copper-blond hair tousled by the wind, bright green eyes lit with joy. They shot up from where they knelt in the water, screaming, "Daddy!"

Cora looked over her shoulder, her a smile blooming across her lips at the man cresting the hill. Miller held out his arms to the children running to his side. Before Cora could join them, the sound of the surf swelled in her mind until it overtook the dream, yanking her from its peaceful embrace.

She lay with her eyes closed, hoping to get back to the life she would never live; children she would never have. She fought to keep the tears from coming, but when they did, she rolled to her side, away from Miller.

He reached out, pulling her close. "I don't want to go back." His breath was warm against her neck.

She raised his hand to her lips. "You have to."

"Come with me."

Despite her sadness, she smiled. "I thought about it, but you know as well as I do, it's not that easy."

"I will never love another like I do you."

His words were daggers slicing her world into pieces. "How can you love someone like me?"

He urged her onto her other side so he could look her in the eyes. "How can I not?"

She melted into Miller's kiss, pulling him down until his weight settled over her. This was one final moment to belong to each other, even if only in body. As long as they remained joined, she could pretend this could be forever. His touch was a merciful escape from the crushing truth of her birthright.

Afterward, she lay with one arm draped over his torso. Her fingers curled around his bicep, hanging on to what little time they had left. At last, she pushed up to a sitting position. "Are you hungry? I can at least feed you before you go back to your aunt and uncle's house."

He pressed his lips to the side of her neck. "I will never pass up a good meal."

She stole one last kiss before throwing on a t-shirt and a pair of shorts before heading for the kitchen. No sooner had she pulled out a pan and set the eggs on the counter when there was a knock at the front door.

On her approach, she saw the wide outline of a man through the frosted oval glass. She barely got the door open before Edwind asked, "Is Miller here?"

She crossed her arms. "Yes."

"What are you doing here?" Miller said, keeping within arm's reach of her.

"I wanted to speak to you." Edwind paused. "Both of you. To apologize."

Cora stepped out of the way. "Come in. I'll make some tea."

Miller went to her side. "That won't be necessary. He can say his peace and leave."

Edwind sighed. "Dino stopped by this morning." He made an awkward motion in their direction. "So whatever happened between you two didn't screw up the grand design, apparently."

"Where is the apology?" Miller demanded.

Edwind crossed his arms. To Cora he said, "I shouldn't have spoken so cruelly to you. I was shocked, to say the least, seeing you kissing my nephew." Miller shifted beside her, and Edwind went on. "Anyway, Darya looked over the notes Cora left behind. The symbols are the same as those on my father's map."

Cora dropped her arms, the excitement of the discovery returning. "Marshall doodled them all over the journals. It has to be important."

He nodded. "It's an island few people know about. Dino and I can fly there. One of us can carry you." He looked at Miller. "I think it best if you return to your mother before we go."

Cora lifted her eyes to Miller. "He's right. The longer you stay, the more likely you'll change everything." Like they nearly did last night. She silently pleaded with him not to make things harder than they already were.

He nodded. "I agree."

Edwind said, "I would like the chance to spend more time with you. Perhaps we can wait a while longer before returning you to ten-twelve."

She urged Miller forward. "Go. I'll come by later to send you back home."

Edwind walked outside, letting Cora and Miller say their goodbyes.

"Fate is cruel," Miller whispered.

She rested her forehead on his chest, breathing him in. "Sometimes we don't understand the path that is laid out for us and what it holds."

"If my path does not lead to you, it is not the one I wish to walk." She pulled back, meeting his stare, and he cupped the side of her face. "But I know what I must do for the sake of my family."

She leaned into him, engraving his kiss into her memory.

"I will hold on to last night for the rest of my life. Know that it is duty alone that forces me to give my children to another woman." He moved his lips to her ear. "I love you, sweet goddess."

She clung to his neck, knowing if she said the words out loud, she wouldn't be able to let him go.

When he was gone, she propped herself up on the door, unable to stop the fountain of tears that flowed down her cheeks. After what seemed like hours, she dragged herself to the kitchen to put away the food that she no longer had to cook. In the bedroom, she stood at the foot of the bed, letting herself bask in the memory of the night before. When that became too painful, she yanked off the sheets to wash them.

On her way through the living room, she was startled out of her thoughts by another knock at the door. A hopeful part of her thought it might be Miller, coming to tell her he was going to defy fate and demand she go back with him. Yet, the outline she saw through the frosted glass was not the man she loved.

She flung open the door and froze. It was a face she never expected to see again. "Emmett? What the hell are you doing here?"

He leaned on the wall with one hand. The foot that Miller had skewered was bandaged and shoeless. "I can't say I'm sorry for this."

She cocked her head to the side. Two men flanked the stone path behind him. A pungent smelling cloth was shoved over her mouth and nose before she could react. It choked her with a sickeningly sweet scent that drowned her in darkness.

"I wish your daftie lover was here so I could give him a little payback." Emmett's voice sounded warbled as she sunk deeper into the dark hole of unconsciousness. "Oh well. The look on your face is fucking priceless."

Whatever he said next was lost in the bleak void of oblivion.

The night sky was clear, every star burning sharp against the velvet dark. Segomo hadn't seen them in so long, he'd nearly forgotten they existed. In the underworld, there were no stars, only faint reflections in the eyes of the dead.

How many times had he taken them for granted, cursing the light they cast through the trees when battle demanded stealth. Now, he understood he had squandered such a blessing.

The taste of freedom was sweet but tainted by the body he wore like an ill-fitting garment, every breath reminding him of what he'd lost. What could never be recovered. The familiar sting of regret was soon drowned out by seething anger. So much had been stolen from him, and Segomo would not be satisfied until Arawn was made to suffer as he had suffered. Once Segomo's mantle was restored, vengeance would be a delicious delicacy he would savor for years to come.

The sound of tires crunching over rock drew Segomo's attention to the black metal beast rolling to a stop mere inches from him. A man exited and limped around the door to stand in the yellow wash of the headlamps. Segomo glanced down at the bandaged foot and didn't bother hiding a satisfied smile. He thought slightly more of Emmett than Marshall, but despised both men equally. Where Marshall was cowardly and soft, Emmett embraced the dragon blood running through his veins, though he lacked the humility and patience Hengist exhibited. Emmett's recklessness would be his downfall.

"I hope Cora didn't give you too much trouble." Segomo crooned.

Emmett shifted, being careful not to put his full weight on the injured foot. "Hardly. That daftie she's fucking had to show off for her."

Segomo reigned in his irritation. "Where is she?"

"In the back. Safe and sound." Emmett motioned behind him. "You don't know how hard it was to keep my hands off her. That girl can make a man beg to be burned alive by her fire. I assume you have a way of subduing her so she doesn't kill us as soon as she wakes."

Segomo felt rather than saw the shadow roll across the ground to his right. A gangly figure stepped out of the blackness as if shedding a second skin. Indech approached them, carrying a familiar pewter torque in one hand. Just the sight of the Qel made Segomo shudder.

"Where is the little goddess?"

The name sounded foul coming from his rotting lips.

"In the back seat. Out cold." Emmett was smart enough not to posture in front of Indech. Maybe there was some sense left in that dragon yet.

Indech moved toward the car, trailing rot and death behind him.

Emmett turned to Segomo again. "What is he holding?"

"A means to keep her godhood subdued so she can't kill us when she wakes."

Emmett's expression brightened. "Well now, that's a bonnie trick, isn't it? Should make her a good bit more willing to submit when I arrange some time. Remind her of the wonderful times we used to have."

Segomo's jaw tightened. The mortal flesh he wore trembled with the echo of divine instinct. His hand flexed where he once wielded a blade so sharp, it could cut through the threads of fate itself.

"Oh, struck a nerve, did I?" Emmett's grin twisted with malice. "Come now, do something about it? I'd love nothing more than to bite your head clean off and piss down your neck."

The car door slammed shut behind them. Emmett turned toward the sound.

That was all Segomo needed. He moved with the grace and silence of a seasoned warrior, drawing the dagger from his side and slitting a thin line across Emmett's throat.

The dragon staggered, clutching at his neck as blood bubbled between his fingers. Taking advantage of his weakened foe, Segomo wrenched Emmett's head back and drove the blade into his heart, assuring a quick death. Hengist taught him there was little that could kill a dragon, but few could survive such a fatal blow. Especially not someone as young and weak as Emmett.

Segomo let the limp body fall to the ground, watching blood flow through fractured rock. There was no regret. No guilt. Only an old familiar thrill of witnessing an enemy perish. He knelt down, wiped the blade clean, and sheathed it in one smooth motion.

Indech stared at Segomo, unimpressed. "I still had use for him."

"He was a liability." He thought about suggesting they do the same to Marshall, but there was a deadline to keep. "We should go."

Indech didn't move at first. "Are you sure keeping Coramagda alive is wise? She is a distraction for you."

"As I've made clear. She is to remain untouched."

Indech ambled past him. "No one will come through this war unscathed. Not even you. Death would be merciful."

Segomo kept his gaze locked on the corpse at his feet.

Perhaps Indech was right. Maybe it was better for her to die rather than have her live in a world torn apart by gods and demons. A whisper of uncertainty swept through him. The all-consuming desire for vengeance that had once raged through him dwindled at the thought of what would happen to Cora. Once he reclaimed his godhood, he would protect her. Even if it meant locking her away.

Chapter 11

"YOU'VE BEEN STARING OUT of that window for the last half hour." Edwind appeared at Miller's side.

Miller pushed off the wall beside the front door, meeting his uncle's gaze. He had expected Cora to be there already. Maybe she defied the gods after all. In his heart, he knew better. She wouldn't put the lives of his descendants in danger for the sake of her own happiness.

"Are you in such a hurry to return home?" Edwind asked.

Turning his attention back to the front walk, Miller frowned. He couldn't rid himself of the sickening dread that twisted his insides. Never before had he experienced such a strong sense of foreboding. "Something isn't right."

Edwind shook his head. "I'm sure she—"

Miller whirled on his uncle. "She would have been here by now. I need to know she is safe."

Edwind glanced over his shoulder at Darya, who sat at the table with the children. "I'm taking Miller into the village. I'll return shortly."

She nodded, and Miller caught a glimpse of discontent in her gaze.

The drive to Cora's place was made in silence. Miller studied the passing faces, hoping to find Cora among them. When they reached her home, he didn't wait for Edwind and bound up the walk to her front door. A shiver ran down his spine when he saw it standing wide open.

Despite being unarmed, he rushed inside, ready to face whatever danger waited for him. He stomped through the house and into the bedroom, but she wasn't there. Back in the living room, Edwind met him in front of the couch. His uncle eyed every wall, each corner. Miller knew exactly what he was looking for, but there was no sign of a struggle.

"She's probably at our place, waiting for us." Edwind murmured, his voice falling short of the conviction of his words.

"Do you smell that?" Miller lifted his chin, taking in a deep breath. "Is aconite still so widely available in this time?"

The color drained from Edwind's face. "I've not seen it used since Darya was abducted in nine eighty-two."

Miller turned in a slow circle. "I should have been here. I should have stayed with her." He ran a hand through his hair, then headed for the door.

Edwind rushed to cut him off. "Where are you going?"

"To search for Cora."

"We don't know where to even begin to look, or if she has been abducted. She—"

"She is in danger," Miller snapped. "I cannot explain what I feel. Please, Uncle Edwind. We must find her." He let his senses drift outward, searching for her presence. "I can't sense her. Not like I should be able to."

When Miller opened his eyes again, Edwind was glaring at him, his expression twisted into horrified disbelief. "Oh, Miller. You stupid fool. You bonded yourself to her. That's how you knew she was in danger."

"I will not be used as a pawn in a bored god's perverse game. Not when the hearts of two people will be shattered in the wake of such selfishness."

"Selfishness—Do you know what this could mean for your future descendants?"

"Maybe it's better this way." Miller's eyes glazed over with tears that reflected the fear and anger coursing through him. "Segomo loses the vessel he means to use to free Tethra. Did you ever consider this is what I am meant to do?"

Edwind slowly shook his head back and forth. "Wiping out generations upon generations of people is not the answer."

The stone holding back Miller's pain cracked, and he threw a hand over his mouth to try to stifle the sob that leaked out. "What have I done?" he rasped. "I've let everyone down. My mother. My father. My children. Cora. I've failed them all."

Edwind took hold of Miller's shoulders. "Perhaps all is not lost. Let's get back to the house and call Dino. If he's still around, there is hope. As for Cora, are you sure you cannot feel her nearby?"

He closed his eyes, ignoring the pain in his heart. "It's faint. Yet I cannot tell you where."

"Then she still lives."

Cora clawed her way out of the heavy blanket of sleep, struggling to reach the surface of consciousness. The warmth of the sun caressed her face and pried at her eyelids. She rolled her head to the side, breathing in the fragrant odor of a flower she couldn't quite identify. The familiar scent took her back to her childhood. To her mother's grove.

Her arms trembled when she raised them to rub at her eyes, trying to force them open only to have the sunlight forced them closed again. She made a disgusted whimper and turned away from the harsh glare, nearly falling to the floor.

After a few tries, she finally pushed herself upright. She rolled her head from side to side, working out the kink in her neck. The world was cast in a gossamer haze, making the scenery sway in fuzzy shadows, but she could make out drab gray stone walls surrounding her.

From outside the window, she heard the sounds of men shouting. There was no urgency in their voices, but she recognized the unmistakable tone of soldiers. Movement at the foot of the bed caught her attention. A man sat with his legs crossed, one over the other. She scrambled backward, halted by cold, hard stone.

After marking his place in the book he was holding, Segomo set it on the table beside him. He watched her with the calm of a man who didn't realize he was minutes from being sent back to the underworld. "I was beginning to think you were going to sleep away the afternoon." His smile was serene; his tone pleasant.

Not in the mood for his off handed humor, she moved to the edge of the bed again. "Was Emmett working for you the whole time?" Her tongue kept sticking to the roof of her mouth. The vibration of her words made her wince from the pain that shot up her neck into the base of her skull.

Segomo's serenity evaporated. "He wasn't my first choice, given the history you two shared, but he was efficient."

Cora went to stand, but the spinning room forced her back down. She put a hand to her head, trying to steady her gaze. "I am going to tear that body apart, you son of a bitch." She meant for her words to carry more of a threat, but whatever he used to subdue her still fogged her mind.

He laughed. "Oh, yes. Mother is quite the bitch, but that's beside the point. I told you to stop mucking around in my business."

"I was never good at taking orders from you."

His grin melted into annoyance. "Indeed. I thought you would have grown out of that by now. A woman of your age should behave with more decorum."

"Why kidnap me? Why not kill me?"

"I found a better way to keep you alive and harmless."

She narrowed her eyes at him, tensing as he approached the bed. He didn't flinch or try to pull away when she lunged at him. A wave of disbelief washed over her at the emptiness where her godhood should have been.

"What did you do to me?"

He reached a hand to her neck and fingered the cold metal that rested there. "You don't know how lucky I was to find one of these so quickly. I thought Morigan returned them to her collection a long time ago."

Cora yanked at the thin torque, but she knew it wouldn't budge. Not without the power of a god to release its magic. Something Segomo didn't have in that body of his. "I don't know who's helping you. I really don't care. Make them take this thing off me. Now."

His expression hardened. "I'm afraid I cannot do that. Not yet."

Her vision blurred again, but she refused to give him the satisfaction of her tears. "Why are you doing this to me?"

"It's for your own good. Don't worry. You won't have to wear it as long as I have. I'm not that cruel." He moved to the domed window. "I remember when Arawn put it around my neck. I was a lot angrier and didn't start begging until much later."

"Is that what all this is about? You're mad at our father, so you're taking it out on me?"

He turned to meet her stare. "Not everything is about you, Coramagda."

There was a knock at the door, and Segomo disappeared into the antechamber. When he returned, he carried a frumpy pale-yellow gown. "It's not what you are used to, but it will help you blend in. I would suggest you not leave your room without myself or the guard I have stationed at your door. The men here are savages."

Cora studied the dress, reminded of the one Darya had suggested she buy. After she refused to take it, he laid it on the bed.

"Where is here exactly?" she asked.

His smile sent her stomach plummeting into her legs. "Somewhere those damn dragons will never find you."

She looked out across an untamed landscape that spread out beyond the stone wall of her prison. The land stretched out, untouched by roads or modern life. No cars. No power lines. Just the dense green of an ancient forest, unbroken and wild. Below, men were dressed in unfamiliar attire. She had a sinking suspicion that she was no longer in nineteen ninety-two.

"I'll allow you to roam unchained as long as you promise not to fight me," Segomo said. "When this is over, I will return you home."

A horrible thought snaked its way into her mind. Who would send Miller home? What if he never returned to ten-twelve?

"Cora."

She turned her head to the side, choosing to stare at the floor rather than look at him.

"Once you are dressed, come downstairs. I have a surprise for you."

She went back to staring at the scenery, lost in the horrors of what kind of future awaited upon her return. She regretted not taking the chance to tell Miller how much she truly loved him, and it left a bitter aftertaste in her mouth, yet at the same time, she was glad he didn't take her words back with him. He wouldn't have to bear the burden of her memory when he found the woman who eventually laid claim to his heart.

The steady ticking of the clock filled the otherwise silent living room. Miller sat on the edge of the sofa, his elbows resting on his knees. He struggled to clear his mind and focus on Cora, but no matter how hard he tried, he couldn't feel her near him. Even if she was taken to the opposite end of the world, he should have been able to get some kind of impression as to where she was located.

Hushed whispers broke through his concentration. He turned his attention to the dining area where his aunt and uncle leaned into each other. Darya glanced at him and smiled before disappearing into the kitchen.

She returned a few seconds later with a cup and slid it in front of him. "Whoever took Cora could be using some kind of magic to hide her from us." She offered.

"Possibly," Miller agreed. "If so, there must be a way to dispel it."

There was a knock at the door, and Darya hurried to answer it. Despite his uncle having spoken to Dino earlier, Miller was relieved to see his descendant with his own eyes. It meant there was still a chance to undo the damage he had done.

Edwind motioned for Darya and Dino to follow. To Miller he said, "Wait here."

"Dino might know people who can help us find Cora," Darya offered. "And you two don't exactly get on together."

Miller frowned before settling onto the sofa again.

He went back to listening to the hypnotic ticking of the clock until his calm was broken by Dino's shrill voice.

"HE DID WHAT?"

Miller stared at the door, daring the little man to confront him.

A small body sat down beside him, and dainty fingers worked into his. "She's still alive," Brigita said.

Miller dragged his gaze away from his uncle's office and smiled down at the girl.

Her stare was as unwavering as her mothers. "As long as Dino is here, she is safe."

He was unsure of what to make of her statement, but before he could dwell on it, Edwind, Darya, and Dino stepped out of the office.

"Miller," Edwind said. "Did you notice anything out of place? Maybe something her abductor left behind?"

Miller patted Brigita's hand before joining the men at the dining room table. "Everything looked as it did when I left her."

Darya sat down beside her husband. "I spoke with Joseph. He is going to Glasgow to use the well."

"It has to be Segomo behind this," Miller said. "He threatened to take action if she didn't stop the search for Marcos."

Darya reached forward and put a hand on his arm. "If he used aconite, surely he doesn't mean to kill her."

"Or he wished to make it easier to kill her."

"She is his sister."

Edwind leveled a hard stare at his wife. "And Cernunnos was your father."

"That's different. He was a sadistic monster."

Dino snorted. "So is Segomo."

"Aunt Cora isn't dead." Everyone turned to the sound of Brigita's small voice. Her hope warmed Miller's aching chest.

Darya and Edwind shared a confused look before Darya asked, "How can you be so sure?"

Brigita crossed her arms, looking away. "I'm not supposed to say."

"Brigita Diane." Edwind's voice held a hint of warning. "What are you not supposed to say?"

"He's never going to trust me again if I tell you. Not to mention what will happen if Ronwen finds out I told you their secret."

Darya moved around the table and knelt in front of her daughter. "What does Ronwen have to do with this? Tell us what you know. Now, young lady."

Dropping her arms, Brigita glanced at Miller, then to her mother. "Before Grandfather left, he told me someone from our past family was coming to visit. He wanted me to tell him when Miller arrived."

"You've been spying for Horsa?" Darya asked.

Brigita looked at the floor. "He isn't allowed to intervene since he's already lived through what has been, but I'm a loophole."

Darya glared at Edwind, then turned back to Brigita, her expression calm again. "Go on."

"Grandfather needed to know when Miller and Cora shared their first kiss. He said it had to happen within a certain time after Miller's arrival to keep everything in order." She looked at her father. "That's why I was so excited when we caught them the other day. It was nearly too late, but everything was still on track."

The ticking of the grandfather clock once again filled the silence of the house.

"That wasn't our first kiss," Miller confessed.

Dino and Edwind turned their gaze on him.

Darya stood. "What does that have to do with your certainty of Cora's safety?"

The little girl pointed to Dino. "He's still here."

Dino shook his head. "And my existence means what, exactly?"

Miller's heart rammed against his chest with both excitement and apprehension. "Cora is my destiny. She is the one I have been trying to get to all this time."

Brigita took her mother's hand. "You're not angry with me for keeping this secret, are you? It could have changed everything if they found out too soon."

"I'm not mad," Darya said. "At you, anyway."

"Don't be angry at Grandfather. He is bound by Fate's laws."

Miller went to the table. "If Grandfather knows about Cora and I, do you think he will tell us where to find her?"

"No." Edwind frowned at the ground. "That's probably why he left when he did. This is our fight now."

"But this is my family in danger if she is killed."

"He trusts we will prevail," Edwind assured him.

"Where does that leave us?" Dino asked.

"I think I know someone who may be able to help." Miller turned to Darya. "Cora's oracle friend, Raquel."

"Of course, I'll ring her up. Though, I'm not sure what she can do. She would have warned us if she knew what was coming."

Dino sat down at the table and drummed his fingers against the hard surface. "All this time, Cora was my ancestor."

Edwind leaned against the wall beside Miller. "I guess it's a good thing she turned down your advances."

Miller settled an icy stare on Dino. "When we find Cora, you can thank her for this life you enjoy and apologize for how you treated her."

Unable to meet Miller's gaze, Dino said, "I didn't know."

Edwind stepped between them. "None of us did."

Darya came into view. "Come on. We are going into the city. Raquel needs Miller to make a connection with Cora."

"Can she not travel to us?" Miller asked.

"She doesn't leave her home." When he still hesitated, she waved to the door. "Do you want to find the woman you love or not?"

He snapped his mouth closed and followed his aunt outside.

The simple yellow dress sat like sandpaper against Cora's skin. Every time she moved, the rough texture clawed at her flesh like hundreds of tiny daggers cutting her from the outside in. She spent too long trying to readjust the fabric so that it fit more comfortably on her body, but nothing could ease the disgust she felt, short of ripping it off and lighting the damn thing on fire. She appreciated that Segomo had chosen a rather straightforward garment with minimal layers. At least she could move freely enough if she decided to make a run for it and wouldn't be too encumbered by heavy cloth.

She stared out the window, watching the mid-morning sun float upward over the trees, contemplating her limited options. The surprise Segomo mentioned still waited for her downstairs, and she dreaded finding out what it was.

She made her way through the antechamber and pulled open the outer door to find a guard sitting across the hall, carving a small idol out of a pale piece of timber. He glanced up, set the tiny sculpture on the floor next to him, and shoved the knife into a pouch at his side before standing. There were no pleasantries exchanged. Instead, he motioned her down the dim hallway toward a set of stairs that rounded downward, out of sight.

The guard stayed a respectable distance behind her, but close enough that if she tried to run, she would be quickly tackled and subdued. Even with her powers, she would have had a hard time out maneuvering him. Despite his demure demeanor, he had the hardened look of a man who had endured a brutal life.

Downstairs, she took a moment to study the meager decor. It was all nearly as drab and lifeless as the pockmarked stones that made up the modest castle. The guard leaned into her. His breath smelled of stale alcohol and cooked meat. "If you are looking for Master Segomo, he will be in the courtyard with the boy."

Her head snapped to the side, eyes wide, pulse pounding. "Marcos?"

She didn't wait for him to answer and took off on a run toward the open entryway. Behind her, she heard a pair of heavy footsteps chasing after, but she wasn't about to slow down. She had to see for herself that Marcos was really there.

The second she was outside, the afternoon sun stung her vision, and she put a hand up to shield her eyes as she scanned the surrounding field. She spotted Segomo watching Marcos struggle with a flimsy bow. A whimper tickled the back of her throat as she took off down the sloped hill toward them. Segomo lifted his head, peered past her, and waved a dismissive hand.

She was aware of the sudden lack of footsteps behind her, but her sights were locked on the boy that was now trying to restring the bow. "Marcos!" she yelled.

His mouth split into an excited grin when he saw her. "Aunt Cora!"

The bow and the loose string dropped to the ground when she wrapped him into a possessive hug. "Thank the gods you are safe," she cried. "I've been so worried."

He wriggled free of her arms, showing no sign of fear. "I'm fine. When I didn't make it through the portal with you, Mister Segomo rescued me from the men at the house and brought me here."

Cora turned an icy stare on her brother. "Is that so?"

"Is Dad with you? He's probably worried out of his mind. You know how he gets."

"He didn't come with me." She took the bow and string, wrapping the silken threads around the taught wood. "There. That should hold."

"How did you learn how to do that?"

"My mother's people taught me many things." She nodded to the target. "Now, show me how good you are."

He walked to the line that had been carved into the dirt, nocking an arrow.

Segomo sidled up next to her. "Had father trusted me, I could have trained you to wield weapons such as that."

"He knew how much you despised me." She studied the surrounding forest. "And how much you wanted to rid yourself of the burden of being a glorified babysitter."

He came into her field of vision. "I never saw you as a burden. Annoying, sure, but you gave me something to look forward to other than the monotony of that place."

She shot him what she hoped was a disgusted sneer. "I'm glad I could be a distraction for you." Then went back to eyeing the fields.

"If you are calculating a plan of escape, I'd advise against it. It's all I can do to keep you out of the lower pits of this place. Hells, it is all I can do to keep you alive at this point."

She speared him with a disbelieving glare.

He shot a glance over his shoulder at Marcos, who was still focused on his target. Turning back to Cora, he said, "Do not fight me."

"I'd rather be shackled to a wall than cower to you."

"It isn't me you should fear." His eyes flicked to the fort. "I brought you here so you could be with the boy. I wanted you to know he was safe."

"For how long? Until you shove that demon inside him?"

Segomo stood up straight and stepped into her. She tried to hold her ground, but despite his mortal body, his presence was still intimidating.

"Do not speak one word of this to Marcos. If you try to abscond with him, or warn of the upcoming ritual, you are dooming him to a fate worse than what he is already facing."

"Worse than being a meat puppet for a Fomorian?"

"Yes. Do we have an understanding?"

Holding back the fear that bubbled just under the surface, she nodded.

"Good." He took hold of her arm, and in a hushed voice, said, "I will leave you to look after Marcos while you are here if you promise not to try something brave or stupid."

She studied the half-dozen men positioned around the outer perimeter of the courtyard. As desperate as she was to get Marcos away from there, she knew better than to attempt an escape so brazenly in the middle of the day.

Turning her attention to Marcos, she said, "Okay, kiddo, I'm going to give you some tips on the proper way to shoot a bow."

From the corner of her eye, she saw Segomo turn and walk away. Despite the urgency of the situation, patience was the smart option. As long as her brother believed she was complacent, it gave her time to formulate a plan of escape when the opportunity presented itself. She just hoped the chance came before it was too late.

Chapter 12

MILLER DASHED DOWN THE narrow alley toward the plain metal door, ignoring his uncle's urging to slow down. Raquel greeted them before they reached her threshold. "I don't have time for your distrust of my kind." She said, taking him by the hand. She dragged him to a small room where two chairs flanked a round table.

"What I believe is unimportant," Miller replied. "I care only to reclaim my destiny."

Raquel squeezed his hand before going to a tall cabinet on the far side of the cramped space. She withdrew a warped copper bowl and a tiny leather satchel, placing them in the middle of the table. "It's about time you and Cora figured out the truth."

"You knew?" Miller asked.

She shook the contents of the pouch into the bowl. "We are all bound by the same laws." She grabbed a small box from a nearby shelf, then settled herself into the chair across from him. "Sit."

He did as he was told, carefully sliding onto the thin cushion, keeping his eyes locked on her face.

She nodded to Edwind and Darya, standing just inside the threshold. "There are cookies and tea in the kitchen. We will be but a few moments."

Miller glanced over his shoulder. Edwind stayed planted in place, arms crossed. Darya reached around him and shut them out, leaving Miller and the oracle alone.

"I don't think even the great and wise Morigan herself could have foreseen this outcome." She struck a red tipped stick along the edge of the box and a single flame roared to life. "Love of one's family tends to blind us to certain truths."

Miller watched with fascination as she dropped the tiny flickering stick into the powder and jerked in surprise when the bowl was engulfed in orange flames, casting the room in dancing shadows. Tendrils of smoke smothered the fire, quickly filling the space between them. His nostrils flared at the soothing scent of aromatic spices.

"Not many creatures can best my gift, but with the bond you now share with Cora, I should be able to find her." Raquel pursed her lips together and added. "Even if it was a reckless thing to do."

"I do not need a lecture." He tried to move away, but she latched onto his wrists with a grip that was surprisingly unyielding.

A thick haze steadily rose into the air, filling the room with a white cloud obscuring everything. "Heed my words, young dragon." Her voice sounded muted and distant in the thick fog.

Her features dimmed and her hair float free of its updo. It swirled around her head as if underwater, drifting with the steady push and pull of the waves of the ocean.

"The tapestry of fate is complex, woven with threads of choices and sacrifices." Despite the close proximity, her words barely carried across the table.

"Speak plainly, oracle. No more riddles."

Raquel's eyes fluttered, as if watching something unseen among the smoke. "The path you seek," Raquel began, her words carrying the weight of eons, "lies shrouded not by darkness but by light. The beast waits in a tempest of hunger, a voracious maelstrom that yearns to devour life itself."

"Why do you speak of Tethra? It is Cora I am looking for. Dammit, Oracle, where is she?"

"The goddess, small yet mighty, will open the way. Tarry not in that which has been, for the sands of time flow swiftly. Your destiny hangs by a slender thread."

Frustration and urgency fueled his movements. He stood, having to hunch over due to the oracles' hold on him. "Where has she been taken? I need a location. A direction."

Raquel's grip tightened to the point it was starting to become painful. "Though your threads are intertwined, your place is not to usurp her fate."

Anger made him yank her forward. "What does that even mean? Where must I go?" A hand landed on his shoulder, and he was no longer shrouded in the heavy mist. The room was once again bathed in faint candlelight.

Raquel sat across from him, her hands folded in her lap, hair pulled back in the same updo as when they arrived. She stared at him with a serene smile, sending a quiver of icy tendrils trickling down his spine. "I was right. You were able to break through the veil. I know where they took Cora."

Movement from his periphery drew Miller's gaze to his uncle, who frowned at him.

"Did you not see what happened?" Miller asked.

"I heard yelling. When I came in, you were standing over Raquel as if you meant to harm her."

Raquel leaned back in her chair. "Miller was doing no such thing. He merely grew impatient. Sometimes, my visions wander."

Turning his full attention to her, Miller said, "What are you?"

One side of her mouth turned up into a smirk, but she ignored his question and looked at Edwind. "Segomo spirited Cora away to a place you would have never found her. I cannot say why he chose that particular place, but she is being held in a fort in Ireland."

"That's not far for us to travel," Edwind said.

Raquel stood and picked up the bowl from the table. "In the year sixteen seventy-four."

The two Wodehal men shared a confused look.

"That's oddly specific," Edwind mused. "You got all that from your vision quest with Miller?"

The smile bloomed across her lips. "Their connection is as strong as you and your druidae."

Miller refused to move out of her way at first.

"Go to her," Raquel said. "Before she does something that cannot be undone."

Cora was reluctant to leave Marcos. While they practiced with the bow, she studied the surrounding landscape, searching for a secluded area they could disappear into when she decided to make their escape. Her hopes diminished when she realized every inch of the valley could be seen from the wooden tower on the north side of the keep. There were at least two guards walking its perimeter at all times. She and Marcos would have to make it the twenty yards to the cover of trees surrounding them. That was a lot of distance to be exposed, even at night. Not to mention, if they made it to the forest, where would she go? There may not be a safe-haven within fifty miles. They'd be running blind in a land just as dangerous as the men who held them captive.

"Did you enjoy your time with the boy?"

Cora lifted her eyes from the ground to stare into her brother's stolen face. "His name is Marcos."

Segomo ignored the comment, motioning for her to continue their trek around the side of what she assumed was the armory. A few of the soldiers carried steel blades that glinted in the late afternoon sun.

She expected him to guide her up the winding path to the front gate, but he kept walking past the other men, toward the outer wall. A shiver of excitement passed over her, tempered with trepidation.

"Where are we going?" She slowed her pace.

Segomo tilted his face to the sky, drawing a deep breath. "I forgot just how good the sun felt on my skin. How wonderful the dirt and trees smelled. The world has changed so much since my time here."

Cora wanted to say something snarky, but she couldn't bring herself to speak. Though his imprisonment hadn't been her fault, she couldn't help the pang of guilt wriggling its way into her heart. There had been a lot of sleepless nights where she questioned Arawn's decision. Despite what she'd been told, she had to wonder if there was more to Segomo's story that her father wasn't telling her.

Segomo looked at her, the melancholy smile falling into a grim frown. "What would you sacrifice for a chance to live again?"

She opened her mouth to tell him that it certainly wouldn't be the life of a child, but there had been times she tried to imagine herself in his shoes. If she was sentenced to an eternity in purgatory, never to see those she loved and cared for, what lengths would she go to for her freedom?

Dropping her eyes to the ground again, she said, "What you're doing is far worse than trading a life for a life. You're resurrecting pure chaos and destruction. Tethra's influence will fester and rot the hearts of those who aren't strong enough to resist, and those who do will be destroyed by his wrath."

"You give that monster too much credit. The world has changed. Mortals no longer believe in the old ways, the old gods. Magic has been replaced by science. Technology is quickly becoming the new pantheon. Indech is a fool to think he can rebuild his empire."

Cora moved into his line of sight, forcing him to look at her. "How many innocent lives will be lost in their pursuit? I may not be the biggest fan of our father and the other gods, but there is a balance that must be maintained."

Segomo studied her face, the muscles around his jaw flexing with each thought. Finally, he turned his attention to the sky again. "You're right. There is a balance. I'm simply tipping it in the direction that benefits me." He nodded toward the fort. "I have arranged for a special meal for us tonight. I doubt it will compare to the delicacies you are used to, but we must make do with what we have."

Food was the last thing she needed. Her mind reeled with the implications of his words. In the depths of her heart, she knew there was no convincing him to let her or Marcos go free. She fast-walked past him, her sights locked on the heavy wood doors leading to her only sanctuary. She felt his presence the entire walk to her room and wanted so badly to scream at him to leave her alone.

She stood in the antechamber, propping herself against the roughly finished wood, not wanting him to see the turmoil warring inside her. "Arawn was right about you."

"Maybe one day I'll tell you the truth about our father. He isn't the benevolent being he's portrayed himself to be."

"Neither are you."

"I never lied about who or what I am. You ignored the truth, clinging to some ridiculous notion of finding goodness where none exists."

She slammed her eyes shut against the harsh words. Her body jolted with the effort to hold in her frustration. Old wounds threatened to open all over again, and she tried to stifle the hemorrhaging emotions before they overwhelmed her.

"Please don't go through with this." She hated the way her voice was so weak and small.

There was a long pause, and she thought he had walked off, but she heard his feet shift against the stone floor and he said, "I cannot stop what has been set in motion."

Frustration turned to anger, and she swung around, shoving the door shut, hoping she was quick enough to push it in the face. She leaned against the rough wood, unable to break free from the grip she had on the handle. She shoved every ounce of sadness into that place where her resentment smoldered until only rage remained. Her body trembled from the force of her rage and she stomped across the room to the window that overlooked the valley.

With no other choice, she resigned herself to play Segomo's game. Let him believe he had cowed her. If he didn't see her as a threat, he would be more likely to let down his guard. When he did, she would pounce on the chance to get Marcos away from there.

Miller sat at the table watching his aunt and uncle share an unspoken conversation. Dino was at the opposite end, drumming his fingers along the polished pine surface.

Unable to take the silence any longer, Miller said, "Who else could the oracle be referring to?"

His aunt's eyes went to the stairs, then immediately back to Miller. "Brigita is just a child. She has yet to fully touch her powers. How can you expect her to tear a hole through time?"

"She will do so in the future," Miller offered.

"When she is older and stronger." Darya looked at Edwind for support.

Edwind shook his head. "Brigita is much too young and fragile to attempt such a thing. I can't allow it. I won't."

Miller looked between his aunt and uncle, but it was Dino who spoke. "What else can we do? You're willing to wipe my entire bloodline out of existence because you won't let your child do what it is she's meant for?"

Edwind took a step toward him but was stopped by a small voice that echoed through the house.

"Is no one going to ask me if I want to help?"

Miller looked past Darya to where Brigita stood at the foot of the stairs. She had her hands planted on her hips in a manner that reminded him of his mother.

"You don't even know how the magic works," Darya said.

Brigita set her mouth in a tight-lipped frown and strode past them to the glass door. Outside, she ran a searching gaze over the forest and set out for a cluster of trees.

Edwind rushed after her. "Where are you going?" When she didn't answer, he looked at Darya. "Is she speaking to the animals?"

"She can't talk to them like Bastian and I do. I don't know what she hears." She then took off after her daughter.

The men stood in a half circle, watching the place where Darya had disappeared into the trees. Minutes passed and when Darya returned, she was holding Brigita's hand. Her expression betrayed the apprehension wrestling beneath the surface. "Brigita, give us some time to discuss our options."

The little girl crossed her arms, ready to argue, but a stern look of warning from her mother made her let out a sharp huff before stomping inside.

To Edwind, Darya said, "Our daughter is far stronger than we could have hoped."

He glanced at the house. "What happened?"

The smile that split Darya's lips told of how proud she was of her child. "She summoned Flidais."

Edwind, unlike his wife, scowled at the news. "Why would she do such a thing? Doesn't she know how dangerous that creature is?" His eyes went wide. "Has Brigita summoned her before?"

Darya shot him a testy look. "Not exactly. Flidais has been visiting the children in their dreams. Like she did me." She put a hand on his arm before he could continue his tirade. "She is their grandmother. Her blood is as much a part of them as ours, but I've made the consequences very clear if she tries to hurt them. It was Flidais who chose our lives over her son."

Miller could tell Edwind wanted to argue, but he simply crossed his arms, conceding to his wife's judgment.

To Miller, she said, "Brigita can't bend time with what little magic she can touch. But she convinced Flidais to send you to Cora."

"She can do that?" Edwind asked.

Darya shrugged. "She is a maiden of the earth. I don't think there's a lot she can't do."

He narrowed his eyes at his wife. "She didn't do this out of the kindness of her cold, wild heart."

"We will talk about that later. Right now, I need to get Miller to Flidais so she can send him to sixteen seventy-four."

Edwind held out his arm. "I'm going with him."

Darya's mouth dropped open, looking from Miller back to her husband.

"I'm not letting him face these dangers alone," Edwind said. "I have to go."

She shook her head. "Out of the question. We don't know when or if they will be able to return. I can't let you take that chance."

Edwind frowned. "And you would send Miller there on his own?"

"Cora is his destiny. Not yours," she snapped.

He reached for her, but she sidestepped his advance.

"My love, I cannot abandon him to fight this battle on his own."

"So, you will abandon your family here?" Tears made her eyes shimmer in the dusky twilight.

Miller took a step forward. "Uncle Edwind, I cannot ask you to leave your home."

"I've made up my mind," Edwind said.

Darya's hands balled into fists at her sides. "You stupid, stubborn man." The ground trembled beneath their feet, and she blew out a calming breath. "I'll forbid Flidais from sending either of you anywhere."

That time, when he reached for her, she didn't pull away from him. "After everything we've been through. The insurmountable odds we've overcome. You know I will come back to you. Nothing will keep us apart. Not even time."

She sank into him. "You better come back to me, you big dumb dragon."

He whispered something into her ear Miller couldn't hear, and a sad smile bloomed across her face. When Edwind pulled away, he said aloud, "Dino will be here to look after you and the children." There was a reluctance to his words.

"Like hell I will be."

All eyes went to Dino, who was standing in the open doorway.

"I'm going to find my son. If that means traipsing through time, then so be it."

Edwind disappeared inside and came back with two swords. "I'm glad my father kept these battle-ready."

Another half hour passed, and Miller stood at the edge of the forest, his hand flexing on the hilt of the sword at his side. It pained his heart that his uncle refused to stay with his wife and children. If Miller could sneak into the portal alone, he would have done just that, but he was at the mercy of the creature that heeded little Brigita's call.

Edwind held his wife in his arms. "I do not like Flidais being so close to the children." His gaze pierced the trees where Brigita and Samuel knelt in front of a shadowed clump of brush.

"She can teach them what I cannot." Darya brought his face around to hers. "I won't have our children grow up like I did, unable to control the magic that could one day kill them."

Edwind nodded. "I trust you, my love." He turned to Miller. "We should get on with it, then. The sooner we find Cora, the sooner we come back home."

Brigita held out her hand to the shadows. "It's okay. You're safe with them."

A dirt encrusted hand reached out, resting in Brigita's small palm. Flidais kept her back to the trees and sidled behind the little girl. "I cannot help you return once the way is closed."

"We know," Darya said.

Flidais cocked her head to the side. "You are willing to send your dragon away, with no certainty of returning?"

"He will return." There was no wavering in Darya's answer.

Flidais led Brigita to a tall maple and set her hand on its bark. "One day, you will be able to do this on your own. Already, you hear the call."

The limbs of the tree began to bend and creak, twisting until there was an oval passage not quite the same height as Edwind standing before them. Specters of white flashed in Flidais' eyes and the opening was no longer empty. An iridescent light shone before them.

"There is your path, younglings."

Dino approached the light, looking over the portal. "You're sure it's the right place?"

Flidais took a step toward him, but Brigita kept her grip tight on the forest goddess.

He pursed his lips together and took in a deep breath before squeezing his eyes shut and jumping into the swirling lights.

Edwind knelt in front of Samuel and said, "Keep your mother and sister safe while I'm gone." He slowly approached Flidais, ignored her presence, and kissed Brigita on the top of the head. "I'll see you soon."

Darya worked her fingers into his. "Come back to us."

Edwind kissed her one last time and stepped inside the light.

Miller paused at the portal, turning to his aunt. "I will make sure he returns. No matter what happens to me."

Chapter 13

M ILLER STUMBLED OUT OF the portal, nearly falling on top of Dino, who was bent over and heaving. Edwind kept his distance from the lurching man, wearing a frown that wasn't exactly sympathetic.

Dino moaned when he stood up and glared at the other men. "How are you two not affected?"

"We've experienced this before," Miller offered, moving through the trees to an opening that overlooked a rocky landscape. The sun sat low in the western sky, dousing them in dancing shades from the surrounding forest. He didn't like the idea of being so exposed in a land he did not know.

Edwind scanned the horizon. "We should find water."

Dino wiped at his mouth and glanced around. "How do we know this is even the right place?"

Cora's presence stirred inside Miller, still faint, but stronger than before. "Cora is nearby. I can feel her."

Dino's eyes narrowed. "You could be wrong."

"If he says she is here, I believe him." Edwind's eyes darted to Miller. "Which way do we need to go?"

Miller stepped back, his form rippling as scales replaced skin and wings unfurled. In seconds, the man was gone, a dragon standing in his place. Edwind and Dino sidled away, making room for the hulking beast. Miller lifted his head to the sky, swinging it in a slow half circle before returning to the two men, human once again. "I sense her the strongest in the west."

"Let's go then," Dino started in that direction.

Miller and Edwind shared a knowing look, then Edwind pointed out a path carved through the foliage to the south. "Perhaps this way would be better."

Dino paused as if to argue, then decided to listen to the men who had more experience in the wilds.

They traveled through the trees, along the side of the mountain. Miller wanted to fly, but Edwind pointed out how dangerous that could be. They didn't know exactly where they were going, nor did they want to take the chance of being seen by anyone. They slowly made their way down the slope to the valley below. By the time they reached the base, the sun dipped into the horizon ahead, casting streaks of shadows at their backs.

Dino's stomach complained nearly as loud as his tongue, so while Edwind gathered wood for a fire, Miller took the opportunity to hunt for food.

"Take Dino with you," Edwind said.

Miller grunted. "I will be more efficient on my own."

It didn't take him long to track and kill a sizable meal. Edwind and Dino sat in front of a roaring flame when Miller returned. Dino raised his eyes, but his gaze breezed past Miller to the darkness beyond the dancing orange light. Ignoring him, Miller threw the three hare carcasses at his uncle's feet before dropping to his knees to prepare the meat for cooking.

Every passing minute wound Miller's muscles tighter. The longer they walked, the stronger his connection to Cora grew. They should continue, but traveling in the dark with no way to study landmarks was foolish. By the time the moon crested the hilltops across the valley, Miller had finished roasting the meat and passed it to the others.

Dino tore off a piece, smelled it, then stuck it in between his lips. His face soured. "It's kind of bland."

"Food is food," Miller said. "It is meant to sustain." Turning his attention to Edwind, he added, "You have grown spoiled in the future."

The elder man laughed. "That we have." He rested against a boulder. "I try to teach the children the old ways. I don't want them to take for granted the conveniences of the modern world."

Miller threw his empty stick into the glowing embers and stared at Dino. "Aunt Darya mentioned that you would have lost Marcos already, if not for Cora. What did she mean by that?"

Dino shifted, staring into the flickering blaze as if they held the answers to the mysteries of life.

"It happened two years ago." Edwind spoke softly. "Marcos had been swimming in the ocean and a rogue wave swept him into the sea by an undertow. It was too much, even for his little dragon body. Cora brought him back from the dead."

"I thought her father wouldn't allow her to do such a thing," Miller said.

A hint of a smile turned up the sides of Edwind's mouth. "She chanced his wrath for the boy. Maybe she felt the connection even then and didn't realize it."

Miller glowered at Dino. "Yet you still treated her with such cruelty."

Dino pushed to his feet. "When your child is taken from you, then you can judge my actions."

Miller stood, readying himself for another fight. Edwind stepped between them before their anger could go any further. "It's getting late. We should rest."

Dino leaned forward as if to argue, but Edwind held up a hand, his eyes tracking something beyond their camp. In the old tongue, he told Miller to grab his sword. Too late, a group of men wearing uniforms and carrying weapons just as vicious as theirs broke through the trees.

There was a glint of flame on metal and Miller picked out a man clutching a particularly distinct shackle. He glanced at his uncle, who gave a slight shake of his head.

A man stepped forward and said something in a language Miller recognized but couldn't understand.

"Do you know what he's saying?" Edwind asked.

The soldier held up a hand to his companions. "You're English?"

Edwind gave a slow nod.

The man eyed their weapons. "You three are a long way from home."

"We aren't part of your conflict," Edwind was quick to point out. "We are here searching for someone. Then we will return home."

He gave a thoughtful grunt. "You do not dress like soldiers, but those blades of yours are made for battle." He nodded to a man behind him. "Unfortunately, you've come at the wrong time. No matter your intentions, we cannot take the chance of letting you wander in our midst until I can be sure you are as benign as you claim. You will remain as our prisoners until we reach the keep."

"We are no threat to you," Miller said calmly.

The general regarded him with a calculated calm. "I must protect my men."

Edwind rested a hand on Miller's shoulder. "It's a reasonable request. I am Edwind. This is Miller and Dino."

After another thoughtful pause, he said, "Rickson."

"Why are you telling him our names?" Dino asked in the old tongue. "We can take them out."

Rickson eyed him. "What is he saying? What language is that?"

Edwind shot Dino a dangerous glare but spoke to their captor. "He was saying it was in our best interest to take you up on your hospitality."

Dino studied both Edwind to Miller, then gave in to the unspoken command to keep quiet.

Rickson motioned to someone behind him. "You will understand if I insist you are bound for the journey to our camp. It lies not far from here."

Edwind agreed with a curt nod.

"Good man."

Twilight blanketed the valley, bringing with it thoughts of Miller. Did he make it back to his own time? Surely, Ronwen could open the way to send him home. Cora's heart threatened to break all over again at the thought of another woman taking her place in his life.

Seeing Marcos today assured her Miller did, in fact, return to where he was meant to be. Eventually, he would forget about her.

Dark thoughts loomed at the edges of her mind. Anger and heartache clouded her judgment, leaving her to wonder if it was worth the struggle. What if Tethra was the lesser evil, given how cruel the gods' games could be?

Marcos's face swam into focus, and she shoved those dangerous musings away. Even if she had to fight to her last breath, she wouldn't let Segomo or Indech destroy an innocent boy. He deserved a chance at love and happiness.

Behind her, the outer door creaked open, followed by heavy footsteps plodding through the antechamber. The soldier Segomo chose to be her guard came into view, his face the same unreadable, hardened slate. She'd overheard other men refer to him as Oscar, but she didn't dare call him by that name.

"You have been summoned for dinner."

She glanced at Oscar. Though his thin lips were set in a hard frown, there was a softness to his eyes. "I'm not hungry," she muttered.

"It isn't a request."

She blew out a breathy laugh. "Of course." She wondered what would happen if she still refused Segomo's demands. How far would she have to push him to invoke the wrath that had gotten him banished to the underworld for the rest of eternity?

Oscar's expression shifted. It was strange seeing pity bloom across his features. "Please, my lady."

She ignored the offered hand and made her way downstairs to the small dining hall, where Segomo and Marcos sat at a long wooden table, bearing the stains of the countless meals and rowdy gatherings, giving her the impression that the fort housed more than just soldiers over the years. Dozens of notches marred the dull surface where no telling how many blades had been stabbed into it.

Cora was barely out of her teens when she had received an invitation to a soiree in a place much like this one. The nobleman who invited her thought he would actually inherit the royal crown. Too bad for him, King Edward V saw through his smarmy niceties and stripped the duke of his title, land and money shortly after.

She skimmed the room, struck by the similarities to the Duke's dining hall. One key difference being the lack of half-naked women filling the guests' goblets. After that night, Cora swore off parties and drinking for a while.

She chose the seat next to Marcos, despite a bowl sitting beside Segomo. A young man, sporting the same uniform as the other soldiers, rushed to the table and moved the soup to where Cora sat, scowling at the surroundings. She poked at the soggy stew, not having much of an appetite. Although, she was impressed by the smoky smell of fresh meat. At least she wasn't being given leftovers.

"Are you not hungry?" Segomo asked.

Marcos stared at his own bowl with much the same disappointment. "It's not as bad as you think. Dad made worse. I can't wait to get back home. I really miss him."

The corners of her mouth flip up into an involuntary smile. She remembered the last time he tried to cook. It was the closest thing to an actual date they'd had, and Dino nearly burned down the house. She couldn't comprehend how a man who made his living making candy couldn't cook a basic meal.

Cora turned an acidic sneer to her brother. "I can't wait for you to go home either."

"For now," Segomo said, motioning to the food in front of them, "can we enjoy our stew? There will be time to discuss our long-term plans later."

As much as she wanted to keep needling Segomo, she didn't want Marcos to be caught in the middle of a heated argument. Relaxing her face into neutrality, she set her spoon to the side. "I thought you said this would be a treat. At least my people knew how to prepare a meal."

Segomo pressed his lips into a thin smile, visibly frustrated by her. "Perhaps you should be in charge of the kitchen from now on."

Marcos sat forward, taking their attention off each other. "I'm supposed to go riding tomorrow." He looked past her to Segomo. "Can Aunt Cora go with me?"

She eyed Segomo. "That sounds like a lovely idea."

Segomo rolled a tiny boiled a potato over his tongue and took his time chewing. His stare bore into Cora, as if trying to see into her mind. "We can discuss that tomorrow." He nodded to the bowl in front of Marcos. "If you are finished with your meal, you can go to bed."

Marcos took in a breath, ready to argue, but Cora distracted him with a hug. "Get some rest, kiddo. I'll see you in the morning."

When he was gone, she turned on her brother. "You can't let this happen. He's just a child."

"It's out of my hands."

"Like hell it is," she snapped. "Take this damn Qel off my neck and let me take him home."

"That is not within his power." A raspy voice echoed from somewhere behind her.

Cora whirled to the side, nearly banging her knee on the table leg. The coarse voice came from across the room where the candlelight didn't quite penetrate. A ruined face appeared from the darkness and rounded the corner past Segomo to stand next to her.

"Who the hell are you?" she barked.

Yellowed eyes were locked on hers when he spoke to Segomo. "You didn't tell her about me?"

"You never came up."

Cora eased away from the grotesque creature. She could smell death and rot on him, eliciting a wave of nausea rippling through her stomach. He had to be the one to trap her in the Qel. Even though she was cut off from her godhood, his power oozed off him like a thick, oily slime that slid across her skin.

"Your brother failed to mention how truly lovely a creature you are, Coramagda." He sat down in the chair next to her, taking her glass of wine. "When my father returns, he will need a queen to rule by his side. You and he would make spectacular children."

Segomo slammed a fist onto the wooden surface, rattling the crude pottery bowls and cups. "She is not part of our bargain. I swear on all of my powers, if you so much as touch a single hair on her head, I will turn your insides to your outsides and let the winged beasts feast on your rotting corpse."

The grotesque demon cocked his head to the side, contemplating the threat. "Bold words coming from an impotent creature stuck in a mortal's body."

"My current situation is temporary."

Indech chuffed out a low laugh, his shoulders shaking once. "There will be more agreeable women to fulfill Tethra's desires."

Cora pushed to her feet, gripping her dress so the men couldn't see her shaking hands. "I think I will go to bed while you two finish with your lovers' quarrel." Indech reached in her direction and she nearly tripped over her own feet to keep out of his grasp, but he merely took a slice of bread from beside her bowl before swinging to face Segomo.

She backed to the door of the dining hall, unable to meet her brother's stare and, for once, was glad to have Oscar at her back, though she doubted he was any match for Indech. Even without the Qel, she lacked the power to stop the Fomorian.

It didn't matter where they went. She had to get Marcos away from here, and she had to do it now. She was adept enough to forage off the land and keep them alive until she could find help. Once she knew where she was, she should be able to search for Hengist or Horsa.

The only thing she had to do now was come up with a plan to sneak past her guard. He wasn't exactly feeble, but he'd be easy to out-maneuver or overpower if she caught him in a vulnerable position. She would do whatever it took to escape before sunrise. Even if it meant taking another man's life.

Miller kept his expression impassive and his movements slight to appear as harmless as possible when the two men led Edwind away. Dino, on the other hand, stood at the bars of the wheeled cart made into a prison. His wide stare was that of an untamed animal ready to strike at anyone walking by. Their guards eyed him with wary trepidation. They wouldn't hesitate to kill Dino if he proved himself a threat.

"Would you get away from there?" Miller whispered. "As much as I would like to see you humbled by these men, I cannot say for sure they would not murder you."

Dino's eyes shot to the side. "How can you be so calm?"

"What other way is there to be? We are in no immediate danger. These soldiers mean no harm, as long as we do not give them a reason to fear us." He sidled up to Dino, turning his attention to the lone man by the fire. He stared at their cage with open hostility. "And there is a hunter in their midst. If you so much as hint at your true nature, we will all be slaughtered for merely existing."

Dino leaned away from him. "A hunter?"

Miller raised a hand to hush him. "Keep your voice down."

"What kind of hunter?" he whispered. "Like a regular hunter?"

"I suppose you wouldn't have such dangers in nineteen ninety-two." Miller leaned into him. "We have been hunted by his people for many years. Centuries, maybe. I cannot imagine the technology they have access to in this time. I certainly do not wish to find out, so keep your dragon put away while we are here."

Giving the flames one last look, Miller went back to his unbothered stance on the other side of the cramped space. "Hopefully, Uncle Edwind can talk our way out of this."

Despite his calm exterior, Miller's insides hummed with fear. He tried to tell himself that as long as he could still sense Cora, and as long as Dino was still there, she was alive. But alive didn't mean unharmed. There was no telling what Segomo might do to her.

Two men walked out of the shadows, past the fire, drawing Miller's attention. Edwind carried himself with his usual calm. His face didn't give anything away when he was put back in the cage. Rickson unchained his wrists, moving with the ease of a man who wasn't worried about his own safety.

When they were alone, a frown worked onto Edwind's lips. "That was an unproductive conversation. At least we aren't in any danger of immediate execution."

Miller tracked the path where the general disappeared. "He knows we aren't soldiers. Why is he still keeping us in this cage?"

"He says it is not within his power to let us go."

Miller shoved his arms into each other. "We do not have time for this."

"What's that about being calm?" Dino teased.

Miller glared at his descendent, but he was right. Emotional reactions would only hinder their objective.

Edwind pretended not to study the hunter. "We have only one dangerous obstacle to fight if we are to escape. Most of these men are easy to outrun, but that hunter already suspects us."

"We need a distraction," Miller said.

Edwind frowned at his feet, thinking.

"I'll do it." Dino spoke the words so softly, Miller almost didn't hear him. "I'm out of my element here. You two have a better chance of finding Cora and Marcos. I'm fast. I can lead them away while you escape. I did it for Cora."

Edwind shook his head. "If you're caught, they will probably kill you. Hunters do not keep prisoners."

"I don't care. Not anymore. I just want Marcos to be safe and Cora has to survive." Dino shoved away tears. "Make sure she and Miller get back to where they belong, so my son has a chance to exist."

Uncle and nephew shared another look and Edwind said, "We need to wait until most of the men are asleep."

"We have to do it now," Dino insisted. "They will be too busy chasing me and you two can escape."

Miller was ready to counter the plan with something more rational, but Dino's dragon was already emerging. Edwind shoved Miller out of the way of Dino's thick tail as it careened past his head. The two men dove for the ground as the cart exploded around them, rolling out of the way of the dragon's claws.

Chaos erupted. The soldiers were quick to chase the dragon that rampaged through their midst. Dino went for the hunter, who grasped at his weapon and shackle. He got the crossbow raised to his waist when Dino swung a massive claw through the air, forcing the other man to roll out of reach of those sharp talons.

Edwind snatched Miller by the shirt and dragged him to his feet. "We must go."

A ground shaking roar drowned out the soldier's shouting. Miller scrambled to his feet, ignoring the urge to turn back and help Dino. He couldn't waste the chance to escape. Still, he didn't like the idea of leaving his descendent to the fate of a hunter.

Rickson barked an order.

Edwind peered over his shoulder, spitting a curse. "He won't be so easily lost." He nodded to the mountain up ahead. "We will be harder to track if we take them in opposite directions. I'll meet you beyond that ridge."

Miller hesitated for only a second before taking to the sky, trusting his uncle hadn't grown complacent in the future.

Chapter 14

Sporadic laughter drifted into the narrow window. Cora paced the length of her room for what felt like hours, waiting for everyone to go to sleep. Of course, there were going to be a handful of men standing guard overnight, but she hoped the majority of them would be dead to the world when she put her plan of escape into motion. After the encounter with Indech, she could no longer sit back and wait for an opportunity to present itself. She had to act now.

Ignoring the steady hum of conversation below, she went to her bed and reached under her pillow for the strip of fabric she'd torn from the bedding. It wasn't the ideal garrote, but it would be sufficient. Her stomach twisted into nervous knots at the thought of going through with her plan. She may be the daughter of death, but she didn't make a habit of dealing it out. Given the chance, she would prefer not to kill anyone. A single, unplanned death could irrevocably damage the future.

Closing her eyes, she sucked in a breath, trapping it in her chest, listening. It was quiet, except for the faintest sounds of snoring. The click of the latch was louder than she anticipated, and she imagined it echoing throughout the whole keep, waking every soul inside its walls.

Oscar barely stirred from his place in the chair by the door. There was a crude wooden mug tipped on its side, empty. She wrapped the fabric around her hands and slipped behind him, careful not to bump into his back. She eased her arms over his head. As soon as it was in position, she jerked it tight against his neck, twisting the garrote with so much force, it bit into her clenched fists.

His reaction was delayed, but he managed to yank her forward, grasping at her forearms. Luckily, Oscar was far too inhibited to find a solid grasp. She wrapped the fabric tighter around her hand. The strangled sounds coming from his gaping mouth made her stomach do a quick somersault.

His grip weakened until he flailed uselessly at her. As soon as he went limp, she dropped the cloth. Trembling fingers fumbled blindly through the wiry hair hiding his neck. She nearly cried out in relief when she felt the flutter of a pulse; he might survive after all.

"I'm sorry," she whispered into his ear.

She crept along the wall to the corner. When she was sure there was no one else around, she fast-walked across the stone floor to Marcos' room. When she peeked inside, he was laying in bed facing away from her. She rushed to the bedside, pushing aside the blankets.

"Aunt Cora?" he mumbled, still groggy from sleep.

She practically dragged him toward the exit. "Come on. We are getting out of here."

He backed out of her reach. "Why? Did something happen?"

"I don't have time to explain. We have to get out of here. You and I are in danger."

"No, we aren't. Mr. Segomo has been keeping me safe here. He's—"

Cora spun around. "Listen to me. Mr. Segomo isn't who he says he is. He took you from your father. He brought us both here against our will."

Marcos still refused to budge, so she squeezed his arms. "Have I ever lied to you?"

He shook his head.

"We have to find a way back home."

Marcos nodded, then followed her into the hall. A faint light appeared from around the corner, and she flung them both against the wall, holding her breath. The flames wavered, then slowly faded into the distance. She tightened her grip on Marcos and continued toward the stairs.

They made it to the bottom step without running into anyone. Despite the absence of people, there was no mistaking the rancid smell of Indech. His stink seemed to seep from the very stone around them. She kept them to the shadows of the main entryway, listening for footsteps. The only thing she could hear were a few men in the courtyard, but they sounded far away in the opposite direction of where she planned to go.

She leaned into Marcos and whispered, "Once we are outside, head to the south, to the cover of those trees. From there, we'll find a safe place to travel."

She slipped through the tall archway, careful to stay hidden. Most of the voices she heard were coming from somewhere out of sight to their right, so she grabbed Marcos' hand and slid along the wall to the left. At the next intersection, she slowed to a stop, about to peer around the corner, when a familiar face appeared in front of her. Segomo's eyes widened, then shot to Marcos. Acting without thinking, she shoved him aside, dragging Marcos toward the outer gate.

Cora made it only a few steps before being tackled to the ground. She tried to elbow Segomo, but he had her arms pinned to her sides. "Let me go." The fear in her voice was sickening to her own ears. She struggled against her brother, straining to find Marcos, ready to tell him to run. Her mind recoiled at the monster standing in his place.

Segomo yanked her to her feet just as Indech strolled toward them. "I told you she would try to take the boy."

Her brother's gaze brushed over her, the fear in his eyes foreign to her. Turning his attention back to Cora, his features hardened into a stony resolve. "Why did you do it, Little Goddess? I warned you of the consequences."

She fought against his hold on her. "Go on. Kill me." Hot tears burned her cheeks.

His grip loosened, but not enough that she could break free. "There will be no killing. Not tonight," he whispered.

Even if she wanted to fight him, she didn't have the strength. He led her to a narrow door and down a set of stone steps, ending in a dank cellar that had been turned into a makeshift prison. Two small cells flanked a single window at the top of the wall. The air was wet and reeked of rotten, mildewed straw.

Segomo pushed her into the cell on the right. The sound of the lock clicking into place echoed in the isolated room, making her flinch. "Maybe a couple of days in here will teach you some humility and make you appreciate the freedom you had."

A wave of resentment shot through her, fueled by rage more than anything else. "You are so blinded by your hatred for Arawn." She rushed the iron bars, knowing they wouldn't budge. "You can't see just how alike you two are."

"I am nothing like him," he spat. "I have never betrayed my own blood."

"Isn't that what you're doing now?"

Silence filled the space between them, threatening to smother her. All the anger drained from his face, replaced with slack-jawed confusion and a hint of regret.

"If you go through with this, you'll be no better than the man you claim to despise. In fact, you will be more of a monster than he could ever be."

His mouth snapped shut as something darker passed over his features. "Careful what you say next, Little Goddess."

The venom in his words made her swallow back a shudder, but she continued. "There is goodness in you. I see it even now."

Her body sagged, and she backed to the cot that lay in the far corner and plopped down on the edge, burying her face in her hands. "I never wanted to leave you." Her voice was as hollow as she felt. "When Arawn found out I meant to travel to your past, to change your fate, he forbade me from ever returning to the underworld."

She lifted her head, expecting him to be gone, but he still stood there, staring at her with an uncertainty she'd never seen on his face before.

"Promise me when this is over, you won't send me back home," she whispered. "I'm tired. Tired of pretending everything is fine when it's not. Tired of being alone." Her words echoed the despair filling every crevice of her being. "I don't want this life anymore. Not when Fate stole my happiness and gave it to someone else."

"What are you asking?"

Her tongue refused to speak the words. After a few seconds, he backed into the shadows of the outer cell and disappeared. Unable to hold on to her pain any longer, so she let go of her grief in a series of shaking sobs, wrapping her arms around herself to keep from breaking apart.

Water crashed against the rock in a steady downpour, splashing onto Miller's feet. His chest heaved and his lungs burned from the exertion of running for what seemed like hours. He didn't dare fly any further. The moonlight would have given him away. He reached out and scooped up a handful of the clean water, sucking down a couple of quick gulps.

He turned his back on the moon, returning to the trek up the side of the ridge where he hoped to meet up with his uncle. Miller's mind drifted to Dino, wondering if he made it to safety. Despite their past, he didn't want one of kin to lose his life. When they found Cora and Marcos, he would scour the land to find Dino, so both father and son were reunited.

A blade slid over his shoulder, coming to a rest at his neck, kissing the soft flesh there. "You are a long way from home, dragon."

Miller was careful to move his head in a slow arc to meet the stranger's stare. He recognized the druid symbols adorning his skin. "Aye. As are my friends."

The man lowered the curved dagger, donning a guarded smile. "Come, your uncle has been waiting for you."

Miller studied the faces watching him from the trees. He followed the armed men in silence. Not long into their journey, the tension eased as their camp came into view through the thick brush.

Edwind was already on his feet, rushing toward them. "You made it out unscathed. Good. I wanted to search for you myself, but Etna refused to let me leave."

Miller glanced past Edwind to an elderly woman sitting at a smoldering fire pit, prodding the glowing logs. The way the flames played on her face struck a chord of familiarity in him. He followed the outlines of the houses that dotted the landscape and was sure he'd seen them before. "What is this place?"

"It is my home." The old woman said, still staring into the light. She lifted her eyes, and their emerald orbs glowed in the orange blaze. "You visited only a handful of times, but you wouldn't remember that yet."

"What is she talking about?" Miller asked, peering at the curious faces surrounding them.

Edwind slapped him on the shoulder. "You may want to sit down for this. It's a lot to take in."

"We don't have time for talk." Miller insisted. "We must find Cora. Dino sacrificed his freedom and possibly his life for her."

"Your woman is safe," Etna rose, throwing a twig into the embers, "for now."

Miller sidestepped his uncle. "How do you know this?"

Despite her short stature, the priestess carried herself with the poise and determination of his mother. "Do you not recognize your own kin?"

Movement from beyond the light drew his attention to someone walking toward them. She shared Cora's crimson locks and fierce smile, but her eyes were the color of the meadows of his homeland. He dropped his gaze back to the old woman. "Who are you?" he asked again.

"My name is Etna. My father is, or will be, your eldest son." She nodded to the newcomer. "Darice is your great, great, granddaughter."

Miller looked at Edwind, who smiled. "I told you."

To Etna, Miller said, "You are my granddaughter?"

She smiled. "And if we wish to keep existing, you must save my grandmother from the sadistic monster who holds her captive."

"Do you know where she is being kept?"

"We've always known."

"Our people have been watching that place for some time now." The man who spoke was the same one that had held a blade to Miller's throat. "There was a young boy brought to the keep. Coramagda arrived soon after. As far as we can tell, they are both being treated well. Neither are in chains."

Miller couldn't understand why Cora didn't use her magic to free herself.

Etna crossed her arms. "We must prepare a way to save them without having to fight the creature that resides there."

Miller frowned. "I will turn that place into rubble if it means getting her back."

Etna's smile reminded him of his mother when she would recount a tale of his grandfather's follies. "I have no doubt you would do just that, but the beast who holds her prisoner is not to be taken lightly. He is much more powerful than you or I. We must—"

Several men charged from the trees. "Priestess." one of them said. "Cora tried to escape with the boy just now."

"Is she injured?" Miller asked.

Etna held up a hand to silence him. "What happened?"

"Her brother subdued her quite easily. She didn't attempt to use her powers."

The old woman stared at the ground for a few seconds. "Did she have something around her neck?"

The young man thought for a moment, then said. "A simple silver torque."

Etna nodded. "I should have known that devious brother of hers would have resorted to such desperate measures to keep her compliant."

"What did he do to Cora?" Miller asked.

She ignored him at first. "Dannin, you and your men will take Miller and his uncle to the castle tonight. We no longer have the luxury of waiting."

"I will go, too." Behind them, Darice tucked a short sword into its sheath at her side.

Etna's mouth settled into a tight frown. "Make sure death is a last resort."

Miller stepped forward, holding up a hand. "I do not think she should join us." He felt eyes turn on him. "Not because she is a woman. It is enough that I risk my lineage. Should she risk her future children for this quest?"

There was a shuffling of glances.

Darice took in a deep breath and laid a hand on his arm. "It is not my destiny to carry on our family line. That was taken from me a long time ago. My death will not make a difference in our thread." She walked past him and joined the other men of the tribe.

Miller looked to Etna for an explanation, but she shook her head, so he let it go.

"Bring Coramagda here, and I can free her from the Qel," Etna said. "Be safe, grandfather."

Segomo stood at the window of his room, frowning at the court-yard below. Images of a past life flashed through his mind, and he was surprised at how crisp those memories were. He could still recall the sweet scent of exotic flowers sprinkled throughout the lush valley of a place he once called home. A pair of honey laden eyes peered at him from over a sun kissed shoulder, a sultry, melodious voice beckoning him to follow.

Amani had been the most beautiful creature he'd ever known. Her smile could shatter the most hardened of hearts. He had been a fool to love her. No one, not even a god, could tame her wandering eye. When she took him and his most trusted general in the same bed, he never questioned her loyalty to him.

Arawn warned him of the fickle nature of mortals, but Amani was different. Or so he thought. When she told Segomo she was with child, he had grand ideas of his progeny carrying on his legacy. Those dreams were shattered when he caught her colluding with his enemy. The horrible things she'd said cut him to the core, claiming the baby inside her wasn't even his. Hate seized his heart and soul until it ate away every ounce of love he had for her and her people. In the end, wrath and vengeance were all that was left.

Only scorched earth remained by the time he had his fill of revenge. His actions led to the destruction of entire bloodlines. Something his family could not ignore. He caused too much damage to Ronwen's precious loom. He had to be punished.

Then came Coramagda. The half mortal goddess that was put in his charge to look after and teach to control her godhood. Her strength was a flicker to his blaze, yet she burned with her own kind of power. For many years, he managed to keep the ravine deep and wide between them. Over the years, the little goddess wriggled her way across with her stubborn tenacity. There was a time he would have burned the world all over again to protect her.

When she stopped visiting, he assumed Arawn had finally poisoned her against him. To learn Cora was forced to stay away—how could he have believed she would abandon him? Knowing the truth made him question everything.

"Why is Coramagda still alive?"

Segomo's muscles tensed, jolted out of his thoughts. He relaxed his expression into neutrality. "I told you, she is not to be harmed."

Indech joined him at the window. "You are letting your heart get in the way of your desire for your freedom."

"That Qel around her neck will keep her submissive. If you murder her, she is bound to find Arawn, then our entire plan is in jeopardy."

"We will not be so easily defeated this time."

"Very well. If you think you are ready to face the wrath of my father, then by all means, kill her. At least I go back to my prison, knowing your fate is far worse than mine."

Indech studied the sky for a few seconds, and Segomo feared he might actually follow through with the threat. Finally, Indech said, "She stays alive for now, but if she tries to take the boy from us again, I shall disembowel her without a second thought."

Segomo unclenched his jaw. "She will not trouble us anymore."

"See that she doesn't. We are too close to achieving what we both want."

As soon as the door slammed shut, he dropped into the chair near the window and pinched the bridge of his nose, willing the images in his mind to go away. Cora's cries echoed inside his head. No matter how hard he tried to ice over his heart, she was the only person who could still make it bleed.

Shouting drew him to the window once again, bringing a blessed distraction from his ever-circling thoughts. He leaned forward to get a better view of the raucous. The scouting party had returned. A bloodied man was being dragged by a short chain attached to a familiar iron collar. Segomo recognized the modern clothes and rushed downstairs to meet the men in the courtyard.

He saw Dino being dragged toward the back of the barracks, but stopped them. "Where are the others?"

Rickson frowned at him. "How did you know there were others?"

"Where are they?" Segomo demanded.

"Gone. We searched the area, but there was no sign of them." He nodded to Dino. "I thought you were a crazy man to send a dragon hunter with us, but—"

"What about the book? Did you find it?"

Rickson motioned to one of his men, who carried a small wooden chest adorned with ancient runes and tarnished silver. A faint hum of magic emanated from the locked box, and Segomo knew they found the right tome. He carefully took the box in one hand and grabbed the chain attached to Dino's shackle in the other.

The hunter rushed forward to stop them. "Where do you think you are going with my prize?"

Segomo leveled a threatening stare at the man, daring him to act. "He is mine. Find another dragon to slay, boy."

The hunter went for his weapon, but the surrounding soldiers made it clear where their loyalty lay. After all, it wasn't he who was paying for their services.

Segomo led Dino into a small room and motioned for him to sit in the chair opposite his own at a small table near the window.

Dino eyed the door, testing the strength of his confines.

Segomo tossed a couple of logs into the dying flames, bringing them back to life. "Careful. I'd hate to have to clean up the mess you will make if you try to call on your dragon."

"I'll kill you all for taking my son." Though his tone held the conviction of his words, Dino's slumped posture told the truth of his powerlessness to follow through on the threat.

"You are but one person in a long line waiting for my head. Now tell me, how did you get here? Who came with you?"

Dino looked away.

Setting the chest on the table near his chair, he went to stand in front of his captive. "I will loosen your tongue, one way or another. Perhaps I should drag Marcos in here to help."

Dino's eyes glistened with fury and fear. "I came with Edwind and Miller."

"The two from the tavern?"

"Yes."

"How did you end up here? To this time? That daughter of Cernunnos is a gifted little goddess, but how could she possibly know where to find us?"

"She isn't the one who found you."

Segomo cocked his head to the side, making a motion for him to go on. Dino nodded to the bottle on the table, eyes watching with hungry anticipation as the glass was filled with a dark, bitter wine.

Dino took his time sipping at the drink, then pushed the cup away. "Apparently, Miller bonded himself to Cora before you abducted her. That's how we tracked her here."

"Bonded?" Segomo backed to the window and stared at the sky. "But she is no dragon."

Dino ignored him, craning his neck to peek into the darkness beyond the threshold. "Where is Cora, anyway? I know she's still alive."

"She is safe. Now tell me how and why this dragon bonded himself to my sister."

"Why does any dragon give themselves to another so completely? Although, he did it before he was aware of the destiny they shared."

Segomo turned a curious stare on Dino. "Destiny, you say?" He knew of his mother's tendencies to meddle in the lives of others and would take great pleasure in screwing it up if it meant pissing her off.

"She is the reason Marcos and I exist."

Segomo's face went slack, thinking he misheard.

Downing the rest of the wine, Dino went on. "She must return to ten-twelve. She and Miller are the mother and father of our bloodline."

"Cora didn't tell me any of this." Was that why she was so desperate to get Marcos away from here?

"That's because she doesn't know about her destiny. None of us did until after you took her."

Segomo's shoulders fell as understanding sweeping over him. When she said Fate stole her happiness, she still believed Miller was meant for another.

"Can I see my son now?" Dino asked, leaning forward.

Segomo gave a slow nod. "I will keep that shackle around your neck to make sure you stay civil."

After sending Dino to be reunited with Marcos, he made sure to assign more guards to the boy's room and took a stroll down the long corridors in the hopes of finding some kind of clarity.

Already, a new plan was forming in Segomo's mind. One that would mean a substantial loss for them in the short term, but it was a sacrifice they would have to make if they wanted to ensure ultimate victory.

By the time he made it to his chamber, Indech was waiting for him in the chair next to the small chest.

"I hear we have guests in our midst." He crooned, running gnarled fingers over the rough surface. "The hunter you stole from is more than a little disappointed about losing his trophy. I will see that he gets it back."

"You will not." Segomo barked.

A pair of glowing eyes landed on Segomo with so much force it squeezed him from the inside out, suffocating him.

"You are a fool." Segomo quaked out between clenched teeth. "You will ruin everything we've worked for." The weight lifted and Segomo picked himself upright.

Indech searched the flames of the candle beside him. "Go on."

"I learned some interesting information about Dino. It seems Cora is the reason you have a vessel to shove your father into."

That time, when the pockmarked face looked at Segomo, there was curiosity in his mangled gaze.

"She and one of the men searching for her are the mother and father of Marcos' bloodline. Kill Cora or her man, and you destroy any hopes of freeing Tethra."

"It would be a tragic loss, but I can wait for another." They stared at each other for a long time. Then Indech let out a disgusted sigh. "I may not be able to kill your sister, but I do not need the boy's father."

Segomo chuckled. "You know so little about the art of war and what it means to sacrifice a pawn to take down the king. When Miller arrives to free Cora, you won't stop him."

"They will not leave without the boy."

"We will let him go as well."

"I cannot let that happen."

"You must do just that, or our plans crumble into dust." Segomo stepped closer. "You woefully underutilize my expertise. Do you think I'm only good for abducting children and chasing down lost tomes? I am a god of fucking war and carnage. My army was unstoppable, not because of its might, but because I understood my enemy's weaknesses. I barely had to shed a drop of blood to bring them to their knees."

Indech rose from the chair. "And yet you lost the war inside yourself, imprisoned by your own father."

The flickering light that danced across the stone walls swayed in time with the sound of the crackling fire between them. Finally, Indech took a step back. "What is this plan you have concocted?"

The smile that split Segomo's lips was one he hadn't worn in a long time. "We will have to give up this battle to win the war, but win it we will if you follow my lead."

Chapter 15

THE MEN MOVED THROUGH the trees with the grace and silence of predators stalking their prey. Miller wanted to take the lead so he could hasten their advance, but he knew Dannin pushed them through the land as efficiently as possible while maintaining a quiet approach. According to the scouts, none of the soldiers had ventured this way.

Miller struggled to suppress fear in favor of stealth. His mind kept spinning images of Cora being tortured, or worse, killed. He was aware that those fears were of his own making. His bond with her was profound, but it didn't grant him visions of precognition.

Dannin slowed, then held up a hand. "The fort is over those hills. I will go with the others and return when it is safe to continue."

Miller cared little about safety. He needed to reach her before it was too late.

Edwind came into view beside him. "We'll wait here."

As much as Miller loathed the idea of sitting idle, he remained with his uncle. With nothing else to do, he studied the glittering sky, unable to appreciate the vast ocean of stars above. Edwind moved a few feet away, staring into the gloom of the trees, thinking of his own family, no doubt. Perhaps regretting the decision to leave nineteen ninety-two so he could follow someone else's destiny.

Guilt pressed down on Miller, clouding his mind. "You should have stayed with Aunt Darya," he said, finally.

Miller didn't expect the smile that split Edwind's mouth. "If my father or grandfather had been allowed to intervene, they would be here as well. Your life, and that of Cora and your future children, are just as important as my family. We all have our place in the tapestry of our kin. I will do everything in my power to make sure you return to it."

"What if I fail?" The words sat on his tongue like a heavy stone. For the first time in his life, Miller felt inadequate. "What if I am unworthy to stand by Cora's side?"

Uncle Edwind's smile twisted into a concerned frown. "How can you ask such a thing?"

"For as long as I can remember, I was expected to take on your role as protector of Didean and its people. I fought against my mother and father, detesting the idea of being made to live in the shadow of a man I didn't know. Now, having met you and Aunt Darya, I'm not sure I deserve to hold that mantle."

Edwind's smile returned. "I often felt the same way. As did Gita. She sacrificed more than any one person should have in order to raise an ungrateful, stubborn boy who rebelled against the duty that lay at his feet. I can never thank her enough for showing me grace when she could have easily and rightfully eviscerated me." He cupped a hand on the side of Miller's face. "You carry the best of both Gita and Saebbi. You are a far better man to bear the weight of that responsibility than I ever was."

A knot of emotion lodged in Miller's throat, making it impossible to argue. Instead, he managed to get out, "I miss my father."

"We will reunite with him again one day."

Dannin broke through the tree line, giving Miller the chance to take a breath and push aside his tears. "The gods smile upon us. Most of their forces have abandoned their posts."

"What of Marcos and Cora?" Miller asked.

"I did not see them among the men. They march to the east. If we are to save her and the boy, it has to be now."

Miller's muscles tightened with both anticipation and apprehension. "Let's hope they do not find Etna and the others."

"The forest protects us," Dannin stated bluntly. "They will not reach us if we do not wish it."

Miller followed his uncle into the trees, hoping the nagging feeling in his gut was merely a projection of his own fear, and not the manifestation of what was to come.

Silence and isolation enveloped Cora in an unwelcome embrace. The cold stone cut into her back, but she hardly noticed. She stared through the metal bars, transfixed by the shadows swaying in the faint moonlight streaming through the narrow opening above her head. Her gaze drifted to the tiny table sitting along the far wall. If she had a slightly longer reach, she might have been able to grab a utensil and at least attempt to free herself.

For now, all she could do was wait for Segomo to decide her fate, hoping he would follow through with her request. If not for the Qel around her neck, she would have taken her own life, but the power of the torque not only took away the wearer's godhood, but their ability to harm themselves as well. Morigan had been quite diabolical when crafting them.

Cora didn't think she could bear facing Dino, knowing that she'd failed to save his son. The heartbreak of losing Miller was secondary to the devastation that awaited not only Marcos, but the rest of humanity if Tethra was set free.

A bitter fury slithered around her heart, squeezing mercilessly at her empathy. Terrible thoughts intruded on precious memories she tried to hang on to. Maybe the world deserved what was coming. Morigan and Ronwen had been screwing with everyone's fate for too long without consequences of their own. They earned every ounce of suffering and fear that waited beyond the bounds of this realm.

Miller's face came into view, banishing those horrific images from her mind. Though his children wouldn't be hers, they were still worth fighting for. As were the lives of Darya and her family.

The unmistakable click of a disengaging lock echoed through the darkness. Cora scrambled to her feet, ready to face Segomo and whatever punishment he deemed fitting. The man that came into view was one she never thought she'd see again. As soon as she was sure Dino wasn't a mirage, she flew across the small space, drawing him near.

"I'm so sorry." Her voice was barely audible through her tears. "I tried to save him."

Dino leaned away, taking her face in his hands. "I know."

They stared at one another as she grasped at the words to express how truly devastated she was at failing them. But there was nothing she could say to make up for her failure. Then the reality of his presence hit her. "Are you alone? How did you get here, or even know where we were?"

He eyed the open door behind him. "As soon as we found out you were missing, Miller sought out that seer friend of yours, Raquel. She used the bond you two share to find you."

"He didn't—What are you talking about?"

Dino gripped her shoulders. "There's so much to tell you, but I don't have time for that now. We need to leave while we have the chance."

Meeting his stare again, she asked, "How did you get past the guards?" She refrained from pointing out his lack of stealth.

"Segomo sent the bulk of the forces on a wild goose chase. He said it would give me the opportunity to get you and Marcos away from here."

At the mention of her brother's name, her body went rigid. "You're working with him?"

Dino reached for her again, but she sidestepped him. "Reluctantly. After I was captured and brought here, he saw it as a way to make things right. You have to believe me."

She shook her head. "This feels like a trap."

"It's not."

"Segomo has too much at stake to just let me walk away. Especially with Marcos. You can't trust him."

"I don't have the luxury of questioning his motives. He gave me the key to your cell and he's making sure we have a clear path out of here." He glanced behind him. "We need to go before some random guard spots us."

The door outside creaked open and Marcos' face peered inside. "The east gate is clear. Hurry."

Seeing Marcos eased the tightness in her chest, but she was hesitant to believe her own eyes. Not after what Indech had done before. "Hey, kiddo," she said, keeping her distance. "You remember that gift I got you for your birthday?"

Marcos looked from her to his dad. "Why is that important now?"

"Just humor me, yeah?"

"It was a Metallica cassette I'd been wanting for months."

Her stomach plummeted with relief, and she let out the breath she'd been holding. There was no way that crusty Fomorian would know about modern music. Yet there was still some doubt in her mind about why Segomo had such a sudden change of heart. Not when he made it clear the lengths he would go to for his freedom.

"Cora."

Dino's voice broke through her indecision. Outside, she scanned the surrounding buildings, surprised at the utter stillness of the fort. The lack of ever present footsteps left a void that seemed to close in around her.

Marcos scurried toward the open gate. Dino grabbed her arm and rushed them across the expanse, pausing at a stack of barrels near the stone arch that promised freedom.

Marcos peered around the barrels, but Cora yanked him back into hiding. "Stay close to your dad."

An arrow zoomed past her head and lodged into the wood, mere inches from her face. She searched the surrounding wall until she spotted the shooter, who was already aiming another arrow in their direction. So much for a clean getaway. She pushed Marcos into his father and hissed, "Run."

She made sure she stayed between Marcos and the soldier as they scrambled through the gate and bolted across the field toward the tree line. Halfway to the forest, she peered over her shoulder, glimpsing a handful of men chasing after them. They wielded bows and newly sharpened swords while she and Dino had nothing.

Under the cover of trees, she pulled Marcos and Dino into a thick cluster of brush. "You two stay here. I'm going to lure the soldiers away. When it's safe, make a run for it and don't look back."

Dino shot up and snatched her by the arm, forcing her to the ground. "I don't bloody think so."

"You have to get Marcos out of here. My life isn't as important as his."

"You couldn't be more wrong." He reached for the Qel and pulled at the metal, but it didn't budge.

She gave him a sympathetic smile. "I wish it was that easy. Only god blood can open it."

"Yeah, but I thought since—" His words were cut short when the soldiers breached the trees.

Dino held Cora in place as he stood hunched over, studying the darkness beyond the brush. "We are going to find our way out together. All three of us. As soon as we lose those men, we can find Edwind and Miller. If they don't find us first."

Her heart thudded against her chest. "Miller and Edwind are here?"

"Yes. Not long after we arrived, we were captured. I gave them the distraction they needed to escape. I just hoped it worked."

A visceral scream of a dying man broke the silence. Farther into the forest, where her sight couldn't quite penetrate, she spotted shadowed outlines of trees swaying in jerky movements against the glittering sky. She stood, but Dino seized her hand.

A flash of red and green passed through a sliver of moonlight, and her legs threatened to buckle beneath her. She broke free of Dino's grasp, taking off toward the sounds of fighting.

"Cora," Dino called. "Stay here."

She ignored him, keeping her sights focused on the shadowed, hulking beasts that darted between the trees. More men shrieked, and she was forced to dive to the side to avoid a body that had been hurled through the air in her direction. When she looked up again, a pair of blazing red eyes stared at her from out of the blackness.

The dragon took one step, then another. On the third, Miller closed the distance between them. Even if she wanted to stop the incoming embrace, she didn't have the strength or the willpower to tell him no. His kiss invigorated her dying soul, and it was finally able to breathe.

"I should never have left you," he whispered. "It will never happen again."

Hearing that simple promise threatened to break her. She lifted her forehead from his, ready to say as much, when a sharp pressure slammed into her back, stealing the breath from her lungs. Her mouth opened, but no sound came out. The world dimmed and her knees buckled at the searing pain boring into her flesh. Miller held her upright, his expression shifting from relief to horror as she coughed, red splattering his shirt.

She pressed her lips together, holding onto a scream when he touched her left shoulder blade. The agony of her wound made her choke on the blood still lodged in her mouth. She thought she heard someone screaming, then the world tilted, and she was in the air, howling wind whipping her hair across her face. When she opened her eyes, she was floating high above the trees, her body cradled in a pair of dark talons, tucked close to the red dragon's underbelly as it soared into the sky.

With the last of her strength, she rested a hand against Miller's scales, comforted by the feel of him before giving herself to death and joining her father in the underworld.

Chapter 16

Sunlight filtered through the sheer sheet, easing Cora awake. She opened her eyes and immediately started giggling at the smiling face staring back at her. Miller brushed his fingers across her cheek.

"Do we have to get up?" she asked.

"The children will be here soon to drag us out of bed." He pressed his lips to hers. "Until then, we can stay for a little while longer."

She nestled deeper into his arms. "I never want to leave."

"We shall be together always."

Darkness crowded the light shining through the windows. She was overcome with a feeling of wrongness. "I don't belong here."

Pain tore through the dream, rendering her awake. The sounds of children's laughter drifted from somewhere in the distance. She raised a hand to her face to shield her eyes from the harsh glare. A warm breeze swept through the window above her head. After another careful breath, she dropped her arm and blinked away the rest of sleep, trying to get a better look at the room.

Footsteps padded to the side of the bed. A tall, slender woman came into view, carrying a cup in one hand and a rag in the other. "Easy, child," said a soothing voice. It carried the tender tone of someone who'd spent many years comforting others. "That wound of yours didn't kill you, but it will pain you for some time."

Cora blinked away the mist from her vision, recoiling at the cup being pressed to her mouth.

"This will help with the pain."

The drink tasted sweet, with a hint of something bitter. After easing back onto the pillow, Cora studied the woman. She had sun-darkened skin, but her eyes were bright and crisp and carried the colors of a summer meadow, eliciting an overwhelming sense of familiarity. "Who are you?"

"My name is Etna." She set the cup on the table in the center of the room.

Cora waited for her to elaborate. When she didn't, Cora said, "Where are the others? Are they okay?"

"Everyone is safe and well. As soon as you are rested, you can take your companions back to where you belong."

Cora pushed herself to the head of the bed. "I'm afraid I can't do that. Not with this thing—" She went to grab the Qel, only to find it missing from around her neck. "Did someone get word to my father?"

Etna paused, then said, "There will be time for answers later."

Cora watched the old woman disappear outside, more confused than before. She tried to sit up, but the pain in her back kept lying flat.

When the door opened again, her heart leapt into her throat and her pulse doubled. Miller strode across the room in two long strides, kneeling beside the bed. He took her hand and brought it to his lips. "I feared I did not get you here in time."

She balled her fingers into a fist, snatching it away from him.

He moved into her and grabbed her hand again, holding more firmly.

She tried to turn away, but he wouldn't let her. "Why are you making this so hard?"

His grin was gentle, as was his kiss.

"Is my heartache amusing?"

"No, sweet goddess. Let me explain myself."

She pressed her lips into a tight, thin line, biting back what she wanted to say next.

"I bonded with you the night we spent together. That's how I knew you were in danger."

She didn't want to believe Dino when he told her, but how else would Raquel have been able to find her? "Do you know how dangerous that was?"

"Would you please quiet yourself and listen?"

She frowned, relaxing into the bed.

"Brigita confessed Grandfather knew about my arrival."

"Horsa knew? Why didn't he tell Edwind?"

Miller silenced her with a raised brow.

"Fine. Listening."

"He couldn't involve himself because he's already lived through what has been. He knew I was coming to claim my destiny."

"I don't understand. Your destiny is back on Didean."

His smile made her heart flutter. "From the moment you fell into my arms, we were set on the path to here; to us." He took hold of her hands again.

Her vision clouded over with tears. "That can't be right."

"How do you think the Qel was removed from around your neck? It is your god blood that freed you and it is our kin who healed you."

Her eyes widened. "That means Dino and Marcos are my family as well."

He nodded, climbing onto the bed so he could reach her lips more easily. She lost herself in the kiss, savoring the softness of his lips. Had it not been for the painful reminder that she had been shot by an arrow, she would have demanded more, but a kiss was good. For now.

He laid her back, careful not to touch her injury. When he tried to pull away, she held him still. "Don't leave."

After kissing each cheek, he settled beside her, resting a hand on the side of her face.

"It would have been nice if Horsa told us about our destiny," she said. "Maybe we could have saved ourselves some heartache."

He brushed a strand of hair from her forehead. "None of that matters now. We are together. I'll never let you out of my arms again." His lips barely touched hers when someone knocked at the door and pushed it open without waiting for an answer.

Dino stood in the doorway, staring at the bed. His cheeks flushed a bright red, and he turned his face to the ground. "I—Sorry. I didn't mean to interrupt."

Cora shifted out from under Miller. "Is everything okay? Did something happen to Marcos?"

Eyes still glued to the floor, Dino said, "He's fine. I wanted to speak to you. I have some things I need to say."

Miller got up on one elbow. "Then say your peace and be gone."

Cora ran a hand over his arm to cool his temper.

Dino lifted his gaze, and his mouth worked into a tight frown. "I would like to eat my crow in private."

"Crow?" Miller frowned. "I do not think Cora wishes to eat—"

Cora pushed herself to a sitting position, trying to keep the pain from showing on her face. "It's fine." She kissed Miller on the cheek. "Give us a few minutes."

He returned the show of affection and eyed Dino on his way outside. "I will return shortly."

When they were alone, Dino grabbed a chair and sat it next to the bed. "I am so sorry for—" He worked his fingers in and out of each other. "Everything. I know I've said horrible things, and I understand if you can't forgive me."

She reached out, stilling his fidgeting. "You were scared. I couldn't imagine having to experience the loss of a child twice."

He had a hard time meeting her stare. "That is no excuse. I was terrified of losing the last piece of the life I once had with Miriam."

Cora tensed. It was the first time she'd heard that name come out of Dino's mouth since his wife died shortly after she gave birth. She hadn't known Miriam that well, but she and Dino were as much in love as she and Miller.

Resting a hand on his shoulder, Cora said, "You are a wonderful father. Miriam would be so proud of you both."

He lifted his head, his eyes glistening with sadness. "What if he was with her, and my selfishness tore him from his mother? What if he was meant to stay with her, not me?"

Cora brushed away his tears. "I wish I knew the answers. One thing I am sure of, when the time comes, she will be waiting for you both."

"I appreciate what you've done for us. You saved my son. No matter what happens, know that everything I do is for him."

The tone of his words struck something inside Cora. Before she could ask him about it, he stood and wiped at his face. "I should let you get some rest."

Cora tried to sit up, to stop him, but the door opened.

Miller sauntered through the doorway with a variety of food, then frowned at Dino. "Have you had your fill of crow?"

Cora cocked her head to the side.

"Uncle Edwind explained to me what it meant."

Avoiding eye contact, Dino nodded. "I suppose I have." Meeting Cora's stare, he added, "I am grateful for everything you've done for us."

When they were alone, Miller sat down in the now empty chair and handed her a piece of bread. "I hope he choked on that apology for how he treated you."

"Nothing good can come from holding on to anger."

"His hatred nearly killed you."

She grabbed hold of his face and kissed him.

"You do not play fair, goddess."

Cora stared at the door, thinking about what Dino said. What if he was right, and Marcos was never meant to be brought back from the dead? Had she wrongly stolen a child from his mother? Now, because of her selfish actions, Marcos might have lost more than his life. If Indech went through with the ritual, it would have destroyed his soul.

Pain throbbed from the puncture wound in Cora's back, each movement a sharp reminder that Miller might be right. She tried to argue when he insisted she stay in bed, at least until she finished eating. He wanted her to rest for a few more days, but they couldn't afford to wait that long. She had to get them home. Her injuries would heal, no matter the year.

Despite his protests, Cora convinced Miller to ready the others for their impending departure. Truthfully, she wanted a few moments to mentally and physically prepare for the amount of energy and power it was going to take to open the way home.

Every time she attempted to draw in a whisper of magic, her heart fluttered sporadically, and the world took on a dangerously unstable waver.

Yet, they couldn't waste precious days waiting for her to regain her strength. Each minute that passed in sixteen seventy-four left them vulnerable to Indech's wrath. Not to mention the unforeseen consequences of meddling in her family's fate. Segomo may have facilitated her rescue, but only because he needed Marcos to keep existing. Neither Indech nor her brother would give him up for long.

As fast as her injured body would let her, she climbed out of bed and went to the door, intending to talk to Dino; to find out if Segomo had said anything else regarding their escape. A cool morning breeze swept over her face, bringing with it the scent of familiar spices and the sharp tang of campfires. A brief stirring of nostalgia made her pause in the doorway. She was struck by the similarity between this place and the forest she grew up in. Aside from their clothes, Etna's tribe could have been her own.

Through a set of simple wattle houses, she spotted Edwind sitting by the communal fire, facing away from her. He was bent forward slightly, muscles tense, probably fighting the urge to drag her out and demand she send him back to nineteen ninety-two.

Guilt gnawed at her insides. He'd been willing to travel through time again, with no guarantee that he would ever return to his family. No matter where she fit in with the grand scheme, her life wasn't worth the risk of her best friend losing the man she loved.

A young woman came into view, kneeling beside Edwind. She handed him a cup of steaming liquid and settled down on the crudely carved seat a few feet away. Her hair burned bright red in the soft light, and there was no doubt that she was one of Cora's descendants. The woman's smile carried the same off kilter slant that Miller and the rest of his kin shared.

The woman said something that was lost in the cascade of conversations humming through the valley. Edwind nodded once before returning to his brooding over the fire.

"What are you doing out of bed?" Miller stepped around the corner, carrying a cup in one hand.

Cora met his gaze, and his expression softened. Watching the transformation from worry to adoration heated her blood. She still couldn't quite grasp the reality that soon she would return to ten-twelve and spend the rest of her life with him on Didean. The thought made her grin.

"I love it when you look at me like that," he whispered.

Tendrils of warmth swept across her cheeks, and she turned her attention to the fire where Edwind was now poking at the smoking embers. "I can't believe he came all this way for me." Her lips curved into a teasing grin. "Or that Darya let him."

Miller handed her the cup. "It took some convincing on his part, but she did relent."

Cora sipped the cool, refreshing water, though she hoped for something with more kick. She wasn't one to day drink, but she could use the numbing effects of alcohol to help mitigate the pain of tearing a hole through time.

Turning back to Miller, she said, "We can't stay much longer. Segomo might have let us escape, but we aren't safe. He will try to take Marcos again. We must get him to Broughied, where he can be better protected."

To her surprise, Miller nodded. "Segomo does not dare harm you or I. Marcos is their ultimate prize." He cupped the side of her face in his hand. "Still, you need rest. If it was will alone that could open a portal, I have no doubt you could do it, but that arrow nearly killed you. Not even our dragons can heal us so quickly. The strain on your body is too great."

"I have to try. I can't put Etna or her people in danger by staying here.

His smile didn't waver. "You underestimate our kin."

"I felt the power Indech wields. It rivals Arawn. He would raze the entire village to take back Marcos."

"The forest protects this place," Miller countered. "I doubt Indech, nor Segomo, can outmatch the forces of nature. Even the gods tremble in the face of Her wrath."

Cora fought a surge of frustration. Miller's logic, though sound, didn't help to ease her fear. He hadn't been in the presence of the putrid well of power that Indech drew from. His ilk was banished to the lowest pits of the underworld for good reason. Fomorians were once seen as gods, but their lust for dominance over the world and beyond twisted them into hellish fiends that gave birth to what modern people thought of as demons. If they found a way to regain their status, no one would be safe.

She didn't get the chance to tell him just how dangerous their situation really was before Etna joined them. "Good. I am happy to see you upright and walking. Come. I wish you to meet someone before you leave."

Cora followed her, glad to have Miller there to help her over the uneven terrain. Etna led them to the fire, where Edwind shot to his feet. His lips were pressed into a tight, thin line. No doubt holding in a demand for Cora to take him home.

Etna held out a hand to the woman with Cora's coppery locks. "I would like you to meet the person who freed you from that despicable torque. Darice shares your gift of life and death."

Darice came to stand in front of Cora, studying her every feature. "I wish I could remember you. My mother told me we met only once when I was an infant. Even then, you sensed my power."

Cora reached for the jewel that hung from a thin piece of twine around the girl's neck. It was the same opalescent pearl that Segomo had given her. "Did I give this to you?"

"You gifted it to your youngest child," Etna said. "Who then carried on the tradition." There was a brief pause, and Cora saw the familiar struggle to hide a painful twinge of regret. "My son was killed before I could give it to him, so it passed to his youngest daughter, Darice."

"But I won't have anyone to pass it along to." Darice wrapped the jewel in her palm. "I plan to travel to Didean. There, I will gift it to my niece when she comes of age."

Cora looked at Miller, then back to Darice. "I don't understand. Don't you want children?"

"I used to. Until the man I loved was murdered by hunters."

Etna laid a hand on Darice's arm. "Jemison was a reckless man who thought he could take on the world."

"I knew the risk of giving my heart to him." The young woman forced a smile. "I've come to terms with my choice."

The somber mood was broken by another loud cackle of children from the woods, and a group of boys burst out into the open, followed by a red-faced Marcos. "It wasn't like that," he yelled after the other kids.

Cora approached Marcos. "What happened?"

More embarrassment worked up his face. The way he refused to look her in the eye spoke volumes.

Behind them, a young woman appeared out of the trees, fidgeting with the top of her dress. "He shouldn't be ashamed of what he saw. It is in the nature of boys his age to be curious."

Etna eyed a man trying to sneak around the other side of the camp. "Dannin, explain."

Dannin's complexion was nearly as red as Marcos.

Miller glanced between Dannin and the other woman. "Oh." He looked at Marcos. "Did you catch them—"

"It was an accident. I swear," Marcos barked. His eyes darted to where the woman had joined Dannin. "I went for a walk and found a spring, and—" He motioned with his hands in the couple's general direction. "I saw them."

Cora had to bite her lower lip to keep from smiling. She knew firsthand the embarrassment Marcos felt. She hadn't been much older when she caught a group of randy men and women engaging in a little pre-celebration one summer solstice. The experience had been both appalling and intriguing to a pubescent hormonal young woman.

"Well, there's nothing to be done about it now." Etna said.

Cora nodded, still fighting to keep the amusement off her face. "I'm sure you would rather talk about this with your dad."

"Or not at all," Marcos muttered.

"Where is Dino, anyway?" Edwind asked.

Etna shrugged. "He wandered off into the trees after speaking to Cora earlier."

"Great." Edwind growled. "That's all we need is for him to get lost and find more trouble."

Cora rested a hand on his arm. "As soon as I'm strong enough, I'll take us back home."

He gave her a comforting squeeze. "I don't mean to rush you. I miss my family."

Etna guided Cora to a lone hut near the edge of the encampment. "Your friend will return soon enough. He should be easy to track if he gets lost. While you wait, I've arranged a bath for you to help with your wound."

Wisps of steam rolled off the surface of the milky water from the round wooden tub centered in the small space. Cora fought to keep from screeching like a giddy teenager after being denied basic hygiene for so long. Since the invention of modern plumbing, she'd grown used to daily showers.

Miller dipped his hand into the bath. "It might be a little too hot."

She ignored his warning and started to undress. "I don't care." She inhaled the soothing scent. "It smells divine. I'm sure I reek, not having had a shower for so long."

Lending his arm, Miller helped her into the tub, easing her to a sitting position. "I hadn't noticed."

She caught a hint of a something playful cross his lips, but all coherent thought left her when the water encased her body. "Oh sweet, merciful goddess. I've never felt anything so incredibly good."

"I'll keep that in mind. It will give me something to strive for."

With her eyes still closed, she reached blindly for his hand. "You know what I mean."

His easy laughter was followed by the warmth of his breath when he kissed her bare shoulder. He rested against her for a long time before moving away.

She opened her eyes to find him kneeling beside the tub. "Aren't you going to join me?" she asked.

The gentle smile turned wicked. "Are you saying I stink?"

"No." She scooped water into her hand, letting it trail up her arm before dripping over her shoulder. "You smell amazing, actually. Though I'm not sure how you stayed so clean after what we've been through."

He leaned forward, kissing her forehead. "I had a chance to bathe while you were recovering. Uncle Edwind insisted I do something to take my mind off your wellbeing for a while."

He started to lean away, but she captured his face in her hands. "Join me," she whispered.

Despite the dim light of the hut, she saw his pupils dilate. His pulse quickened where her pinky rested against his neck. "I don't know if that is wise, given how injured you are."

Holding his gaze, she said, "Why are you fighting so hard not to make love to me?"

"I want nothing more than to lose myself inside you for the rest of our lives, but I dare not risk hurting you further."

She stared into his eyes, where golden flecks glinted against rich green. "Would you stop if I asked?"

"Of course."

She pushed to her feet, bringing him up with her so she could lift his shirt over his head with her good arm. "Then trust me to know my limits."

He unfastened his pants, struggling to keep his balance when removing his boots. All the while, his simmering gaze never left hers. When he was naked, he stepped over the rim of the tub, drawing her into his body, careful not to touch her upper back.

She eased onto his lap, welcoming the shiver that rippled through her as he slipped inside. The sharp sting with each measured thrust was easy to ignore, drowned beneath the rising tide of need. His hands slid down her sides, fingers gripping her hips with hungry insistence as he pushed deeper.

A low, vibrating rumble echoed through the water, sending a shiver along her spine. She let out a hoarse moan, embracing the approaching storm of pleasure.

His mouth parted, but she silenced him with a ravenous kiss, bracing herself against his chest as she ground against him, demanding more. With each roll of her hips, his fingers sunk deeper into her flesh until he shuddered beneath her.

A sharp cry filled the space between them that could have been mistaken for pain, but only pleasure flooded her body.

Minutes passed and her pulse slowed, synching with Miller's as they lay chest to chest.

"See?" She lifted her head and kissed the tip of his nose. "I didn't break."

He brushed her hair from her face. "You are quite resilient." Carefully, he scooted from underneath her, grabbing a cloth from beside the tub. "Come here so I can look at your wound."

Tamping down the urge to tell him she was fine, Cora whirled around, sending waves of opaque water rippling outward. "It doesn't really hurt anymore." As soon as she spoke, she sucked in a breath at the feel of his probing fingertips.

"I see." Miller kept his voice steady; tone soothing.

She glanced over her shoulder. "It's still tender."

His lips twitched as if he wanted to smile. "You aren't in any danger of reopening the puncture, but you will be bruised for quite some time."

Cora pulled her knees to her chest, losing herself to the rhythmic movement of the rag on her back. "I don't know if I'll be a good mum."

He urged her around to face him. There was a tightness in his mouth and eyes, though the love he felt for her was ever present in his gaze. "How can you say such a thing?"

Miller didn't understand how foreign such tenderness was to her. "What if I don't know how to love them?"

"You will love them with the ferocity of a thousand suns. No one will fight to protect them, teach them, care for them like you will. Look what you did to save Marcos. You would have given your life for him."

Though his words eased the aching inside her chest, she couldn't help but feel unworthy of the gift of motherhood. "I was so young when I was taken from my family. Arawn tried to show affection, but I don't think it's in his nature to truly care for anyone but himself. It's the same for most of the gods. Maybe immortality slowly erodes their hearts."

Miller pulled her into his lap. "You are not your father or your brother. I will spend the rest of my life showing you what it is to be loved and cared for."

His kiss melted away the remaining apprehension that lingered inside her mind. Holding her close, he said, "I shall forever be grateful for your presence in my world."

"I love you." The words felt strange on her tongue, yet at the same time, she wondered how she went so long without them.

"And I love you. In this world and beyond."

Cora rested her head against him again, content for the first time in as long as she could remember.

By the time they reached the communal fire, Dino was sitting among the others, though he kept to himself on the far side of the stone circle. Marcos was near one of the houses, admiring a polished serrated knife Dannin was showing off.

Edwind and Etna spoke quietly at the edge of the trees. When he spotted Cora and Miller, he beckoned them over. "There have been whispers of people searching the woods. I think it is better if we leave sooner rather than later."

Cora nodded. "I know what I have to do."

Etna approached them, holding the bloody remains of Cora's clothes and the onyx blade Segomo had stolen from her. She was surprised he returned it, but how else was she supposed to get home? "I recognized this as soon as I saw it. You were adamant that the dagger stay on Didean." She nodded to Darice. "She is the only one since my father who has been able to feel its true power."

Cora took the death blade while Miller tucked her clothes under his arm. "I'm glad it's in a safe place. It is dangerous in the wrong hands."

The group moved to an empty space away from everyone else. "I may need your help." Cora said to Darice. "I don't know if I'm strong enough to hold the portal open on my own."

The young woman gave her a wide-eyed look of terror. "I can't wield that kind of power."

"If you heard the call of the blade, you can tap into its magic. Take my hand." Cora's movements were steady as she sliced through the air. A familiar tingle seeped into her skin, sapping away what little energy she'd mustered. Darice squeezed Cora's hand, imbuing her own magic with Cora.

Edwind stood at the precipice of the portal, but nodded to Dino and Marcos. "You go through first."

When it was Miller and Cora's turn, she took in a deep breath, ready to take on the full weight of the portal. Miller wrapped an arm around her, pulling her forward. The familiar lurch of reality splitting pulled at every fiber of her being, and if not for the solid body beside her, she felt like she would have spun out of control, lost forever in the swirling light of that place in between worlds. As soon as her feet touched the soft sand on the other side, Miller drew her into his arms, holding her steady against the disorienting pull of gravity.

In the distance, she heard a woman's voice breaking over the waves. Darya raced down the shallow slope toward them, Brigita and Bastian on her heels.

Cora glanced up the beach for Dino and Marcos. When she saw them standing a few feet away, she was able to breathe a little easier, knowing they had all made it safe and sound back to where they belonged.

"Come." Miller's voice was warm against her ear. "Now you can rest and heal."

Chapter 17

SEGOMO STARED AFTER CORA as she walked up the hillside. He wrestled with conflicting emotions. Guilt bubbled up from the pit of his stomach, and he tried swallowing it back down. Only the weak allowed themselves the luxury of regret. Every choice came with consequences, therefore he acted with intention, knowing ahead of time the price he'd have to pay.

Despite the certainty he felt, a terrible sense of foreboding made his skin prickle at the agreement he forged with Indech. At the time, it was the best option they had. A simple trade to ensure both he and the Fomorian got what they wanted.

Now that he knew the truth about Cora's absence from his life, he questioned his decision. He wasn't so sure their arrangement was worth the terrible fate awaiting the world. Yet, there was no undoing the grave bargain. Lives were forfeited. Souls were swapped. What choice did he have then to see it through to the end?

A hand landed on his shoulder. "Dad, are you okay?"

Segomo glanced to the left, where Marcos was staring at him with a worried expression on his young face. Despite his efforts, he couldn't help but feel sorry for the boy. What awaited him was a fate worse than death. Worse than what Segomo endured. He frowned at the boy's hand, then pursed his lips into a thin line. "Of course. I think I'm still rattled from the journey home."

When Marcos hugged him, Segomo had to force himself to return the gesture, but found it even harder to release the boy when he tried to pull away. Not that he cared for Marcos in any significant way, but it felt so familiar, like the times Cora clung to him when she was scared or sad. She showed him an unconditional love that no one had ever given him.

Shoving the guilt away, he eased out of the embrace and began the trek up the hillside to the house, where the others had gathered at a small table outside. Edwind hugged his children close, while his woman stood at his back, resting her hands on his shoulders. A surge of jealousy hit Segomo so fast and so hard, his footsteps faltered before trudging forward again.

Had things played out differently all those eons ago, he may have had the chance to experience the love of a wife and child. If not with Amani, then perhaps another woman would have shown him such tenderness.

Segomo glanced over his shoulder at the fading sun, knowing Indech waited for him to follow through with their bargain. When he returned to the smiling faces at the table, he reminded himself of the true purpose of his guise. Yet, giving Marcos to Indech was no longer an option. Not anymore. The world was better off with Tethra trapped in his prison. But Segomo still yearned for his freedom.

He leaned against the railing, listening to Edwind and Miller recount their journey. Since Segomo knew of the events that led the trio of dragons to sixteen seventy-four, when it was his turn to speak, he managed to muddle his way through, careful to use the same mannerisms he observed in Dino.

"I don't know about you three," Edwind said, gently removing his children from his lap to stand. "But I cannot wait to eat proper food."

Segomo kept his distance, knowing he had to act before it was too late. "Cora."

She paused at the door, glancing over her shoulder.

"May I speak to you for a moment?"

Her smile didn't falter. "Of course."

Miller moved a hand to her back, refusing to leave her side.

"Alone," Segomo added.

She nodded for Miller to go inside.

Ignoring Miller's narrowed stare, Segomo kept his focus on Cora. When they were alone, he clasped his hands in front of him, fighting the urge to drum his fingers on the wood surface of the railing.

"Is everything okay?" she asked, joining him at the edge of the deck.

He stared at the steady push and pull of the sea. "Soon, you will return to Didean with Miller."

She followed his gaze. "When I'm sure Marcos is safe from Indech, yes." Her smile warmed him and chipped away at his resolve. "It's still a lot to wrap my head around," she went on. "I mean, am I cut out for that kind of role? I don't know how to be a parent. What if I screw up my kids?"

He eyed the people beyond the windows. "I think your—we turned out just fine." He pushed off the railing. "The point is you are will have the life you deserve. You will be happy, yes."

Her expression softened, and her grin bloomed even wider. "Yeah, but I'll miss you guys."

He closed his eyes and drew in a deep breath. When he opened them again, his face was a blank slate. "I am deeply sorry, Little Goddess. I wish there was another way."

Cora blinked at him, her expression falling into a mixture of confusion and horror.

"I have come too far to give up this chance to escape my prison."

She took a step back, reaching for the dagger.

He leveled a stony stare on her. "Are you willing to risk damaging this body?"

Cora's eyes glistened in the dusky twilight as she tried to hold on to her fear. "How did you do it?"

"I offered Dino a means to save his son. He is a noble man, willing to give his life for those he loves."

"You tricked him."

"Not at all. I won't let the boy be used in such a heinous ritual. And Indech, well, he may be a formidable foe, but he is easily manipulated."

Cora's eyes flicked to the side, eyeing the others through the windows.

"I want my freedom. That's all I care about," Segomo reiterated.

When she looked at him again, tears spilled over her lashes. "I can't do that."

He drew himself up straight. "We both know the power you wield. Once I am reunited with my body and free of the Qel, you can put Dino back where he belongs. Everyone wins."

"You don't understand. Arawn forbid me from ever returning to the underworld."

Segomo looked over her shoulder. So far, no one was watching them, but he knew Miller would return soon. "You may not be able to open the way, but your blood runs through Dino's body. With your help, I can get us there."

She shook her head. "The others would rather see you returned to your prison."

"Yet you wish to give the boy back his father." He held out his hand, and when she didn't move, he leaned forward. "I may not have my godhood, but I have Dino's dragon, so weigh your options carefully."

The moment her fingers fell into his palm, he pulled her down the steps, toward the beach. There, she drew the dagger from her jeans, staring into the black abyss of its blade before lifting it into the air. Segomo had forged it with his own two hands. His power thrummed through the otherworldly steel. Even after he had been imprisoned in the underworld, he could still hear its beautiful song. He was the one who suggested Arawn to gift it to Cora. He wanted to know she carried a weapon that would protect her from the dangers of a world she never asked to be a part of.

Segomo grasped her hand, pouring what little of Cora's godhood resided in Dino's blood into the dagger. The air gathered like a heavy blanket, swaddling them in a suffocating cloud of magic. He guided her arm, the blade cutting through the veil between this world to what lay beyond. She hesitated before the last line was complete, but he forced her to finish.

Behind them, someone shouted her name. Miller sprinted toward the swirling lights. She tested Segomo's grip, but he swooped an arm around her torso and dragged her through the portal.

The palatial estate loomed against a dull blue sky while soft, white clouds drifted overhead despite the lack of wind to move them along their path. The surrounding fields were dotted with twisted trees that belong to a long-forgotten time. Tall, golden blades of grass swayed in the nonexistent breeze.

Cora hated the fragmented feel of the underworld. She wondered if Arawn made it so bleak and disjointed on purpose. Segomo often wore a scowl when he would stare out of the window of his study and she couldn't blame him. He had been forced to endure the dreary landscape for centuries.

She crossed the threshold into a sparsely decorated foyer. It still held the distinct smell of fresh peonies, Segomo's favorite flower. She never had the heart to tell him their fragrance turned her stomach. Everything looked exactly as she remembered. Not a single speck of dust or wear touched the pristine surfaces, which wasn't surprising given that time had virtually no meaning in her father's domain. A thousand lifetimes could pass in the mortal world, but in the underworld, it felt like mere days.

Segomo was gentle but firm when he urged her forward. "We must hurry. Before Arawn becomes aware of our presence."

He led her up a set of spiraling stone stairs to the second floor. It didn't matter that she hadn't been there in decades. She remembered the first door on the right was his bedroom. She would sneak in there some nights when she couldn't sleep. He pretended to be frustrated with her, but never once did he make her go back to her room. He would let her take his bed while he found somewhere else to stay for the night, if he even slept at all.

She didn't know what to expect when he opened the door. His body lay on its back, eyes closed, his expression locked in an unnatural serenity. Segomo shared the same red hair as she and Arawn, but his eyes were his mother's smokey quartz so clear and bright, they looked liked polished gems. And just like Morigan, his stare had a way of piercing one's soul, reading their innermost fears and desires. It was an ability Cora used to covet. Had she been able to see the true intentions of those around her, perhaps she could have avoided so much disappointment and heartache.

Segomo approached the bed, studying himself. "It is somewhat surreal seeing my body through another's eyes."

Cora glanced at the open doorway. She thought about making a run for it, but there was nowhere for her to go. Running blind through the underworld was dangerous. When she turned around, Dino—Segomo stared at her, a hint of regret clouding his gaze, and she said, "I'm sorry I abandoned you."

His face hardened and his mouth lifted into an icy smile. "Don't be. It is our family legacy, turning our backs on the ones we love."

"I never—"

He waved a hand at the bed, cutting off her reply. "Remove the Qel."

"Segomo."

"If you want Dino back, you'll do as I say." There was a desperation in his voice, and she wondered if it was the fear of Arawn, or what he set out to do.

In the end, it didn't matter. As much as she hated her brother's actions, she still held onto the hope that he wasn't the terrible monster everyone made him out to be. That he had been unfairly punished. If she was in his shoes, would she have agreed to the same deal with Indech?

Cora approached the bed. The ethereal metal of the Qel hummed beneath her touch. Having been forced to wear one, the feel of the icy steel made her shudder. It only took the slightest of tugs to undo the torque. There was an audible click, and the air stirred as Segomo's godhood broke free. His power pulsed around him like a living being, stronger than Indech. Stronger than Arawn.

Segomo moved to the other side of the bed. "Throw it across the room."

Reluctantly, she obeyed.

He laid down next to the body.

For a long time, she stared at Segomo, the real Segomo, weighing her options. What if she refused to put him back? Would he kill her? Go after Darya and her family?

"Please, Cora. I just want to be free." Hearing that plea come from Dino's mouth shattered her heart.

If it meant the chance to bring Dino back from the dead, she would do anything Segomo asked. Taking in a deep breath, she rested her hands on each man's chest. In the back of her mind, she questioned her own abilities. Knowing what happened when she fused herself to Teodor made her afraid to attempt such a delicate and dangerous act. As soon as she pulled on her magic, Segomo's soul heeded her call.

The hand that lay on Dino's chest heated to an uncomfortable degree, and her skin glowed a bright red. When her hold on Segomo was secure, she was acutely aware that she had the power to end him right then and there. She could snuff out his existence with a thought. A shiver ran down her spine at the notion of doing something so unbelievably cruel. No matter what evils her brother had done to deserve his punishment, she was not him.

After another few heartbeats, she eased his soul into its rightful place.

The second Segomo stirred, she scrambled to the far side of the bed where Dino's body lay in deathly stillness. She leaned over him, cupping her hands against his face. Closing her eyes, she let her senses wander through the underworld, searching for his essence, but he wasn't there. With Marcos, it had been easy to bring him back. Why couldn't she do the same for Dino?

"Where are you?" she whispered. Waves of icy dread washed over her. "I can't find him. Why can't I find him?"

Segomo was already standing, his body poised to leave. "When I'm gone, call on Arawn. He will give Dino back to you."

Her gaze dropped to the bed, her vision clouding with sadness and regret. "I tried to tell you. He won't allow it. Not again."

Segomo reached for her, but she pulled away from him. "You got what you wanted," she snapped. "Get out of here before I bring Arawn here to imprison you."

A few seconds passed, and when she looked up, he was gone. She collapsed onto Dino's quiet chest. "Please forgive me."

Grief consumed her, and she lost herself to it. Not only did she fail to save Dino, she let loose a being of rage and revenge against her own family. How could she possibly face the others, especially Marcos, after what she had done?

A hand brushed the side of her cheek, and she sat up to find Arawn standing next to her. He looked the same as the last time they saw each other, except pity took the place of anger.

"Please, bring him back," she begged.

His expression mirrored her heartache. "I turned a blind eye when you stole from me before. I cannot do so again."

"Why not?" Her anguish hardened into something darker. "You've let others escape their fate. What about Darya?"

"It wasn't her time to join me."

"It's not Dino's time either."

He looked to where the Qel lay by the open door. "Everything is as it should be."

She followed his gaze. "As it should be? You knew this would happen? That Segomo would bring me here to free him?"

"We are too much alike, Segomo and I. Unable to admit when we are wrong, refusing to relinquish our pride. It had to play out as it did."

Her mind reeled at the implication of his words. She pushed to her feet, ignoring the hint of childlike fear that still remained in her psyche. "Did you know he would use my family and blood to gain his freedom?" When he didn't answer, she grabbed his arm. "Let me bring Dino back to his son."

Pity vanished, replaced with cold indifference. "I cannot. Now return to the destiny that awaits you."

Bile crawled up her throat, threatening to upend her stomach. "How can you be so cruel? What does my destiny mean if I can't save my own flesh and blood? Why give Marcos a life at all when all he will know is pain and loss?"

A familiar animosity muddled his features. "Do not speak of Fate so callously, Coramagda. She does not look kindly on such things."

"I don't give a fuck about Fate. I don't give a fuck about destiny, and I certainly don't give a fuck about you. Let the world come undone. Let it all unravel."

Arawn leaned into her. "Careful how you throw such threats about, girl."

Something inside her snapped. For the first time in her life, she drew on the magic from which she was born and struck him across the face with every ounce of power she could muster. The veil of calm slipped, and she caught a glimpse of the monster hiding behind the glowing embers of his icecap eyes. He raised an arm, and the Qel flew from the corner of the room to his open hand.

"Go on," she hissed. "Lock me away like you did Segomo. Maybe after countless centuries of isolation and misery, I will be driven to the same desperate madness and trade my own fucking freedom for the life of a goddamned innocent man!"

The ground quaked as her rage threatened to crumble the stone beneath her feet. She stared at her hands; the glow of her magic staining them red. It might as well have been Dino's blood.

Arawn didn't put the Qel around her neck, but tucked it into his belt.

She pushed past him toward the door.

"I am sorry." Arawn's tone was calmer now.

She paused at the threshold, refusing to look back. "You will be. All of you."

Once bold steps began to falter and slow the closer Cora got to the lower pits of the underworld. Finding her way wasn't hard. Her desire for vengeance led her right to the place she wanted to be. Vile whispers slithered inside her mind, wrapping her thoughts with their sickly pleas and sweet promises. If only she would release them, they would give her the means to restore Dino.

The idea of setting those abominations free had seemed like the best option when she stormed out of Segomo's prison. Now that her anger had eased, and rationality took hold again, the burning need to punish her father waned, edged out by despair.

She came to a stop at the top of a barren hill overlooking a rather innocuous looking iron door. There were no guards stationed outside. There was no need. The gateway could only be opened from this side, and only the god of the dead could unlock it. But his blood ran through Cora's veins. It would heed to her call.

Minutes passed—or maybe hours—and she stayed rooted in that spot, unable to make herself take another step closer to that place of infinite agony and chaos. She didn't have it in her to doom humanity in such a horrific way.

"You shouldn't be here."

The stranger's voice startled Cora, and she scanned the desolate wasteland until she spotted a shadowed figure on the other side of a tall boulder a few yards away. She should have known Arawn would dispatch one of his death knights to find her. His psychotic minions wouldn't hesitate to subdue her by any means necessary.

She relaxed her body, preparing for whatever fuckery he was about to set into motion. "Did Arawn send you here to abduct me, or kill me?"

"Neither." The man stepped around the rock into the muted light. Though she didn't know him, something about the knight felt familiar. He held out his empty hands, showing he was unarmed. "I mean you no harm."

"Then you won't stop me." She forced herself to take a step in the direction of the iron door.

The Death Knight moved with unnatural speed, blocking her path. "You're letting your rage sway your morality."

She huffed out a breathy laugh. "Morality? You and your brethren are a bunch of crazy psychopaths that thrive on death and carnage. Morals don't align with your existence."

His lips spread into an amused smile, making her anger falter. "Some of us still hold on to our humanity."

"You're an idiot, then. None of it matters. The gods, fate, destiny. We are all just pawns in a big fucking game where nobody wins."

"Is that what you really believe?"

She drew herself to her full height, but the man still towered over her. "Yes."

"What about your family? Your husband?"

The impact of his words rocked her back on her heels. She was so consumed by her pain and anger, she almost forgot about the life that had been promised to her; the man who loved her despite everything. Miller's face swam into her mind's eye. His slanted grin gripped her heart until she thought it would burst. "He's not my husband. He still has time to find another woman to love. Someone more deserving of his devotion."

"There is no other woman more deserving of my son's heart than you."

Plump tears fell over the dam of her lashes, streaking down her cheeks. She recognized the same gentle features that Miller had inherited from his father. "Saebbi?"

"When I took on the mantle as one of Arawn's knights, he showed me a vision of my family's future and the line of descendants that would spring forth from the seeds planted here." He laid a hand on her belly.

Cora's gaze dropped to her stomach, forcing more tears to fall.

"Your bloodline echoes throughout all of time."

She shook her head, pushing his arm away. "Look where it leads."

He lifted her face, his own stare brimming with emotion. Before he could reply, she heard a familiar voice echo from somewhere beyond the dunes behind her. In the distance, a man's silhouette crested a hill, and a terrible fear gripped her.

"Miller?" Was he dead? Did something happen to the others? Did Segomo go after her friends?

Before she could ask any of those questions, he dashed forward, scooping her up in his arms, crushing her mouth with a kiss that left her confused and breathless.

"There you are," he whispered, the warmth of his breath tickling her lips. "Arawn told me I must hurry, before you did something you would regret."

"My father brought you here. Then you're not dead?"

His eyes traced the outline of her face. "I am very much alive. We know the truth about Segomo and Dino."

Her insides twisted with a fresh wave of anguish. "I tried. I couldn't save him."

Miller halted her rambling with another kiss, then said, "No one blames you."

She rested her forehead against his chest until he went rigid. When she lifted her head, he was staring past her to where Saebbi stood watching them.

"Father?" Miller released Cora and stumbled forward.

Arawn appeared beside her. "Will you return to the life fate has set forth for you?"

Keeping her voice neutral, she said, "Sure, if you bring Dino back from the dead."

"I cannot restore his life. It is out of my hands."

She swung an angry glare at him. "You are the keeper of souls. Nothing is out of your power."

"We all must abide by certain rules."

"Fuck your bloody rules." She muttered. "You only follow them when it suits you."

Arawn let out a weary sigh. "After you took Marcos from me, Ronwen went to great lengths to weave his thread back into the tapestry. I will not ask her to do so again." He dropped his gaze to the ground. "I fear it was the decision to save him that paved the way for Indech to release Tethra."

She stared into his eyes, trying to think of something that would compel him to return Dino to them.

His expression softened. "Death is part of life. It comes for us all, eventually."

"What will happen to Marcos? He's all alone now."

A hint of tenderness softened his features. "Morigan has shown me a glimpse of what is in store for Marcos. He will grow to be a fine man and father children of his own."

Knowing that happiness waited for him gave her a sliver of hope that he would forgive her one day. "Why did you take Saebbi as a knight?"

"He did it for my mother." Miller took her hand. "He thought it would give them a chance to be together for as long as she lived. He didn't know the price of his choice until it was too late." When he lifted his eyes, they were alive with anger and focused on Arawn.

"I did not lie to him. He knew the consequences of the mantle."

"Surely Gita will accept him as he is." Cora said.

Miller glanced over his shoulder. "I believe so, but he is too ashamed to face her." Turning back to Cora, his resentment dissipated. "I was able to tell him goodbye. At least I can give peace to my mother."

Cora snaked her arms around his waist. "I need to give Marcos that same peace before we return to Didean."

Miller drew her into a tight embrace, and she rested her head against him, reveling in his comfort. A salty breeze swept her hair away from her face and when she looked up again, they stood on the beach in front of the Wodehal home. Cora's chest constricted around her lungs. She was devastated about the thought of witnessing Marcos' grief over losing his father.

Chapter 18

Cora's profile reflected the pain behind every word she spoke. From his place by the glass-paned door leading to the veranda, Miller could hear her soft voice drifting across the expanse, though he couldn't make out what she said. Marcos had his back to her, his head bowed. He clung to the railing as if his life depended on the strength of his grip.

Darya joined him at the window.

"What will happen to the boy now?" he asked.

"We'll look after him, of course. He's been like a big brother to the children."

An angry voice cut through the barrier of glass between them. Marcos was mere inches from Cora's face, his eyes blazing. Miller recognized the anguish simmering behind the rage.

He rushed outside as soon as Darya opened the door.

Marcos glanced sideways. "I know she can give me back my dad, but she won't."

"I tried," Cora said, reaching for him.

He jerked away. "You did it for me."

Miller stepped between Cora and Marcos. "She speaks the truth. Arawn will not allow your father to be saved. You were an exception."

The boy's eyes glistened with unshed tears. He leaned to the side, looking past Miller. "Please, Aunt Cora. Bring him back." His voice cracked and Cora's muscles tensed.

Miller put a firm hand on his shoulders. "I know the pain you feel."

"Do you?"

Squeezing gently, Miller said, "I lost my father, too. The anger festering in your heart cannot undo the past. Cora is not the one who took him away from you."

Marcos looked from Miller to Cora. His mouth twisted into a frown, then jerked out of Miller's grasp and bolted down the steps toward the beach.

Cora started to go after him, but Miller held her back. "Let him grieve."

"I feel so helpless."

Miller pulled her closer, wishing he had the words to ease her sorrow. But some pain only time could heal.

"Who is that?" Darya asked, her eyes locked on the white sands below.

Miller and Cora turned, and she went rigid. He recognized the staccato beat of terror in her pulse. She slipped from his arms before he could stop her.

"Get away from him!" Her voice rang out, sharp with panic, echoing down the slope.

Marcos glanced over his shoulder. There was no fear on his young face. Only sadness.

Miller sprinted down the hill past Cora, reaching the beach first. The twisted monstrosity standing near Marcos flicked up his hand, and Miller slammed into an imperceptible wall.

Cora slid to a stop at the unseen barrier, pressing her palms against it. "Don't you dare touch him." She ran along the barrier, searching for an opening, but it encased Marcos and the Fomorian completely, cutting them off from the outside world.

Cora came back around to Miller as Daray reached them. Her eyes were wide with disbelief. "I can't get in," she said.

Black talons swiped through the air, bouncing off the invisible wall, followed by Edwind crashing to the ground. Darya rushed to his side to help him up.

Cora's palms glowed against the unseen barrier as she searched for a breach in Indech's magic. "Don't listen to him. He only wants to use you." Her body trembled with the effort to hold herself in place.

Marcos looked over his shoulder at her. His lips moved, but Miller couldn't make out what he was saying.

Cora shook her head. "It won't be you that brings him back. If you allow Tethra to take you, he will destroy your soul."

Crimson light flared, and Cora was thrown through the air. Miller caught her before she hit the ground. When he looked toward the water, both Indech and Marcos were gone.

Cora let out a weak wail. On her next breath, she cried, "He's going to give himself to that monster to save Dino."

"We will find him." Miller promised.

"How?" The fear in her voice sliced into him.

"I'll call my father." Edwind said. "Fate's laws be damned." To Darya, he asked, "Can you get a message to Grandfather?"

"I don't know where he is."

"Have Flidais find him."

Darya hesitated, then nodded, her expression hardening. "Look after Brigita and Bastian. Don't let them leave the house."

Miller helped Cora up the embankment. Once inside, he settled her onto the couch, intending to speak with his uncle, but she squeezed his arm.

"He's too strong." Ice-blue eyes shimmered in the dusky light. "We can't defeat him on our own."

The glass door of the veranda burst open, and everyone gaped at the man who ran inside.

"Where's Marcos? Where is my son?"

Cora shot to her feet, nearly tripping over the couch to reach Dino. The impact of her hug rocked them both off balance, but he held her steady. She cradled his face in her hands, letting go of the tears she had been hanging on to. "I begged Arawn for your life. How—"

The door swung open again.

Segomo sauntered inside wearing a pleased grin. "I bet my mother didn't foresee this little ripple in her precious plan."

Miller shot across the expanse between them, but instead of snatching Cora out of the way, he grabbed the dagger at her back, then positioned himself in front of her, ready to fight the unwanted intruder.

Segomo's eyes narrowed before turning a devious smile on her. "Mother chose a good man for you. Though not a smart one. He doesn't recognize when he is outmatched in both skill and power."

She saw the tensing of Miller's muscles and the slight shift in his stance. "Try me." He growled.

"Someday, perhaps. But today is not that day."

Cora put a soothing hand on Miller's arm but kept her eyes locked on Segomo. "You have brass walking into this house."

"I came back to give you what Arawn would not. Our father isn't as all-knowing as he believes." Segomo's expression darkened. "It cost me a favor to a psychotic dragoness, but my intention was never for you to lose Dino forever."

"That's right," she countered. "You intended to use his son as a meat puppet for a deranged demon." The surrounding air stirred with a dangerous energy. If he thought she was going to be bullied by him, he would soon find out just how much she'd learned during her time away from him.

Segomo studied Cora, taking in the subtle shift around her body. "Someone has tapped into more of her powers. Amazing what a little fury can do for a person."

Crimson light flared against her palms. "You want fury? I'll give you fury."

His body blurred forward, took hold of her arms, and Cora no longer stood in the Wodehal house, but on a grassy cliff overlooking a verdant valley. A torrid wind whipped at her hair, threatening to sweep her away. She glanced around, trying to get her bearings, but nothing looked familiar. A dense smoke rose into the air from the ashes of the village below.

The stench of death burned in her throat. "Where are we?"

"You said you wanted to know what happened that drove our father to imprison me." Segomo pointed to the smoldering ruins below. "Go on. See for yourself."

She watched the rising plume of gray wisps, wishing she couldn't smell the rancid odor of burning wood and flesh. Though her mind begged to return home, the desire for the truth urged her down the steep slope, winding its way down the side of the cliff.

Dozens of charred bodies were displayed on the ground as if they had been trying to flee the carnage that destroyed their lives. As much as she didn't want to look at the dead people, she couldn't help but notice that a lot of them were children. She stumbled past a family of four, clutched together, forever locked into their last embrace, burned beyond recognition.

Every razed home she passed, she witnessed more bodies; more families preserved in their final horrific moments. Ahead, a familiar silhouette appeared from the smoke. Segomo was on his knees, bent over a corpse covered in blood and ash.

Cora approached him, careful to keep her distance.

"Each person who died that day is a black mark on my soul." His voice was low, almost a whisper.

"Did you kill all these people?"

"Not by my own hand." He turned his head to the side, staring at her feet. "But I let it happen."

Cora inched closer, getting a glimpse of the dark-haired woman cradled in his arms. "Father punished you for letting them die?"

He looked away. "I made a promise to protect them. Yet I abandoned them when they needed me the most."

"Why did you abandon them?"

He gently ran his fingers over the woman's bloodied cheek. "I was betrayed by Amani and her father. They thought his meager army was invincible, so when their enemy gathered for war, I left them to their fate. I forbid my death knights to intervene as every man, woman, and child was slaughtered and burned."

Segomo pushed to his feet, surveying the surrounding massacre. "Hengist was the only one to defy my orders, but even he wasn't strong enough to stop the inevitable alone."

Cora was horrified at what she was hearing. "You let all these people die because of betrayal?"

He whirled on her. "It is far worse than that, Little Goddess." His words sliced the air between them. "Jarl poisoned Amani against me. He couldn't stand the thought of my offspring usurping his power. Amani flaunted her lover in my face when I came to warn them. But even that didn't stoke the flames of my fury. When she told me she killed the child in her womb; my child, so that she wouldn't have to bear an abomination, I lost myself to my rage."

Segomo closed his eyes and drew in a long breath. His body deflated when he let it out.

"All those innocent people. They didn't kill your baby. They didn't deserve to die like this."

He dropped his gaze to the dead woman on the ground. "I made Jarl watch his daughter and his entire clan perish. I wanted him to spend the rest of eternity knowing it was his actions that doomed them to their fate. Even after everything he took from me, I couldn't bring myself to kill him. Instead, I handed him over to his enemy."

Cora scanned the charred remains of a once thriving village. As horrified as she was to witness the devastation her brother allowed to happen, she couldn't quiet the voice that sympathized with him. She wondered how far she would go to avenge the death of her family. Now she understood where Dino's visceral anger came from. Something she would experience for herself when she became a mother.

"This is the truth you wanted so badly to know." Segomo's words cut through her thoughts, and she was finally able to meet his stare.

"Why show me this now?"

"I need you to understand where my pain comes from. Why I fought so hard to keep you out of my heart. After imprisoning me, Arawn tried to mend the divide between us, but there was no room for forgiveness in either of our hearts."

He reached out, and she instinctively flinched away, which heightened the bitterness in his face. "You and your friends are no match for the forces you are up against. Let me help you."

Did she really want his help, knowing the horrid acts he allowed to be wrought on these people? The answer was simple. To save Marcos, she would gladly accept whatever aid Segomo could give.

Steeling herself against his touch, she put her hand into his. "Alright."

The brutal scenery vanished, and her stomach rolled at the momentum of her feet, landing on solid ground again. The air was clean and crisp, filled with the salty brine of the ocean. Segomo let go of her just as three dragons landed with heavy thumps on either side of them. The earth hummed with power at Darya's approach.

"Are you hurt?" She asked Cora.

Cora only managed a faint shake of her head. Discovering the truth about Segomo made her question everything she thought she knew about him and Arawn. The feel of Miller's hand gave back her voice. "I'm fine." She met Segomo's hard stare. "We need his help."

The steady clink of the spoon against the delicate teacup was soothing to Cora's troubled thoughts. She focused her eyes on the swirls of cream dispersing with each rotation of her hand.

Once in a while, she would look up and study the four men sitting around the table. They spoke in hushed voices, looking over the map Horsa had given Edwind. From what she could hear, they were arguing about the best way to reach the island without being seen.

An impossible feat, according to Segomo, and Cora agreed with him. Indech was expecting them. He'd be a fool not to. But a front assault wasn't ideal either, given the army the Fomorian amassed.

Her thoughts then turned to the horrific scene Segomo showed her. No matter how hard she tried to hold on to her anger, and despite Segomo's role in everything, she knew the truth now. That knowledge didn't absolve him from his terrible deeds by any measure. Still, Cora couldn't dispel the nagging voice in the back of her mind questioning her own morals if she was put in a situation like his.

"You're going to stir the heat right out of your tea."

Cora glanced to the side, where Darya stared at her with concern. Relaxing her mouth, Cora said, "Sorry. I guess I'm still a little shaken from earlier." She didn't dare tell anyone the truth until she had time to process everything and decide how she wanted to proceed with her brother.

Watching him interact with the other men was bizarre. He had been relegated to the far end of the table while everyone else sat in close proximity to each other. It was amazing how a common enemy could get Dino and Miller on the same side.

Darya leaned onto the counter, gently taking the spoon from Cora's hand. "Were you really going to unleash all those monstrous souls on the world?"

The question made Cora's cheeks warm. "Had it not been for Saebbi, I can't say for sure." Then she shook her head. "No. I don't think I would have had the nerve. I was just so angry."

"You had every right to be furious. I would be too." Darya glanced at the table, then back to Cora. "Is Saebbi really a Death Knight?"

"It was his choice. I wish he would let Gita make the decision whether to welcome him or not. He did it for her, after all."

"If we could talk to him, maybe he would change his mind." Darya looked at her husband. "Do you think he will speak with Edwind? They were as close as brothers once."

"I can ask Arawn to bring him here, but it's be up to Saebbi to accept." Cora took a sip of her tea, relishing the warmth as it slid down her throat and into her belly. She watched Miller for a few seconds, and said, "Something Saebbi mentioned has been bothering me."

Darya's unrelenting stare made her even more nervous. Cora eyed the table one last time, lowering her voice to just above a whisper. "He spoke as if I'm already pregnant."

Darya sucked in a breath and put a hand to her mouth. "You're pregnant?" The words were muffled behind her fingers, but spoken loud enough for everyone to hear.

A chair scraped across the wooden floor, and Miller came around the table to the bar. "You are with child?"

Cora winced, wishing she'd kept it to herself.

Miller lifted her chin up, and she could have cried out at the sight of the smile that split his face. "How can you know this?"

She shrugged. "Your father insinuated as much, but he didn't come out and say I was pregnant."

"If anyone would know, it is a Death Knight." All eyes turned to Segomo, who sipped his tea, unbothered by the eyes on him. "Who better to detect life than the instruments of death?"

Miller's kiss made her swoon, and her knees went weak.

Segomo cleared his throat. "We should get back to rescuing the boy."

Miller's smile stayed in place. "We know what must be done. The only change to the plan now is that Cora will stay with Darya."

There was a collective shuffling of feet. Cora moved out of his arms. "Why would I stay here?"

"You're carrying our child. I will not let you—"

"Miller," Edwin cut him off. "If I can give you any advice as a future husband and father to be, do not finish that sentence."

"Oh, let him continue," Segomo cooed. "I wish to see the bloodshed."

Miller glanced at his uncle. "You understand my concern." Then turned his attention back to Cora, who glared at him as she struggled to hold on to her volatile emotions.

She knew where his fear stemmed from, but that didn't mean she would put up with his antiquated ideas. Stepping around him, she went to the table. "Anyway, you said Indech is expecting us, so sneaking onto the island is out of the question. Nor can we rush in, not knowing what we are up against."

Segomo shrugged. "Unfortunately, we don't have much of a choice. No matter where we land, his minions will know."

"What's stopping you from just popping in and grabbing Marcos?" Cora asked.

A frown wrinkled his otherwise smooth face. "Indech isn't particularly smart, but he is cunning. He has himself well warded against those who can potentially muck up his plans. He left himself vulnerable by focusing on keeping me out, though. He doesn't see you or your companions as a threat."

Miller stormed past them, the slam of the door making her flinch against the terse silence. His footsteps shook the veranda as he stomped down the steps, heading to the beach. Cora tried to ignore his outburst, but her guilt wouldn't let it go.

She caught up to him on the white sands at the edge of the ocean. Each time she reached for him, he stepped away from her, still refusing to meet her gaze.

"What do you want from me?" She asked, finally.

He whirled around, his eyes sparkling with unshed tears. "I want you to be safe. I want our child to be safe."

"You want me to sit in this house and do nothing to fight for the life of our family? To not fight by my man's side? I would never ask that of you." She took his hand and placed it on her lower belly. "I will be safe. We will be safe with you."

He drew her in his arms. "I want nothing more than to have you with me always, but what we are about to do is dangerous. I can't stand the thought of something happening to you and our child."

She leaned back, taking his face in her hands. "I am the daughter of death himself. My brother is one of the most feared gods ever to walk this realm and beyond. My husband will burn through any man or beast stupid enough to threaten his family."

The corners of Miller's mouth worked up into a smile. "I am not your husband yet. That will come when we are finished here."

She kissed him one last time. "Since you followed me through the portal, I've been dreaming of our children. Twins. A boy and a girl."

His eyes widened. "Twins?"

She nodded.

He wrapped himself around her. "Promise me you will not put yourself in harm's way."

"As long as you promise not to get yourself killed."

When he leaned away, there was a mischievous smile tilting his lips. "I know someone who can bring me back if I do."

Chapter 19

SEGOMO STOOD ON THE bow of the sailboat, pretending not to watch Cora and Miller. She held one of his hands on her belly and whispered into his ear before kissing him on the cheek. Maybe it was his imagination, but her aura seemed radiant in the waning light. Yet there was a darkness staining the edges of her glow. She carried within her the same potential to destroy as she did to create. Something he'd seen in her long ago.

Turning away from his sister, Segomo studied the endless horizon, losing himself to his thoughts. He wondered, given the chance, would he have been a good father? He spent many wasted years imagining what would have happened if he had chosen differently. The loss still stung his heart, and he had to choke back the familiar rage that swirled inside him like a torrential storm at sea.

"You made your choice, little brother."

The haunting bravado of that soprano voice startled Segomo and his head snapped to the side to find a face he could have gone through the rest of his existence never seeing again. "I know the game. You and mother dearest like to pretend we have choices when they are but mirages of the predetermined prisons you've chosen for us."

Ronwen crossed her arms and leaned against the railing. "Had you not abandoned those people—I tried to give you the only comfort I knew how."

"You allowed them to take everything from me. I didn't need your words. I needed your—" He clamped his mouth shut, refusing to let her see his regret. "You are a fool to show your face in my presence. I could end you where you stand."

Her expression shifted from neutrality to bemusement. "You just got your freedom. Don't piss it away on meaningless threats." She glanced to where Cora and Miller stared across the sea. "You've left me with a difficult decision to make."

He watched her with cold indifference, but the prickle of uncertainty chilled his blood. "Is that so?"

"Do I let Dino live and weave his life into the tapestry or take back what you stole from Arawn."

Segomo followed her gaze, his stomaching clenching at the thought of the pain Cora would have to endure yet again. "Do what you must. At least I did my part in trying to keep the man alive. She cannot blame me for his death this time."

Ronwen turned her piercing stare on him. "You care deeply about how Cora perceives you." When he didn't answer, she went on. "I wish I could undo the past. No one deserves that kind of anguish."

He glanced away. "At least someone in this family will have the life they deserve."

"It's not too late for you."

Her words stoked a long-held resentment. "Whatever our mother thinks to do to meddle in my affairs, tell her to not waste her time. I've had enough of your interference to last throughout the ages."

Ronwen spread her hands and shrugged. "Your destiny has always been out of our control. From the moment you took your first breath, your thread was indecipherable."

Hearing that confession didn't help quell his simmering anger. "Is that why you all fear me so?"

"We never feared of you, little brother. We feared for you."

His gaze snapped to Ronwen. A ball of unfamiliar emotion lodged itself in the back of his throat. Her revelation drove home the tragic reality of his existence. "I never asked for this life."

She smiled, her dusky eyes sparkling against the sinking sun. Her visage dimmed until she slowly faded into the horizon. Then she was gone, leaving him staring at the rolling waves.

"Who are you talking to?"

Cora stood a few feet away, looking at the place where Ronwen had been. "No one. I was thinking out loud." He looked past her to Miller, who was watching them both, his body tense, ready to leap forward to protect her at the first sign of trouble. Segomo wondered how long it was going to take before she proved to that damn dragon just what a capable goddess she really was.

"What's so funny?"

Segomo forced the amused smile from his lips. "Nothing. How are you feeling? I am not familiar with the needs of a woman in your condition. Whatever you want or need, I can bring to you."

"I'm fine. I wish everyone would stop treating me like I am some wilting flower just because I'm pregnant. Which, by the way, I don't know that I am. It's too soon for anyone to say for sure." She crossed her arms. "Am I even ready to be a mum? Will I be a good one?"

"This is probably a conversation you should have with Miller."

She looked over her shoulder, her expression melting into adoration. When she turned back to Segomo, she said, "When this is over, no matter the outcome, you shouldn't stick around. Neither here nor ten-twelve. Maybe one day I can forgive you and Father for what you've done, but I can't ask Miller and the others to do so."

The man who had watched Cora grow from a scrawny little girl into a strong goddess wanted to reach out and beg her not to abandon him again, but he, of all people, knew the struggle to keep one's heart guarded against the sting of betrayal. He nodded, holding his own torment locked behind a mask of serenity. "I have a whole new world to rediscover. I will have better things to do than worry myself with your life."

"Good. As long as we have an understanding."

A shadow passed overhead, then the boat rocked from side to side. Edwind pierced Segomo with a steely stare before joining Miller near the aft.

Segomo grunted. "I hope your friends know they are not likely to survive this little adventure. You should have stayed behind with the druidae."

"It's sweet of you to care, but we are more capable than you give us credit for."

He shrugged, hiding the disappointment that surged through him. "Maybe you are right. For your sake, I hope so." He had no intention of letting anything happen to her, even if it meant dragging her to some forgotten corner of the world until all of this was over.

The sunlight dimmed, turning the once vibrant setting into a dull gray. All around them, a dense fog rolled across the ocean's surface until it enveloped the ship in its impenetrable gloom. He could barely make out anyone on board, it was so thick. Pushing his magic outward, he split the veil, encapsulating the deck in an invisible barrier that the thick cloud couldn't penetrate.

Everyone was on high alert. Edwind and Dino were now at the bow, glowering into the gray nothingness while Miller positioned Cora in between him and the companionway leading below, as if to push her down there at the first sign of danger.

"Is this your doing?" Miller asked Segomo. "Are you trying to hide us?"

Segomo shook his head. "This is Indech's doing. He thinks to confuse me in the mist."

Edwind moved along the railing. "Can you get the ship through?"

Before Segomo could assure the youngling of the might of his powers, the world around them came alive with a loud screech that resonated throughout his blood and bones. The first hit sent a sickening crack through the hull, and Cora barely caught herself before she stumbled past the companionway to the other side of the deck. The vessel groaned like a dying beast, the planks beneath her feet buckling.

Miller spun around, snatching her from the edge just as another impact tore through the ship. The mast snapped, sending ropes whipping through the air. A jagged piece of wood shot past Cora's cheek, close enough that she whipped a hand to her face, checking for blood. Luckily, the splintered wreckage missed her.

"Hold on!" Segomo roared, digging his fingers into the railing as their world tilted violently. The sea lashed back, hungry, insatiable.

The deck beneath them gave way. One second, Cora was standing—the next, she was plummeting into chaos. A tangle of broken wood and flailing limbs, the ocean rising like a great, gaping mouth to swallow her whole.

"Get her to safety!" Segomo's voice cut through the pandemonium.

Miller caught her mid-fall. With a powerful beat of his wings, they shot into the air.

Dino and Edwind followed, their wings unfurling into the mist, but Segomo stayed.

Another hit split the ship down the middle as water rushing into its broken heart.

Perched at the top of the shattered mast, Segomo looked down at the churning abyss below, gripping the rope of the sail rig like a warlord surveying the battlefield. His sword flared into existence, casting eerie silver light across the wreckage. For a moment, the ocean was still. He stared into the water, his heart pounding with excitement. Letting go, he dove head first into the dark waters, hungry for the coming battle.

The ship dropped from sight, disappearing into the thick fog below. Cora clung to Miller, the security of his grip around her torso doing little to ease her panic. Even though she trusted him completely, the speed with which he had lifted off the deck and the blinding gray nothingness that surrounded them left her panicked and scared. She hoped he had a relatively keen sense of direction to at least get them back to the safety of the mainland.

They drifted through the sky, Miller's massive wings methodically moving up and down, slowly cutting the air as he kept them at a steady height. Cora thought she heard voices below, but the heavy waves crashing against land drowned them out. Without warning, the world dipped, and her stomach lurched at the sudden drop. She hugged his talons, worried he would lose his grip on her.

After a few seconds, she saw the tops of trees peeking through the haze. Miller made a full, slow circle around a small clearing before bringing them to land. Her legs wobbled from both fear and relief to be standing on solid ground.

Miller searched her over for injuries. "Are you hurt?"

Not trusting herself to speak, she shook her head, then checked their surroundings. Nothing looked familiar. This had to be the island.

A few more seconds went by, and when nobody leapt out of the fog, Miller's shoulders eased slightly. "I think we are safe for now."

Safe was far from what they were, but she was relieved not to be in immediate danger. "Did you see where Edwind and Dino flew off to?"

He narrowed his eyes at the blanket of gray above. "They came this way. Perhaps they landed somewhere else on the island."

"We need to find them, but running blindly through an unfamiliar landscape isn't the smartest choice."

"I agree. Stay at my back at all times."

She hooked a finger into a loop of his jeans, and his face relaxed into a smile.

The haze wasn't as thick on land, but she still couldn't see but a few feet in any direction. A profound silence settled over them as they cautiously made their way deeper into the forest. Miller's presence was a reassuring anchor in the storm of her anxiety.

From somewhere in the distance, she heard a piercing roar, and the treetops thrashed back and forth. Miller curled his arm around her waist, pulling her closer. Cora poised herself to attack whoever or whatever came after them.

He slowly backed away from the sounds of splintering wood. A tall figure rushed out of the mist, coming to a stop in front of them.

Edwind pulled his nephew into a brief hug. "I hoped you two found your way safely."

"Did you see where Dino landed?" Cora asked.

"I lost track of him in the fog."

Miller surveyed the surrounding haze. "I have no doubt he made it to the island. I just hope he is safe."

Cora turned in a slow circle. "If he is here, he will find Marcos. With or without us."

"Is there any sign of Segomo?" Edwind asked.

Despite the dire situation, she laughed. "Indech's minions can't kill him. Even the ones who have retained their full strength."

"I cannot say I will grieve if he happens to fall to one of those Fomorians." Miller said.

Edwind glanced around again. "My sense of direction is useless in this damn mist."

"It's a good thing I'm here, then."

All eyes turned to the man stepping out of the gloom. Segomo eyed Miller, his smile lacking warmth. To Cora he said, "I am sorry if I disappoint by surviving." His clothes clung to his body from having been doused in the ocean, but there was not so much as a single scratch on him.

Cora's face warmed, but she refused to give in to the guilt that nibbled at her insides. "I wouldn't say I'm disappointed, exactly."

His expression didn't change. "I can rid us of this fog. It's a rather juvenile distraction, but I should have expected it from Indech."

Miller held up a hand. "Leave it in place. Perhaps we should use it to hide ourselves, as Indech uses it to veil the island." He settled a stoney stare on Segomo. "If you are trustworthy enough to lead us in the right direction."

Segomo's mouth pursed into an angry scowl. "What choice do you have, really? I just hope you are competent in battle."

Cora watched an unspoken sparring of wit and will pass between her future husband and estranged brother. Had they not been in mortal danger, she would have expected them to start measuring certain male body parts. She stepped in between the two men, focusing her attention on Segomo. "Can you get us to Indech?"

Segomo tore his gaze from Miller and his tight features softened when he looked at her. "Relying the on the accuracy of the map, there is a dolmen near the heart of the island. If there is one place that holds enough power to complete a ritual as complex and dangerous as Indech is planning, it will be there."

He was right. Not many of those ancient standing stones were left in the world. She turned her attention to Miller. "We don't have the luxury of doubt right now." Her gaze swept over her brother. "No matter the horrors he's inflicted, he is a man of his word."

That seemed to satisfy Miller. "Shall we continue, then? I don't know how much time we have left."

"What about Dino?" Edwind asked.

"He sacrificed his own life to keep him safe," Cora said. "He will do it again without hesitation."

Segomo held out an arm. "This way."

Miller was reluctant to take the lead with Segomo. He didn't trust the psychotic god to not betray them once they reached Indech. He proved the only loyalty he had was to himself. What if Indech offered him another pact that was too tempting to pass up? Would he make his sister, someone he claimed to care for, watch Marcos be destroyed from the inside out?

Cora's presence calmed Miller's nearly fractured nerves. It was comforting to know that she would be spared, no matter the outcome. Indech wouldn't dare risk her death and the loss of his vessel. If Cora was already pregnant, Miller's life wasn't necessarily safe. And he would give his last breath to make sure his descendants lived on in the past and the future.

Miller caught sight of a cluster of trees swaying back and forth to their left. Even with his enhanced vision, he had difficulty discerning the shadows that passed between the thick trunks. He gripped his sword tight, ready for an attack.

A grotesque severed head rolled from the dense fog, bouncing off Cora's feet. A pair of malformed eyes stared at the sky, wide and unseeing. Miller tracked the ichor as Dino emerged from the mist. Dino's skin and clothes were covered in the same black ooze that still leaked from the demon's gaping neck. He gripped a wicked curved blade in his left hand. There was a glint in his eyes that Miller recognized as one of maniacal rage. Dino's body heaved with the same frantic intensity as the twisted grimace on his face.

Cora approached the distraught man, holding out a hand to him. Miller moved forward, but Cora shooed him away.

"You're safe now." Her voice was calm and steady. "Put down the sword." She wrapped her fingers around the wrist that held up the weapon.

Dino blinked a couple of times, then lifted his arms, staring at the gore covering his skin and clothes. His hand flexed open, dropping the blade to the ground. When he looked up again, his demeanor was no longer that of a fierce warrior, but that of the man Miller had met when he arrived in nineteen ninety-two.

"Are we too late?"

Cora ignored the blackened blood staining his clothing and wrapped her arms around him. "It's not too late."

Dino shook with silent sobs. Miller's heart ached for him, knowing he would one day become a father himself. He felt a glimmer of the fear Dino experienced. For the first time since arriving in this new world, Miller saw his descendent as an extension of himself. Of Cora. Of the countless generations waiting to be born.

Miller approached them. "Let's find your son and take him home."

Dino released Cora and backed away, nodding.

Edwind and Segomo joined them, both men studying the decapitated head. Edwind looked at Dino, his expression guarded, but there was a hint of pride in his eyes. "I didn't know you had it in you. Maybe you carry more of our blood than I realized."

There was a ghost of a smile that broke through Dino's anguish.

Segomo punted the severed head into the trees. "Yes, yes. The quiet dragon has proven himself to be quite formidable." He stared into the bleak gray of the sky. "But the time of the awakening is near. We must hurry if we are to save the boy."

They didn't get far before the mist began to recede, rolling across the ground as if an unseen force was sucking it back into whatever maw it escaped from. Miller and his uncle shared a worried look.

"Are you doing that?" Cora asked her brother.

"Not I," Segomo said, "but whoever is responsible reeks of the underworld."

Edwind searched the surrounding trees. "Perhaps Indech knows it is useless to try to hide himself."

"This is not Indech's doing." Segomo insisted.

Cora was inclined to agree. The power that permeated the air was the same magic that ran through her veins.

A group of shadowed figures manifested into solid matter a few yards in front of them. She recognized the black blades poised to strike and onyx tipped arrows, nocked and ready to fire. Faces solidified into recognizable features. Some of the Death Knights she knew; most she did not. The formation of the warriors split in two, letting a familiar face through their ranks.

Edwind stepped past Miller, coming to a stop in front of Saebbi. They stared at each other for a long time. Each man was unable to convey the words that sat on the tips of their tongues. Finally, Saebbi's stoic expression bloomed into a wide grin. "I think I like you better with short hair."

They threw their arms around one another for a brief hug. When Edwind pulled away, he shoved half-heartedly at his friend's shoulder. "You stubborn damn fool. Why would you accept such a mantle?"

The smile never left Saebbi's face. "It is my destiny."

Edwind made a disgusted sound. "Bah. Destiny my eye. I know why you did it, and now you are too cowardly to confront the reason for your choice."

Saebbi's smile was replaced by a scowl. Both men glared at each other when Miller stepped in between them. "As much as I agree with my uncle, and as happy as I am to see you again, Father, why are you here?"

Turning to Cora, Saebbi said, "Arawn is giving you his army to fight by your side. He is forbidden to intervene, but we are obligated to follow our overseer."

She eyed the other knights. Having seen what they are capable of, she knew very well that they had no interest in the living or the dead. Their only motivation was fighting and winning. Still, Saebbi was right. They are bound to the will of their commander.

"I'll accept their help, but only because you lead them."

Saebbi's grin caught her off guard. "It is not I who gives their orders. You command us now."

Miller's wide-eyed stare matched her own. She took a step back, shaking her head. "I'm no leader," she whispered.

"That is not for you to decide," Saebbi said calmly. "The mantle has been given."

Cora's blood chilled in her veins at the thought of commanding an army of her own. She was a protector, not a warrior.

Saebbi offered her a faint, grim smile. "You need but speak your orders."

A single, slow clap pierced the silence, breaking up the somber mood. Segomo put himself in between Cora and Saebbi. "Oh, this is delightful. The Little Goddess is going to lead Death Knights into battle. Surely, we would fare better if they were led by someone who has experience in the art of war."

Turning his attention to Segomo, Saebbi said, "Your father is no fool. Giving you power over his army again would have dire consequences."

"Cora is no warrior," Segomo scoffed. "Her heart leads when it should remain silent."

Saebbi didn't relent. "Do you suggest we abandon her as you abandoned your people?"

That wiped the smirk off the war god's face. His features darkened into something dangerous. "Be careful how you speak to me. It is my blessing that gives you your powers. If not for me, none of you would exist."

"And if not for you," Cora snapped, "countless generations of people would still exist."

Segomo let out a slow breath, studying Cora as if committing her face to memory. He opened his mouth, then hesitated just long enough for anticipation to flicker in her eyes.

A stoney mask slid into place. "Well," he said, rolling his shoulders back. "It seems I've outlived my usefulness to you." His smile was light, but the bitterness behind it ricocheted between them.

Cora sucked in a breath, and Miller saw her pulse pounding in the side of her neck. Before she could react, he was gone.

The silence that followed his departure was deafening. Cora stared at the ground, her muscles coiled tight as she fought to control her emotions. Miller went to take hold of her hand, but she shrugged out of his grasp. The guilt and sadness pulled at her features, but that soon gave way to resolve. She turned to Saebbi, a faint glow tinting her skin. "Your orders are to stop Indech and save Marcos. Nothing else matters."

When Miller reached for her again, she latched onto him. Their gaze met, and his body hummed with the chaos of emotions flashing across her eyes. "You are doing the right thing." He murmured.

"I know." She looked over her army. "If Indech missed his father so much, we will make damn sure they were reunited for eternity."

Chapter 20

Guttural grunts and rapid clicking echoed around them. Cora's pulse pounded in her ears, making it hard to gauge where the sounds were coming from. Saebbi and Edwind scanned the trees, holding their pace steady. At one point, Saebbi made a quick movement with his hand and shadows blurred out of sight as the Death Knights melted into the fog. High-pitched squeals filled the air but were cut off mid scream.

A woman appeared in front of them. Her dark armor hid the black blood that had been sprayed across her face and arms. "The dolmen isn't far." She spoke in a language Cora hadn't heard in decades. Not since her time in the underworld. "We must move quickly." The Death Knight pointed to a pulsing red glow in the distance. "It has begun."

Thunder rolled overhead, and through the blanket of fog, she saw a light growing ever brighter, ever closer. Cora doubled her pace, ignoring Miller and Edwind's protests. "If he has started the ritual, we don't have any time to waste."

Dino jogged to her side. "What's the plan?"

That was the hundred-thousand-dollar question, wasn't it? Stop Indech. Rescue Marcos. Nothing else matters. "We are going to save your son."

His expression hardened into resolve. "Good plan."

Even before they broke through the trees, Cora heard chanting. The voice uttering those vile words of power grated on her psyche, sending waves of nausea through her. She pushed herself faster until she breached the mist. The air thinned, making each breath a struggle. Her heart stuttered when she saw the number of men and beasts encircling the dolmen. Through the sporadic movements of the Fomorians, she spotted Indech with his hands raised toward the swirling fiery cloud expanding in the distance. Marcos stood by his side, his eyes transfixed on the doorway being ripped open between their world and that of Tethra's prison. Fingerlike shards of light arched outward, as if clawing at reality to spread the portal ever wider.

"We're too late." Dino's voice shattered her paralysis.

Before she could speak, there was a loud crack of thunder that boomed overhead, shattering the clouds and revealing a growing circle of darkness within the roiling gateway. Dino was right. The prison had been breached.

She looked behind her to where Miller stared at the sky. Knowing that she may be carrying his children made her choice even harder. Glancing back at Dino, she worked her fingers into his. "I need you to trust me."

He frowned. "The last time you told me that, things didn't work out the way you planned."

She held his gaze until he looked away.

"Tell me what I need to do."

Her smile felt heavy. "If we destroy the dolmen, Indech loses his conduit. But he's not going to just let us stroll up there and knock it down." She studied the valley, assessing the best path to take.

Saebbi appeared at her side.

"We need to topple the stones," she said.

A serene smile lifted Saebbi's mouth, and she caught a glimpse of her father's influence in his eyes. As much as he claimed to retain his humanity, his mantle still held sway over him. He nodded once to her, then made a quick motion with his hand. The Death Knights flanked her and Dino, weapons at the ready.

Miller's touch, though comforting, couldn't dispel the gnawing dread eating at her insides. She stared into his eyes, silently pleading for him to assure her everything was going to work out in their favor.

Another crack of thunder rolled overhead. The gateway spread ever wider, and to her horror, the dolmen began to glow. The archway between the two stone pillars rippled, revealing a dark, desolate landscape beyond. Indech stopped chanting. He pointed to the doorway, and after a brief hesitation, Marcos walked forward.

Dino shot down the embankment before Cora could stop him. Fear drove her to chase him, ignoring Miller's shouts at her back. All she could focus on was reaching Marcos before he made it through the gateway.

Chaos erupted around her as both man and beast charged. Dino was in his dragon, recklessly swinging his claws and tail, clearing a path to the dolmen. More than once, Cora came close to being hit with a flying body part, but she easily dodged each incoming piece of debris. She tapped into her power so she could keep up with Dino. Miller shot past her, his red scales rippling in the eerie light above, joining Dino in the rampage.

They were a mere few yards from the dolmen when her worst fears came true. Marcos hesitated for only a heartbeat before plunging into the prison. If her throat hadn't been constricted by the terror that threatened to rip her apart, she would have screamed. Dino, however, had no such problem. The air resonated with his piercing roar.

Indech whirled around, his muddy eyes tracking the descending chaos. He stepped in front of the doorway, ready to defend the dolmen. He raised a hand holding a long, curved blade, only to have it evaporate into a cloud of black mist. His face twisted and puckered, first in shock, then anger.

One of the Death Knights leapt over a group of grotesque beasts, bringing down his onyx sword, striking the soft earth, lodging the scimitar into the ground. Indech appeared behind the knight, kicking him with so much force, he was sent rolling through the air, crashing into a nearby boulder. The sound of bones snapping was nearly as loud as that of the raging battle around them.

By some miracle, Cora made it to the dolmen before Dino, but he got to her just as she reached the standing stones. His forward momentum carried them into the gateway together.

As soon as they crossed the barrier into Tethra's prison, her world spun out of control, and she rolled across barren soil peppered with rock until she finally came to a stop, her body screaming in pain. For a long time, she lay on the ground, her arms and face tingling where the jagged earth had scraped away her flesh.

The stagnant smell of death and ash filled her senses. The odor made her stomach lurch and roll and it took every ounce of willpower to keep the rising bile from escaping. She pushed herself to her hands and knees, studying the unnatural terrain. A sickly pale sky loomed overhead. There was no sun. No moon or stars. Only an infinite gray nothingness. The isolation of that place was suffocating, and she shuddered at the thought of having to spend an eternity here.

In the distance, a looming jagged mountain jutted from the ground, the highest peak disappearing into the thick, opaque gloom of clouds. A thundering voice rolled like an avalanche across the open field of rock, sending Cora to her knees. She'd never heard the language, but it held a power far stronger than even her father. Behind her, the glow of the doorway promised a way out.

A man's pained groan drew her attention to her left. Dino pushed himself upright, an arm wrapped around his waist. "Holy hell. That was a rough ride."

She scrambled to her feet and rushed to his side. "Are you alright?"

He stood and nodded, studying the desolate landscape. "Where's Marcos? Oh, God. Did that monster get to him already?"

"Dad?"

Cora spun around, searching for the source of the voice. Marcos came into view from the other side of a pile of what appeared to be small, pale stones. It took her a few seconds to realize they were bones.

The sounds that emanated from Dino's mouth might have been words, but they were lost in the gut-wrenching howl of a scared father. He grabbed up his son, wrapping him into a protective embrace.

Cora limped forward, mussing Marcos' hair. "What the hell were you thinking, kid?"

The stark terror in his eyes cut her deep. "I just wanted my dad back."

Her vision warbled and blurred, but she refused to let the tears fall.

Another agonizing groan shook the ground beneath them. Nothing could have prepared her for the abomination that strode toward them from the bleak haze. A single, black eye searched the landscape from in the middle of a misshapen, boulder-like head. Gray cracked skin blended into Tethra's horns, and bony protrusions jutted out all over his massive body. Each step was accompanied by a heavy thump, thump, thump, sending tremors through her veins.

An oppressing fear gripped her, leaving her rooted to where she stood. For the first time since arriving on the island, she was faced with a terrible sense of hopelessness. There was a reason it took all the gods to banish Tethra. His was an ancient magic that predated the very essence of human life itself. His might, unfathomable. Whatever meager power she could wield would be but a nuisance for something as indomitable as him.

Then he stopped. That solitary obsidian eye locked on them. Cora's skin prickled beneath the weight of his suffocating gaze. Beside her, Dino's breath came in short, heavy pants.

Tethra tilted his head, studying them with inhuman stillness. If not for the subtle movements of his eye, he could have passed as an extension of the gray mountain behind him.

"We need to get out of here." Her heart pounded so loudly, her words felt distant to her own ears.

Dino pushed Marcos at Cora. "You two go. Do whatever you have to, but make sure the dolmen is destroyed."

She shook her head, refusing to budge. "Not without you." Her eyes darted from Tethra back to Dino. "If you're inside when the gateway closes—"

"Someone needs to stay behind. He can't be allowed to break free." His lips trembled into a sad smile, and he looked at Marcos. "Keep Cora safe, yeah?"

Marcos shivered against her. "Dad—"

Tears spilled onto Dino's cheeks as he took in the outline of his son. "I'll always be with you. Just like your mum."

Desperate to make him see reason, she said, "You can't kill that thing. Tethra will destroy you with a thought."

Dino clasped her hand. "I don't have to defeat him. I only need to distract him until you close the door to his prison."

Cora shook her head again, but he pulled her into him, pressing his lips to her ear. "This isn't your destiny." His arms loosened, and he held her face in his hands, tears washing away dirt and ash. "We are."

"Dad." Marcos clung to his arm. "We can make it. Together."

Giving one last pleading look to Cora, he took off into the air toward the Fomorian God.

Marcos started to pull away from Cora, but she tightened her grip on him, forcing him to look at her. "Don't let his sacrifice be in vain."

In that moment, she watched as a scared teenager released his fear and embraced the strength of the man she knew he would someday become. Looking at his father one last time, Marcos took off toward the gate, gripping her hand like his life depended on it. The sensation of falling was brief, and she landed hard on her back, staring into the hollow place beyond the dolmen.

The world around her spun as she was jerked upward, coming face to face with Indech. Blazing yellow eyes tore into her mind, sending shards of pain through her head. The Fomorian squeezed with just enough force to keep her subdued, yet still able to breathe. To Marcos, he said, "Go back in there, young dragon. Or I will destroy everything you love, even your very existence."

A familiar cry broke through the chaos raging around them. She latched on to Indech's arms, but it was futile. He was immune t her power. Despite herself, she laughed.

Indech's sneer mutated into a grim, malformed smile. "Are you amused, Coramagda?"

Her eyes tracked the two dragons that flew toward them. It took only a few seconds for them to reach the dolmen, and with surprisingly little effort, toppled it to the ground, closing Tethra's prison once again. The shockwave of the magic holding open the gateway rippled outward, sending them flying through the air. Pain exploded inside her head when it made contact with a nearby boulder and struggled to cling onto consciousness, but she lost her grip on it, sliding into blackness.

Reality flickered like a candle in a storm. Each attempt to open her eyes was met with a kaleidoscope of blurred shapes before darkness claimed her again. It was the desperate clutch of strong fingers against her palm that finally anchored her awake. The touch was as familiar as her own heartbeat. Marcos clung to her hand, his emerald eyes wide with a fear no child should know.

But they were alive. Somehow, against all odds, they survived.

She rolled her head to the side, muscles screaming in protest, and searched the sky above. Relief flooded through her when she saw receding clouds revealing a calm twilight beyond. The supernatural mist choking the island dissipated into the atmosphere, leaving behind air that tasted of ash and ozone. A deep rumble vibrated through the earth beneath her, drawing her attention to the shattered remains of the dolmen. Pieces of ancient stones trembled and shifted, sending cascades of pebbles and dust raining down as something fought its way to the surface. Her heart leaped with wild hope—Dino? Had he somehow survived?

That hope was destroyed when a malformed hand burst through the debris, fingers twisted like gnarled tree roots, skin mottled with patches of sickly death. Cora's throat constricted on the scream building in her lungs as she scrambled backward, pulling Marcos into her arms and pressing his face against her shoulder.

The sound of Indech wrenching his mangled body from the rubble was like a symphony of breaking bones—wet pops and sharp cracks that sent shivers down her spine. When the Fomorian rose to his full height, his flesh rippled and reformed, healing as it distorted further from anything human. He fixed them with a snarl that revealed rows of rotting teeth, matching his crooked black lips.

The air itself seemed to ignite as Miller materialized between them in a flash of crimson scales and fury. He bellowed a battle roar, sending tremors through the ground, scattering the remaining debris. His thick tail whipped around like a meteor, but Indech moved with impossible speed, leaping clear of the strike.

There was a sickening thud of stone against scales as the Fomorian sent a boulder into Miller, rolling him sideways. The dragon's massive body carved a furrow in the earth. Indech already had another heavy boulder raised above his head, ready to crush Miller's skull. Without conscious thought, Cora surged to her feet, her dagger seeming to materialize in her hand as she charged.

The collision sent them both crashing into the rubble, the stone flying from Indech's grasp. White-hot pain exploded across her back as jagged rock edges tore at her flesh. The impact drove the air from her lungs, leaving her gasping like a landed fish. Before she could recover, thick fingers clamped around her throat, lifting her until her toes barely brushed the ground.

Indech's eyes blazed with an otherworldly light that bore straight into her consciousness, forcing visions of such horror that her soul recoiled. Worlds burned inside her mind's eye. Realities shattered as the screams of countless beings across countless dimensions filled her head. With a terrifying casualness, he shot his free arm behind him, catching Miller mid-lunge. The dragon-turned-man had his sword raised for a killing blow, yet Indech flung him aside like a discarded child's toy.

The Fomorian's grip tightened around Cora's throat. She clawed at his fingers, but it was like trying to bend iron bars. "Your survival is no longer necessary," his voice grated against her thoughts like rusted blades scraping bone. Black spots dotted her vision as she gasped for air that would not come. "I will bathe in your blood and that of your kindred until the very stones are soaked with the memory of your screams."

His jaw began to unhinge, stretching far beyond what any natural anatomy should allow. But where a tongue should have been, an obsidian blade emerged, black as a starless night, and severed his jaw in a spray of dark blood. Indech jerked backward, his grip loosening enough for Cora to tear herself free, gulping precious air.

The demon turned, his body still moving even as death claimed him and the Fomorian's head toppled from his shoulders. As his corpse crumpled to the ground, Segomo stood revealed, the obsidian sword gleaming with otherworldly malevolence.

He met Cora's shocked stare as she lay there massaging her bruised throat, choking on her own breath.

"I will never abandon you," he said softly, his voice carrying the weight of eons of guilt.

Miller appeared behind Segomo like an avenging spirit, roughly shoving him aside with a boot. In the next instant, he stood Cora upright, his chest heaving with the aftermath of battle.

Segomo rose with fluid grace, brushing debris from his clothing with elegant motions. Cora tried to throw herself between them, terrified of what her brother might do to Miller, but he merely offered a knowing smile and a single nod before vanishing.

She frantically searched the battlefield until she found Marcos. The boy stood before the ruined dolmen, seeming both fragile and somehow ancient against the backdrop of destruction. "He sacrificed himself. For me," he whispered, his voice thick with understanding far beyond his years.

Cora hugged him. "He loved you more than his own life," she murmured into his hair, tasting salt on her lips, whether from sweat or tears, she couldn't tell. The wind picked up, carrying away the last traces of magic and death, leaving behind only the bitter taste of victory and loss.

Across the horizon, a line of silhouettes shimmered into view. Saebbi stood at the forefront of the Death Knights. The tender smile on his face was a stark contrast to the gore that coated his clothing. As quickly as they appeared, they faded into the receding mist.

Miller joined her, lending his support and helping them to their feet. Edwind came to a stop at the outer edges of the collapsed Dolmen. He stared into the rubble, his mouth pulled into a tight frown. His gaze swept over them, and Cora's heart clenched at the sadness there. She knew that despite their differences, he didn't want Dino to be cursed to that fate.

Edwind started for them, but the sound of rock scraping against rock drew their attention to the mound of stone. A hand appeared, covered in dirt and blood. Edwind dropped to his knees, flinging stones away until he could get a grip on the arm that jutted upward.

Cora was too shocked to believe what her eyes were seeing. Dino's battered form emerged, his face bloodied and haggard. Marcos ran to his father's side. Despite his injuries, Dino welcomed the incoming collision with a pained grunt, his smile never wavering.

"How?" It was the only word that Cora could think to speak.

With the help of Marcos, Dino hobbled over to where she stood. "I was ready to face Tethra. The next thing I know, I'm buried underneath rock."

The how wasn't important. What mattered was Dino survived.

Miller tucked a finger under Cora's chin, pulling her gaze to him. "All is right with our kin. Can we go home now? I want so badly to make you my wife."

"After you tell Darya and the children goodbye," Edwind insisted.

Cora nodded, unable to put into words how much she dreaded their goodbyes. Her chest tightened at the prospect of leaving her friends, but she knew her life would soon be full of love and joy with the family that waited for her in the past.

Chapter 21

CORA WASN'T SURPRISED TO find an undamaged sailboat waiting for them when they reached the dock. She wondered if, had things not worked in her favor, if the unnamed dragons that left it there would have joined in the battle. From the stories she'd heard, Hengist was still rightfully bitter toward Morigan and welcomed every opportunity to throw sand in her ever-watchful eye. Horsa, on the other hand, chose a different approach. He took Fate's daughter as a lover.

The journey to the mainland was made in uneasy silence. Weary faces tinted with relief stared back at her. Once Miller was sure she was comfortable, he went to speak with Edwind. Their hushed conversation floated over the wind, pushing the sailboat through the choppy water, allowing her to catch a word here and there. Dino clung to Marcos, half-expecting some vile creature to rise from the ocean depths and try to take him away again.

Despite their victory, a subtle unease still gnawed at her nerves. Segomo was still out there. Where or when, she didn't know. She just hoped he kept his promise to stay out of their lives. Yet there was no denying the part of her that regretted all those years she'd missed with him. He was the first person in her life that showed her unconditional love, even if it was disguised as indifference.

A gust of wind cut across the bow, bringing with it the smell of fresh peonies. Cora expected Segomo to appear beside her, but it wasn't his dark, storm cloud eyes staring back at her. Though she had never met Morigan directly, Cora knew enough about her to recognize the suffocating aura emanating from Fate.

"Not many creatures slip past my sight." Morigan's voice was more delicate than Cora imagined. Almost maternal.

Despite that, shards of fear swept through Cora. Was Fate there to punish her for freeing Segomo? Would she snatch away her destiny with Miller?

"I didn't have a choice." Cora tried to keep her voice steady.

What she wasn't expecting was the way Morigan's expression relaxed, yet still held the sharp edge of judgment. "Oh, but you did. You could have refused Segomo and let Dino remain in the underworld. You could have destroyed my son's soul while you still held it in your hands."

Cora shook her head, ready to defend her actions, but Morigan leaned closer, whispering, "Because you cleaned up your own mess, things will stay as they are instead of how they should be." The tenderness disappeared from her features. "I shall not be so forgiving if you or your kin defy me again."

Cora was scared to move, to breathe. Evoking her father's wrath was one thing, but to do so with Morigan would be idiotic, to say the least. "I understand," was all she could manage.

There was no warmth in Morigan's smile. "I hope so. You may think me cruel, my judgments unfair, but now you know the consequences of disrupting the balance that I maintain." Her gaze slid down to Cora's stomach. "You will soon realize what sacrifice truly means."

Then she was gone, leaving Cora staring at the glistening surface of the ocean as the ship cut through waves. She glanced to the side where the others were still blissfully unaware of the visitor among them. Miller felt her stare. When he turned to face her, his lopsided grin melted away the last of her fear.

Broughied's shore came into view, like a beacon of hope in a raging storm. It was then Cora was finally able to take in a full breath.

They had survived.

They made the walk from The Dragon's Rest in silence. Cora squeezed Miller's fingers, needing the extra assurance that he was really there. She expected to wake at any second to find herself back home, on her couch, still searching for a way to find Marcos. Miller's presence grounded her in reality, cementing his place in her life and her destiny.

Cora heard Brigita's voice on the breeze before she saw the little girl racing down the hill to the beach. Edwind took off on a run, meeting his daughter and lifting her into his arms.

When Brigita saw Marcos her face lit up. "You saved him."

Darya wasn't far behind, with Bastian trying his best to keep up. Her gaze swept over the tired and bloody faces, coming to rest on Edwind, who joined his wife and son, slumping into her.

Dino took Cora by the hand. "I don't know how I can thank you for saving Marcos. For saving us both."

She slung her arms around Dino and Marcos, engraving their presence in her consciousness. Knowing the legacy that waited in the wake of her and Miller's life made the reality of having to leave them bearable.

Darya approached them. "Would you like to have one last meal before you go home?"

Cora looked to Miller, his smile sending shivers down her spine.

"I wouldn't mind some of those flat round breads," he said.

"Pancakes." Edwind reminded. "A fitting final feast together."

Despite the horrors they had witnessed and survived, laughter soon filled the Wodehal house. The smell of warm syrup and butter was a stark contrast to the battlefield they had left behind. A tentative joy rippled through the dining room, slowly at first, then building. Like they were rediscovering how to be happy again.

Cora traced the rim of her glass, watching Bastian perched on Miller's lap, stuffing a too-big bite of pancake into his mouth. Miller didn't seem to mind; he just ruffled the boy's hair, smiling between bites.

Dino stood, cup in hand. His grin faltered slightly as he looked between them, and when he spoke, his voice was rougher than before. "To those who dared to fight for what is right, no matter the cost. To the sacrifices made, the lives saved, and the bonds forged that will outlast the sands of time." His throat bobbed, his grip tightening on the drink. "And to you, Cora and Miller, who showed us that even in the face of darkness, hope can shine through."

A heavy silence followed. Then, one by one, glasses lifted.

"To Cora and Miller!"

Cora swallowed against the lump in her throat, a warmth spreading through her chest that had nothing to do with the alcohol she'd just consumed. Miller leaned closer, brushing a stray lock of hair from her face.

"To family," she whispered.

Epilogue

THE VALLEY HUMMED WITH laughter and life, preparing for the fall harvest. Cora stood at the outer wall of the castle, watching two men instruct a group of children how to clean and dress down a hare. Miller held one of the smaller girls so she could participate. One by one, each child was allowed to take part so they could practice with the knife.

"I remember when Miller was that age." Gita ambled down the slope of the path leading into the village, wiping her hands on the apron tucked around her waist. "He was a handful, even so young. I was scared he would cut himself, but Saebbi promised nothing bad would happen."

Gita's emotionless expression softened into something more tender. "He kept his promise. He made sure our son was safe."

Cora went back to watching Miller. Beside him, Saebbi helped guide the hand of a little boy who was eager to get his turn.

Gita squeezed Cora's arm. "You do not know how happy I am that you brought them back to me."

"It was the least Arawn could do. I'm just glad Saebbi got over himself and returned of his own free will. I was prepared to drag him here, even if it meant beating the stubbornness out of him."

One of Gita's brows raised. "And I would have gladly helped." She looked over her shoulder to the keep. "I cannot imagine Saebbi being absent from the lives of his grandchildren."

Cora followed her gaze. The twins had been asleep for a couple of hours. Soon they would demand to be fed soon. For a little while longer, she watched her husband.

Every day she woke to his smiling face and fell in love with him all over again. Turning, she excused herself and made her way inside.

At their chamber door, she rested a hand on the iron latch. The twins cooed softly, patiently waiting for Cora to return. Their contented babbling made her grin. The last three months were a blur of feedings, sleepless nights, and an endless barrage of dirty nappies, but she had never felt so whole and loved as she did with her family.

The first thing she saw when she entered her room was a man standing near the fireplace, holding one of her babies. Shadows flickered across his face from the dying fire. A faint smile lifted his lips before he laid a gentle kiss on her son's forehead. "There are no more two perfect beings than your children."

Cora's breath caught. Miller's sword was gone from the chest at the end of their bed. She silently chided herself for making such a big deal about having a weapon so close to the children.

Segomo strolled to the bassinet and set Brin down beside his sister. "I know you will give them the love we were denied."

When he stepped away, she rushed to the bassinet, looking them over. They were content, staring at her in anticipation of their coming meal. She turned, eyes narrowing on Segomo.

"How dare you show your face in our home? I thought I made myself clear. I never wanted to see you again."

If her words hurt him, she couldn't tell. "I meant to be gone before you found me."

"Why are you here? What did you do to my children?"

"I gave them my blessing. No mortal weapons can harm them in battle. Their flesh will defy the strongest of steel, and their blood will refuse the bite of arrows. As it will be for their children, and their children's children. It is why Dino survived when I yanked him from Tethra's prison. He proved himself a fierce warrior that day."

Cora stared at her brother, trying to force out the words she'd been wanting to say to him since their time on the island. But there was so much anger and pain left inside her heart. Nothing good would come from hanging on to such bitterness. So she chose to do the one thing that came the hardest.

Before she could talk herself out of it, she approached him, sliding her arms around his waist and squeezed like she used to do when she was a child. "If I never see you again, I want you to know that I forgive you."

After a few seconds, he returned her hug. "Be happy, Little Goddess."

Then he was gone.

The door to their room opened, and Miller stepped inside. His gaze went to where the twins babbled at each other. When he looked at Cora, his expression turning to worry. "What's wrong?"

She searched for the right words to tell him the truth, while also assuring him Segomo meant them no harm. "The children were given a wonderful gift."

Miller inched closer to the bassinet, peering at the babies. "Did your father visit again?"

Arawn's unannounced arrival shortly after the birth had been a surprise to the both of them. Miller hadn't exactly been welcoming.

"It was Segomo," she admitted.

His eyes widened, and he bent over the twins, picking them up, one at a time. "Why didn't you call for me? What did he do to them?"

She rested a hand on his back. "He bestowed his blessing."

Miller held Niara close to his chest. From the way his anger withered into annoyance told her he knew what that meant. He stared into his daughter's eyes, the smile returning. "I do not care that he has blessed our children. He isn't welcome here."

"He knows that. I don't think we will ever see him again."

Miller drew Cora into him, kissing the top of her head. Niara began to fuss in his arms. Brin soon followed his sister's lead.

Cora picked up her son, heading for the chair near the window. Miller leaned against the stone wall, cradling Niara so she could see the fields beyond. As Cora listened to her husband explain to their three-month-old infant the intricacies of life on Didean, she wondered how she had been able to survive as long as she did without the joy that her family brought her. Knowing what awaited them in the future, the lives that would be lived, the love that would be given, she was finally content with her destiny.

A Word From The Author

THANK YOU FOR READING *DESTINY Awakened*. I hope you enjoyed the journey as much as I cherished creating it. If you have a moment, I'd be grateful if you could share your honest review on your favorite platform. Your feedback means the world to me!
www.cahollister.net

<u>Also by C. A. Hollister</u>
Destiny Unbound: Laws of Fate Book 1
Imperfect Illusions

About The Author

C.A. Hollister's roots are deeply planted in the rich soil of a small North East Texas town, where family gatherings buzzed with the warmth of shared stories and the joy of cooking together. This nurturing environment sparked her imagination, leading her to create her own unique universes from a very young age. In her storytelling, she blends the familiar with the fantastical, weaving tales that resonate with raw emotion and explore the universal longing for connection and love. Her approach to writing marries the everyday with the extraordinary, inviting readers into worlds where magic touches the mundane, and where characters' desires and heartaches echo our own.

www.ingramcontent.com/pod-product-compliance
Lightning Source LLC
Chambersburg PA
CBHW071539110726
47908CB00007B/1938